I0594365

STEALING TIME

Rebecca Bowyer

Story Addict Publishing
MELBOURNE, AUSTRALIA

First published 2021 by Story Addict Publishing.
P.O. Box 11, Croydon, Victoria 3136 Australia
storyaddict.com.au
Copyright © 2021 by Rebecca Bowyer.

Publisher's Note: This is a work of fiction. Names, characters, places, and incidents are a product of the author's imagination. Locales and public names are sometimes used for atmospheric purposes. Any resemblance to actual people, living or dead, or to businesses, companies, events, institutions, or locales is completely coincidental.

Book cover design by RockingBookCovers.com
Book Layout ©2015 BookDesignTemplates.com
Printed by IngramSpark
Stealing Time/Rebecca Bowyer -- 1st ed.

ISBN 978-0-6485323-3-0 (pbk)
ISBN 978-0-6485323-4-7 (ebook)

A catalogue record for this book is available from the National Library of Australia.

To all those who'd desperately like a few more hours to magically appear in their day.

CHAPTER ONE

Varya

Varya looked up from the stove and smiled as her friend deposited her handbag on the hall stand and shrugged off her jacket.

"Long day?" she asked.

"You could say that." Zoe slumped onto a bar stool beside Daniel and peered over his shoulder. "History?"

Daniel frowned and rounded his shoulder, blocking his device from his mother's view.

"Just a novel. With Greek gods," he mumbled. Without taking his eyes off the screen, he pushed the stool back from the counter, stood up, and wandered out of the kitchen.

Zoe smiled and watched him leave, perfectly navigating around furniture and through the doorway to his bedroom, without even needing to lift his eyes.

"His peripheral vision must be extremely well developed." She turned back to Varya. "So, honey, what's for dinner?"

Varya threw a tea towel at her. "Nothing, if you keep that up."

"Well, it smells good. Thanks for looking after Daniel. Need me to do anything?"

"No, it's fine." Varya turned to the stove.

Zoe studied her back. "How was your day? Everything okay at work?"

"Work's fine."

"They found a cure yet?"

Varya smiled faintly. "Not yet. Getting closer."

It was Zoe's standard attempt to penetrate her friend's thought bubble. Somehow, it always worked, always got her attention.

One day there would be a cure for disease that had taken Varya's four-year-old son. Varya hoped she would be a part of the discovery; it was what she'd spent twelve-hour days working towards. But some days, cleaning benches, noting observations and laying out instruments didn't feel much like contributing. The process of medical research was so damned slow.

"How about you? Save any lives today?"

Zoe's face clouded. "We lost a kid today. Five-year-old little girl. Cancer."

"I'm sorry." Varya wanted to hug her but knew better than to try to offer physical comfort. Zoe needed her space, to be able to maintain her composure in the face of tragedy. It was the only way she managed to continue working as a pallia- tive care paediatrician at the Gillard Memorial Hospital.

"She was ready to go. We were having trouble managing her pain in the end. She was tired." Zoe paused and swal- lowed. "It's the parents, afterwards, that's the hardest part to deal with. It's a relief for the child, when death comes, but the parents... they're the ones who get left behind. Their suf- fering never really ends."

Varya gripped the bench to stop the world from spinning and slow her own breathing.

"But you know all this, I don't need to tell you." Zoe met Varya's eyes and they exchanged a moment of raw pain before Zoe shook her head.

"But that's all far too morbid for a Monday evening. When can we eat? I'm starving."

"Lemongrass and chilli stir fry tonight," Varya announced, a little too loudly. She turned away from Zoe to stir the sizzling contents of the pan.

"Smells wonderful. Chicken?"

She shrugged. "They were out of beef again. Maybe next month, they reckon. I get lectured every time I ask for it, you know. Bad for the environment, plant-based beef substitute tastes practically the same..."

"Chicken is good. Or tofu, even. So long as we can still get a steak every now and then. A girl needs her steak, you know, no matter the emissions." She went to the fridge and pulled out a half-empty bottle of white wine. Varya shook her head as Zoe held it up to her, eyebrows raised.

"Might help you relax a little. A glass a day won't harm you."

"Vineyards are better for the environment than beef, at least," said Varya, ignoring her friend's offer as she pulled bowls out from the cupboards.

"How are you sleeping these days?" Zoe sat at the counter and poured herself a small glass, taking a small sip and studying Varya.

"Fine," said Varya, without meeting her eye.

"You seem tired, is all."

"Well, alcohol won't help that. It'll just make me more tired." Varya turned back and started to serve the rice, two scoops per bowl. Then she moved them to the pan and scooped the meagre rations of chicken on, drizzling extra sauce over the top before placing the three bowls in a row on the counter.

"Daniel! Dinner!" she called out, before making her way around the counter and taking her place two seats away from Zoe.

The two women watched as Daniel came loping out, his impossibly long, skinny limbs flailing around in alarming proximity to the door frame. He slumped down in the chair between them and shovelled food into his mouth with alarming speed.

Zoe smiled and shook her head. They ate in silence for a few minutes. She took her opportunity to pounce as Daniel paused in his shovelling to take a drink of water.

"So, anything interesting happen at school today?"

Daniel looked up at her in mild surprise, as though he'd forgotten she was there.

"A kid's gone missing, one of the kids in the other class. Ben Williams."

Varya put her fork down and tried to swallow her mouthful but her throat had already started to clench.

"Missing?" Zoe pushed her hair back. "You mean he's away, sick? Or he's moved schools?"

Daniel shook his head. "Nope. Never came home last night. Police are out looking for him. His mum was at the school this morning, crying."

Zoe and Varya exchanged an anxious glance.

"That poor woman," murmured Zoe.

"Do they have any idea where he might have gone?" asked Varya.

Daniel shook his head. "Nope. They've tried everyone. CCTV footage, all of it. He's vanished somewhere between school and home."

"Well, I'm sure he can't have gone far. Maybe he went camping, or just decided to have some time to himself. I'm sure he'll be found soon, okay?" Varya scooped up a spoonful of rice and held it between her bowl and mouth purposefully.

Daniel looked at her, expressionless.

"Sure," he muttered. He continued eating, sneaking curious glances at Varya from time to time.

It had seemed like the right thing to do, offering to help Zoe care for Daniel. Sometimes Varya wondered whether she'd tried too hard over the years, whether her near-constant presence might make Zoe feel pushed to the side, or whether Zoe had seen it as a ready excuse to bury herself in work. Caring for other people's children while Varya cared for hers. Both women worked non-standard hours. Between them, they ensured Daniel always had someone to greet him at home after school.

Zoe had lost her husband to a rare autoimmune disease and needed help to care for Daniel while she continued working shifts at the hospital to support them. Varya needed to be near someone who understood the grief she suffered at losing her son. She couldn't work twenty-four hours a day at the lab, not without raising suspicion. Especially in the evening hours, time stretched out. She'd felt like she was rattling around her own apartment, after her husband had left.

After Kir was gone.

Varya had taken Kir home from the hospital towards the end. The known treatments had failed. The experimental ones had been stopped in their early stages. There were no clinical trials for Kir to be enrolled in, no final attempts, no long shots. His condition was rare and, as such, the bean counters who held the medical research purse strings had deemed there to be insufficient public interest to invest in a cure. The dollars were being spent on furthering stem cell research for more common childhood cancers.

And so, Kir had come home.

Zoe had watched it all happen. She'd worked on the same ward, but with different patients. She'd spoken in soft tones to Varya in the tearoom. She understood the pain of being told your loved one didn't deserve a chance to live. They bonded over their anger at the system's failure. Before Kir was discharged for good, Zoe gave Varya medications to keep him comfortable. Medications which, she told her newfound friend—out of ear shot of other staff—if Kir became too distressed, could end his pain altogether at the right dosage. Zoe whispered a number in her ear. Varya clenched her fists, fought back tears, and silently noted it.

By then, Kir's father had left, taken a promotion up at the naval base just outside Canberra. Sebastian and Varya had fallen out over their son's medical treatments. The months of illness had taken their toll on an already strained marriage. Kir was not going to live, Sebastian told her, what was the point of putting him through the pain and distress of more treatments when it was fruitless? Sebastian wanted to spend the final days with his son as happily as they could, and then move on. Varya was determined to eke out every extra day she possibly could with the only son she would ever have. One child per woman, that was the law to contain the population and preserve precious and dwindling natural resources.

They had to try, she said.

No, they didn't, he said.

In the end, he left. He took a week off after quitting his job in Melbourne and spent his own final days with Kir, the way he wanted to.

And then he was gone. Varya hadn't heard from Sebastian since. Not during the dark days when Kir shivered in the hospital bed at Gillard Memorial with tubes attached, not when she held his head through the night at home while he vomited the contents of his tiny four-year-old stomach onto the mass of towels she kept by his bed.

And then Kir was gone, too.

Later that evening, after the dishes were stacked in the dishwasher and Daniel had retired to his room to chat to his friends and shoot things in his online gaming world, Zoe poured herself another glass of wine and sat, staring at the subway-tiled splashback. One hand rested on her mini screen. Varya gave the bench one final wipe and came to sit next to her friend.

"I'm sure that kid'll be alright."

Zoe turned to her, frowning. "Are you?"

"He's probably just wandered off. You know what kids are like these days."

"I do. And usually they leave some sort of sign before they decide to take off. A note. A packed backpack. They take their screens with them." Zoe cut herself off and lifted her glass to her lips, taking a large gulp of wine.

"He didn't take anything with him? Daniel told you that?"

Zoe had spoken to Daniel in his bedroom while Varya was cleaning up from dinner. The conversation fragments that drifted into the kitchen had started out fluid and upbeat, then became monosyllabic and sparse. By the time Zoe had returned to her seat at the bench she was withdrawn and silent.

"No, Daniel didn't tell me. I read it online." Zoe tapped her screen, staring at it but not focusing.

This was not a good sign, thought Varya.

"There hasn't been a child abduction in over a decade," said Zoe. "All that stopped, it was supposed to have stopped with the arrests, the destruction of the technology, the improvements they made to the Rest Time Chips. They're tamper-proof now." She rubbed at her neck as the words rushed out, swirling together in a cloud of anxiety.

Varya frowned and stared at the back of Zoe's neck, the tiny scar visible now, with her hair swept to the side. She knew her own neck carried a similar light pink nick, where her Time Chip had been inserted. Sixty-five years, that was the maximum time allowed to each person in modern-day Australia. Assuming they stayed out of trouble, worked their allotted hours, and had one child—only one—to get the maximum Time Chip extensions granted.

But ten years ago, some people had become greedy. They'd discovered a way to steal time from other people. And who had more time to be stolen than a young child? For several months, the time thieves had terrorised the eastern seaboard from Maroochydore to Melbourne. Until Varya had helped to stop them.

She didn't want to think about those dark times when children couldn't be let out of their parent's sight for even a second. She shuddered at the memory of children suddenly reappearing on the doorsteps of frantic households. The footage of joyful reunions shattered just seconds later as the child collapsed in their parent's arms—the years, weeks and minutes stripped away from them. It was a bittersweet torture, this precise theft of time. The time thieves left just enough time for one final greeting; just enough time to build up hope again before the child was then torn away forever, the Time Chip's termination sequence activated decades too early.

After two or three such traumatic returns, the parents of newly abducted children had become wise. They just held onto their babies for dear life when they came back, clutching them while they were still warm and could hug them back.

After several dozen abduct-and-returns, the grief was immediate. In one infamous case, the mother refused to open the door to her returned child. CCTV footage showed a thirteen-year-old girl banging her fists on the door, shouting for her mother to let her in. Her father later revealed that he ran from the backyard into the house, where his wife sat with her back against the front door, sobbing uncontrollably. She simply couldn't face watching her daughter die. The father had tried to move her, but she wouldn't budge. When the banging subsided, she raised the handgun she'd concealed at her side, and shot herself.

Varya shook her head. "Kids go missing for other reasons. It's not always about time. He might have had an argument with someone and wandered off and got lost. You know how unpredictable pre-teens can be."

Zoe clutched the stem of her newly re-filled wine glass. "Oh, come on, Varya. Daniel's in his room. He can't hear us, there's no need to sanitise this. Besides, even he doesn't believe you. He's nine years old, he's not a baby."

Varya flinched. She knew Zoe was right, but she wished she could still tell Daniel whatever made-up version of events would make him feel safe at night, and have him believe her.

When had that changed? Two years ago, three? They grew up so fast, lost their faith in adults so quickly. Then again, when adults lied on a daily basis—often even to themselves— it was hardly surprising.

"Fifty-five years on the clock, he had left. That's a lot of years to sell, a lot of money, and a big motive." Zoe looked at Varya. "What's to say it's not happening again?" Her voice held an uncharacteristic note of panic.

Zoe had worked in the emergency department in the early days when the time thieves had been less precise. Half a dozen children had been returned with enough time left on their Chips to make it to the hospital. Their parents would rush them in, screaming for the Time Chip to be taken out. Zoe and her colleagues had been powerless to do anything except give the family some privacy in their final moments. No Time Chip had ever been removed without causing death to the host. At least the children's deaths were peaceful ones, as the initiators were designed to provide, unlike some of the traumas inflicted on other children brought into the E.R. But what could be truly peaceful about the death of a young child who had barely had the chance to live?

Eventually the perpetrators had been caught. A criminal cell harbouring a fourth-dimension physicist who had worked on the time exchange projects and couldn't let go of the prospect of immortality or—at the very least—old age. He and his co-conspirators had been put to death the old-fashioned way: by lethal injection. The time theft technology they'd used had been retrieved and destroyed. Varya knew Ben Williams couldn't have been taken by time thieves. The Rest Time initiators were absolutely tamper-proof and the consequences for developing technology to override them were both swift and brutal.

Besides, there was nobody left who even knew how to effect a time transfer. Except for Varya. And her former Time Corps colleague, Reginald Baker.

Varya focused on Zoe's wine glass and decided she was thirsty after all.

CHAPTER TWO

Marisa

"It's not about how much time you have available to you, it's about how you use that time to its full potential."

"Bullshit," Marisa muttered to the well-suited television presenter as she fanned out forty hours' worth of time tabs on the low table in front of her. "Time is money, and money has always been able to buy more time." Although usually what people meant was that you could pay someone else to clean your house, or get your groceries, or execute any one of your millions of smaller chores, to free up time for yourself. So then you could spend that extra thirty minutes a day doing a high-intensity workout to keep your body healthy instead, and twenty minutes meditating to keep your mind healthy, and ninety minutes reading or doing crossword puzzles to optimise your brain synapses.

Marisa nodded in satisfaction, collapsed the time tabs back into a neat pile like a seasoned card shark, dropped them into a small matchbox and handed it to the waiting teenager. The girl turned the box over in her soft, slender hands and pushed out the drawer with a candy-pink nail.

Inside were layered small, clear blue rectangles. The girl reached in with her index finger and stroked the pile until she managed to separate the top sheet. She held it up to the light and inspected it.

"And this thing can freeze time?"

"No." Marisa shook her head. She always found it difficult to explain the mechanics of the tabs without going into unnecessary detail. "Not freeze. It will sort of slip you into a pocket of time. Time will continue in nanoseconds outside of the pocket, but for you it will feel like four hours." She turned her back to the wall screen and held out her hand expectantly.

The girl ignored Marisa's outstretched hand. "But I can study, and nobody will see me?"

"Nobody will notice. You have your own bedroom?" Marisa tossed her head towards the main house, across the glittering pool. She saw a drape twitch and wondered just how private the pool house was, not that she was really concerned about discovery. At worst, the girl's parents would confiscate the time tabs for their own use and maybe suspend their daughter's generous allowance for a while. They wouldn't dream of turning her over to the authorities for illegal fourth-dimension activities. That would jeopardise their own supply. The corner of Marisa's mouth twitched but she managed to remain serious and professional as she gestured meaningfully with her empty, upturned palm. This silly girl believed she'd found something her parents knew nothing about, something that was all hers. She couldn't know that her own mother had called Marisa herself and had been dropping breadcrumbs for the past week to try to bring her daughter to Marisa. The girl was young and idealistic. She thought she wanted more from life than the opulent luxury into which she'd been born. She wanted to study international humanitarian law and run away to help the refugees in third-world countries. Ah, the heady socialism of youth, thought Marisa. She watched the girl finger the time tabs in wonder.

The girl nodded. "Yes, I have my own suite." She pulled a wad of crisp notes from behind a set of mugs sitting on a nearby shelf. She placed them in Marisa's palm, careful not to touch her skin.

Marisa felt her eyes start to roll and took a deep breath. "Okay, then in the evening go into your *suite* and lock the door behind you. Hold your study materials against your chest, like this." Marisa crossed her arms and hugged her own torso. "Make sure they're well pressed against your body, then place one time tab under your tongue and let it dissolve."

The girl frowned, disbelieving. She held the transparent blue rectangle up to the light again and sniffed it.

"Can I use it to go to class?"

"No. You won't get an internet connection either, it'll seem far too slow. So, hard copy or offline screen copies only if you're studying." Marisa nodded and stood. Open secret or not, she wanted to be gone before she was seen. Visiting the girl's mother under the guise of soliciting donations for the Minor Miracles Foundation was an easy cover. It would be harder to explain a covert visit to a teenage girl.

"Remember, one sheet per four hours. Don't take more than one at a time or you'll be stuck in the time pocket for eight or more hours. That's a long time to be tapping your fingers for." She leaned in briefly and opened her eyes wide. "Don't tell anyone you have them, keep them safe. And study hard, make your family proud, even if they don't agree with your choices."

The girl blinked, then nodded, and slipped the matchbox into her pocket.

Marisa slipped out of the door, walked quickly past the pool, and let herself out through the back gate. She noticed the main house drape drop as the gate clicked. Out on the quiet, leafy street she popped the boot of her car and checked for onlookers before she punched in the mobile safe code and added the cash to her small pile. Cash days were irritating. She far preferred legitimate donation days. The sums were larger, transfer was digital, and there was no need to be inconspicuous. But cash had its uses for their operation. It was harder to trace and more freely accepted on the black market for the ingredients required for the manufacture of time tabs.

"And we're done for the day. Time to head back to the bat cave." Marisa snorted at her own joke as she flipped the car on and told it to take her home. "Okay car, increase volume to level seven." She closed her eyes as the car pulled out from the kerb and the tones for the four o'clock news sounded.

"*In today's news, the government has introduced a Bill to increase the available life extension for procreation of a single child from five years to seven, in an effort to stabilise birthrates, which are declining too steeply. And police are calling for information from the public to help them locate a nine-year-old boy who went missing from the quiet suburb of Waterdown...*"

"Bloody politicians, fiddling around the edges. It won't help!" she shouted to no one in particular. "Okay car, play some music."

"Your favourite tunes, on shuffle," responded the calming voice of the car's AI. The reporter's voice was replaced by the pop and twang of the latest techno hit.

Marisa tapped the back of her head against the seat a couple of times before putting her feet up on the dash and closing her eyes again. In her opinion, the only thing that would help was dismantling the entire Time Chip system and rebuilding society from scratch. But she'd given up on revolution long ago. Now she longed for nothing more than working enough extra hours to grant her the time extensions required for her to live until the ripe old age of sixty-five, and earning enough money that she could retire ten years earlier than that and spend the rest of her days lying on a beach somewhere on the Sunshine Coast.

She wasn't completely heartless, though, she told herself. Soliciting "donations" for the Minor Miracles Foundation, a genuinely honourable cause, was a worthwhile way of keeping busy. And besides, the job came with plenty of benefits, she mused as she patted the leather dash of the car with her Italian-designed boots.

CHAPTER 3

Varya

Later than night, Varya returned to her own small apartment. She'd moved there after her husband and son were long gone, soon after she'd opened the Minor Miracles Foundation. It was close to work, far from her spacious former family home. She lay her palm on the panel inlaid next to the doorframe and kept her face steady, eyes open. The fingerprint and retina scan took a few moments, then the locks clicked. There were six of them, two for each side of the door not held by hinges. She pushed the door and it swung open silently. She stepped through, breathed in the sterile scent and placed her handbag down on the couch. The apartment had come fully furnished and she'd done little to personalise it. There were no cushions, no throws, no rugs, no lamps. She continued briskly down the hallway, past the kitchen, and stopped at the first door beyond it. She placed her palm on another panel and waited. Pushing the door open, she smiled.

This was where Varya kept the most valuable of her valuables.

Everything from her old life had been left behind in the move, except for the contents of this tiny room. The clothes in the hamper, the drawings tacked to the wall, the low shelves full of picture books. She'd transferred them all to this room exactly as they'd been left in the old house.

Varya returned to this room every night, without fail, to visit with her little boy who was no longer here.

She held out both palms this time and stepped forward.

"Mummy, will you come back next week?" he asked tonight.

"I'll be back tomorrow, sweetheart. I come every day."

Kir creased his four-year-old brow, testing out where his worry lines might carve their groove into his face in years to come.

"But you'll come next week too?"

"Yes, I'll come next week too." Varya smiled sadly. She knew it was normal for young children to have no sense of time, but Kir had even less sense of the beats that marked the days than most. When day is day and night is day and each visit of hers felt like just a few minutes apart or sometimes hours, it was impossible for him to learn the difference between seconds, minutes, hours, days. The units of time and the passing of them had become meaningless for him. He could spend as much time as he liked, and his account would simply refill. He never moved forward. He gained knowledge but no wisdom because his childlike brain couldn't process. Facts were all a jumble inside his head. Blades of grass and vast cities held equal importance in his mind.

But perhaps that was for the best, Varya reflected, given Kir's situation. Children are unique in their ability to live in the moment, to enjoy each flower stem, and to question the ladybug climbing up it. When you're sealed inside a timeless world, living in the moment is what will keep you sane.

Varya looked at her mother, who watched Kir, with a fond smile. It was a gift her mother had retained throughout her life, this ability to enjoy what was right in front of her. It was a peaceful existence, Varya reflected, though one that needed protection from other, more practical people. Such as herself.

Varya heard rapid banging in the distance, muted, but still there. She sighed and stood.

"I should go," said Varya.

Kir nodded solemnly.

"Yes, Mummy. You go and find me a cure for my poor body." He put his little hand against his chest. Varya pressed her own hand gently over his, cupping it against his chest.

"I will. Don't you worry, I'll find it."

Elena cocked her ear and glanced in the direction the sound came from, back from where Varya had stepped through the shimmering air. Elena nodded at her daughter.

"You go. We'll be fine."

"I think we're nearly there."

Elena smiled. "There's no rush. We have plenty of time."

CHAPTER FOUR

Back in her apartment, the banging grew louder and more insistent. Varya took one last look at Kir's bedroom, arranged just as he had left it five years ago. A mass of coloured pipe cleaners twisted into bracelets on the crafting table; the Legos tidied away into their container—too difficult for a tired, sick little boy to play with any longer—and a dozen stuffed toys lining the bed, within easy reach whenever comfort was needed. Then she stepped out of the bedroom and shut the door, pressing her palm against it, and waiting for the whoosh and click which indicated her son and mother were safely secured.

She checked the security camera before unlocking the apartment door to Marisa.

"Sheesh, took you long enough. What were you doing, painting your nails?" Marisa swept past Varya and headed straight to the kitchen, flicking on the coffee machine. "I've run out at home and the local store doesn't know when they're getting another shipment. The border's been closed again, too many climate refugees leaking through. I'm dying for a cup of hot, velvety caffeine."

"You'll be up all night if you have one now," warned Varya, glancing at the display on the refrigerator. 20:55. She pulled two cups down from the top cupboard, nonetheless.

"That's okay, we've got work to do. I've got several new clients for you tonight." Marisa rubbed her thumb and forefinger together suggestively. "Rich ones. Seriously rich. Ready to make big donations to your cause in exchange for a few extra hours."

Varya regarded her warily. "Not my cause. You didn't tell them about me, did you?"

"No, of course I didn't." She grinned and splayed both hands out on the table, puffing out her chest. "Besides, it does my marketing good for them to think I'm a mysterious agent working for the poor sick kiddies. Either that or I'm a one-woman genius working for myself. I'm not sure they really care, as long as they get their receipt for their legitimately tax-deductible donation." She leaned in, her bosoms pressing against the table as she pouted her lips. "Either way, I'm the woman who can give them exactly what they want, all while taking their hard-earned money and making them feel good about it."

Varya ran her tongue around her teeth and raised an eyebrow.

"You use that line on all our clients?"

Marisa laughed. "Now they're 'our' clients?" She shrugged. "I only use that line on the stupid ones with more billions than brains."

Varya sighed and sat down at the kitchen table. Marisa fascinated, impressed, and exasperated her in equal measure. She'd met her at a seedy bar on the city fringes.

Varya made the pilgrimage there each night after Kir was gone, just to sit and be somewhere entirely different. She would sip her gin and tonic at the bar, watching people come and go, imagining them to be in equal amounts of pain. Imagining them to be suffering unimaginable losses, just like her. It was somehow comforting. Marisa was the one who topped up her drink each night, who succeeded in drawing her story out of her, bit by bit.

It was Marisa who suggested Varya could do something with her talents, albeit under the radar, to help other families avoid her pain and loss. To search for cures for the rare diseases that the government refused to fund research for. It was Marisa, too, who offered to help as foundation fundraiser. And as Varya started to make enquiries and arrangements to set up the Minor Miracles Foundation, and to think through funding options, she began to take her suggestion more seriously. She'd watch Marisa change her demeanour like a chameleon. Flirty bantering with the local men on a Friday night to persuade them to upgrade their order to the best steak rather than just a burger because, well, they'd earned it, hadn't they? Cajoling angry truckers wielding pool cues to step down, calm down, or the drink they had just hurled at the wall would be their last at this bar. Charming travelling businessmen by expertly building complicated - but manly - cocktails and charging them double for the pleasure of watching her work.

One night she'd taken Marisa to a local restaurant and put a proposal to her. Marisa quit work at the bar the next day and had been with Varya ever since. Over time, Varya had grown to trust her wholeheartedly. A personal assistant and confidante, all rolled into one. Marisa had made herself utterly indispensable and irreplaceable.

But some days, when Marisa shed her many faces and relaxed into her natural, slightly rough, demeanour, it still rattled Varya. She'd become used to the gentler, quiet rhythms of the lab.

Now, she flipped open her laptop and looked at Marisa expectantly. "Okay, so tell me the details. What do you need?"

Marisa held up both palms. "Nah-ah. Coffee first. Then we'll talk. My poor damned brain can barely add up the zeros, let alone calculate the time tabs without a double shot of caffeine."

"You should think about taking a few tabs yourself, catch up on some sleep. Then you won't need so much coffee." Varya stood to retrieve the pot from the machine. She divided the black liquid between the two mugs and carried them both over to the table.

"No, thanks. A dealer shouldn't partake of her own wares. Something about pissing where you sleep..." She blew on her coffee and then took a sip. "Mmm, that's my drug." She closed her eyes in satisfaction.

Varya sat and waited, watching the steam rise from her own mug.

"So, how've you been, anyway?" asked Marisa.

Marisa liked small talk. Varya preferred silence but tried to indulge Marisa where she could.

"Good. I'm good. You?"

Marisa shrugged. "Same, I guess. Always too much to do, never enough time, you know how it is."

"Busy," said Varya with a nod.

"Busy," agreed Marisa. She took another sip of her coffee and tipped her head from side to side, rolling her shoulders and cracking her neck. "Ah, for the good old days when people worked eight-hour days, hey?"

Varya snorted. "Wow, you really are taking a nostalgic trip down ancient history lane, aren't you?"

"Yeah, well, a girl can dream, right?"

"You could work an eight-hour day if you wanted to, you know. Plenty of people do."

Marisa frowned and rolled her eyes. "They do. But I'd rather live past fifty-five, thanks."

"Yeah, maybe." Varya wasn't so sure that it was worth it anymore - working an extra four hours a day, twenty hours a week, to get the Rest Time Extension granted. At thirty-four years old, fifty-five seemed a long way off to her. Living until sixty-five could mean another thirty-one years of moving through the world without her son. She shuddered at the thought.

"Hey, do you still get the time extension for Kir, even though he's...?" Marisa asked, before widening her eyes and jerking her head back. "Oh, God, sorry, that was incredibly insensitive, even for me. Shit, what an idiot. I'm sorry. Are you okay?"

Varya shut her eyes briefly and sucked in her breath, inhaling the yeasty scent of the coffee. She forced a smile.

"Yes, I'm fine, it's okay."

Marisa took another deep drink from her now-cooling mug. "Good," she said quickly. "That's good." She reached down and swung her backpack up onto the table, pressed her finger against the lock and waited a second for it to snap open. Dragging her screen out, she laid it out on the table between them and tapped and swiped.

"Okay, so that rich bitch from the bank that we've been supplying for years, spoke to her niece—who's an antiques dealer—and she needs to do a bit of image reinvention after some affair she's alleged to have had with a high-profile suspected art thief. So, she's pretty keen on making a sizable public donation to the Minor Miracles Foundation. Plus, she wants the time tabs to help deal with the jet lag after her international scouting trips."

"Scouting trips for antique trades or heists?" asked Varya with a playful smile.

"Do you care?" Marisa looked up from the screen with an expression that told Varya that *she* certainly didn't.

Varya shrugged. "Not really. Not while she's solvent and feeling generous. There are bigger problems in this world than holding people to account for stealing overpriced paint on canvas." She opened her laptop again and started to type. "So, she's going to use it for sleep?"

"Yep. She wants twenty four-hour tabs."

Varya nodded. "Okay, that's fine. Next?" She looked up. "And I don't need the back story for all of them, we'll be here all night. Just purpose and batch details will do."

"Fine, have it your way. But you're missing out on some juicy gossip, my friend."

"I'll live."

"Kid's about to flunk out of law school. Heading into the final semester. Wants one hundred four-hour time tabs so he can study without it impacting on his social life." Marisa paused and looked up at Varya gleefully, awaiting her reaction.

Varya had stopped typing and was sitting, tapping the edge of her keyboard thoughtfully. She started typing again and muttered, "I take it the parents are footing the bill, otherwise he'd just pay someone else to do the work?"

"Bingo!" shouted Marisa, pumping both of her arms into the air. "It's like you were at the meeting yourself. I don't know why you even bother to employ me."

Varya looked up and frowned at her, then continued typing.

"He can have fifty four-hour slips. Tell him if he can prove his grades have improved through his own efforts, I'll make him another twenty for free."

Varya looked up questioningly when Marisa didn't start on the next order. She sat there, arms crossed, grinning.

"You don't care about heists but you're happy to rip cheating law students a new one. You sound like my fucking mother."

"Your mother was clearly an intelligent person who valued hard work. Next on the list." Varya looked up again, questioningly, when Marisa stayed silent. She frowned, tracking back over what she'd just said, as she took in Marisa's folded arms and unimpressed glare.

"My mother's still alive, you know," said Marisa.

Varya sat back in her chair. "I'm sorry, I just assumed..."

Marisa shrugged. "It's okay. We're not close." It clearly wasn't okay. "I'm forty-seven, it's a reasonable assumption that my mother's headed off into her Rest Time. But she hasn't. She was only fifteen when I was born."

Varya did some quick calculations. "Still a few years left, then."

Marisa nodded. "Yeah. Only a few, though."

They both sat in silence. Varya wondered whether it was a comfort or a grief brought forward, to know the exact moment when your mother would die.

"Okay, so, next on the list... Aaaw, you're gonna want to know the back story for this one. It's hilarious."

Varya smiled tiredly. "Alright then, let's have it."

CHAPTER FIVE

"Hey."

Varya ignored the low, soft voice next to her, just as she ignored most things while she immersed herself in her daily work at the lab. She pushed a sample several millimetres to the left and adjusted the zoom of the microscope.

"Name's Connor."

A sheath of printed paper dropped down on the bench in front of her with a dull thud. Varya looked up, startled. Was he talking to her? She looked from side to side to check, but the bench was empty for several arms' lengths on either side. People didn't speak to her, as a rule. Most staff were long-term hires and knew better than to even try. She glanced at the stack of prints, then up at the intruder. She squinted at him for a moment before silently bending her head back over the microscope.

He didn't leave.

Varya kept one eye firmly on the barrel of the microscope and snuck a glimpse at this man with the other. Dark blue denim jeans and worn work boots protruded from the too-short lab coat. He shifted his feet so they both firmly faced toward her. Varya sighed. She raised her head to inspect his face and experienced a slight jolt of recognition. Those eyes. Clear blue, electric white streaks, seemingly shrunken irises. She zoomed her focus out and swept his body. He seemed slightly embarrassed now, his cheeks had flushed a soft pink. She relaxed as she realised that the rest of his person was foreign to her.

"Varya," she said, with a quick nod, before bowing back to her microscope.

Connor sucked in his breath. "O-kay, then. Nice talking with you, Varya." He picked up his pile of prints and walked on. She looked up sharply as she heard the same dull thud, this time at the work bench several feet to her right. He was looking directly at her, and grinned. She raised her eyes up-wards briefly, then closed them, shook her head, and went back to work.

"Don't mind her, she's very friendly, really," she heard Jolene say in a stage whisper. "Just don't interrupt her while she's working. She gets a little cranky."

"Duly noted."

Varya rubbed her eyes. She looked over at Jolene, who had placed her hand lightly on the newcomer's arm and was now moving to place her other hand on his back and wished her all the best. Varya found it hard to imagine herself wor-rying about small, mundane things like flirting.

Her back hurt from having sat at the chair for three hours already. Maybe a small break would be a good idea. The sam-ple cells on her strip all started to blur together after a while. Why did it have to take so long? Why couldn't finding a cure be like it was in the movies, when an antidote to a viral pan-demic could be developed in just two days, before the heroine had to suffer the pain of losing the newfound love of her life? Instead, this curing process took months of painstaking trial and error, scanning and logging samples, analysis, running it through machines, waiting for growth and mutation. Then failing and beginning right back at square one. Hours and days and weeks and months and years. So much time, so little progress. But they would find the cure. As long as the money kept coming in, as long as the funding was there.

"Varya."

This time Varya turned instantly to the sound of her name and saw Professor Langford standing beside her. Her long, grey hair was swept back in a low, loose bun. Her usually still and precise hands fidgeted.

Varya frowned. "Professor?"

"We need to talk."

Varya flinched inwardly and shook her head slightly.

"Not…"

"About the test results. It can't wait. Please come through to my office now."

Varya frowned but nodded and stood. Langford led the way out of the lab, down a corridor and, giving the empty hall a final sweeping glance, into her spacious office at the end. Varya entered and waited for Langford to close the door.

"This had better be important," Varya hissed. "I've told you, we can't be seen to be working together."

"We do work together," Langford retorted. "And in that context, I'm your superior. So, sit."

Varya, temporarily deflated, sat on the chair, and waited. It had been a long day, a long week. The years passed so quickly, but the days went on forever. And she was tired, always so tired.

"I'm sorry, Janet, it's just... hard. I wish it didn't have to be like this."

Langford nodded.

"What is it? Have you... found something?" Varya dared to hope for a moment.

"No, I haven't. I'm sorry."

Varya slouched in her chair further and scratched the side of her nose. She looked away, trying to compose what she knew was a disappointed frown on her face. Langford reached her hand out to Varya across the desk.

"I'm trying, Varya. But this isn't my field of expertise. I really think it's time to bring in somebody new."

"But I trust *you*, Janet. This isn't something I can just ask anybody to help me with. I'd end up hauled before the Courts faster than I could say 'fourth dimension'." She leaned in and took Langford's hand. "You can do it; I know you can. I've seen your work on neurological preservation and reversals. You just need more... time."

Langford smiled wryly. "Ah, time." She withdrew her hand and sat back. "That's what I need to talk to you about. My time is running out. I don't like to think about it, or talk about it, but I've only got a few hours left. Today is my last day."

"You're leaving?" Varya was alarmed. The Minor Miracles Foundation had been Janet Langford's whole life since it had opened. She'd arrived even before Varya most days. Staff speculated that Langford slept in her office. Varya knew she didn't. Janet may have arrived before her each morning, but it was Varya who turned out the lights of the facility most nights—when she wasn't looking after Daniel.

Janet's brow furrowed now in a way that made Varya want to fidget, too.

"Varya, child, how old do you think I am?"

"I... I don't know."

"It's my birthday today. I'm sixty-five years old. My time on this earth is almost up."

"No." Varya let out a small moan before she clapped her hand over her mouth.

"Hush now. There are ears everywhere," said Janet sharply. Then, in calm, raised tones, she recited, "I am grateful for the time I've had. I wouldn't want to covet that which others don't have either. Sixty-five years is long enough to walk this earth, to use her resources. It's time to cede the space to somebody else." Janet leaned forward again and picked up a pen, turning it over in her hands. Varya swallowed and rubbed the back of her neck, running her hand along the vertebrae, wondering if the bumps she could feel were bone or microchip. They buried the Time Chips so deeply it was impossible to tell without an ultrasound.

"I've prepared a full update for you on my research. I've left the notes so you can brief the next scientist on the project after my Rest Time. But, Varya, I do think it's time to look at calling on the expertise of your ex-husband's department. They might have already solved this particular problem. It's not the kind of thing they'd publicise, but I'm sure he'd tell you."

Varya nodded. "I know," she murmured.

"So, you'll get in touch with him?"

"I'll think about it. There's no rush."

"And your mother? Is she in a rush?"

Varya glared at her. "Is that all?"

Langford sighed. "Yes. That's all." She stood and turned as though to walk around the desk to Varya, but then stopped and held out her hand instead. "It's been an honour to work with you, it really has. I hope you find everything you're looking for."

Varya nodded stiffly, rose, and shook the proffered hand gently, holding it longer than she thought she should. She would be one of the last people to clasp this woman's hand while blood still coursed through her veins. Varya met Janet's eye and held her gaze for a moment.

"Thank you," she said. She bit her lip and opened her mouth, then closed it again. "Thank you." And then Varya left the office, closing the door behind her.

CHAPTER SIX

When Varya next looked up from her work, it was to discover that the lab was almost empty. What had broken her concentration was a figure standing in front of her. The static electricity he created by standing so close had displaced the air around her and made her look up.

Connor grinned at her.

"Finally. I thought I was going to have to tap you on the shoulder and risk getting my fingers bitten off."

Varya looked around at the empty lab and frowned.

"Is it that late already?" She was used to the way time stretched and shifted now, with her ever-increasing use of the time tabs to get everything done. But she was careful to never take them at work. Never in a public place.

Connor's expression softened. "No, it's a Rest Time Celebration."

Varya's face fell slightly before she swallowed and forced her expression to be blank, feigning indifference. Nobody could know of her deeper connection to Janet Langford, or her true status at the Minor Miracles Foundation. They had to believe she was just another lab tech.

"Who?" she asked.

"Professor Langford, the one with the long grey..."

Varya waved him away impatiently. "Yes, everyone knows who Professor Langford is."

Connor held his hands up in surrender. "Okay, well, I just thought you might want to..."

"Yes. Thank you. I'm coming." Flustered now, she gave her bench a quick once-over, replaced a sample into a glass container, turned the microscope off, and nodded to Connor. She followed him out of the room and down the long hallway to the breakout room.

Professor Langford had chosen to have her Rest Time Celebration at the laboratories. She'd never had children or married. Her work was her entire life, time extension credits well-earned. Connor and Varya padded into the room quietly and joined the back of the crowd.

A large electric clock counted down the minutes and seconds. Twenty-three minutes until Rest Time. A young woman sobbed quietly but theatrically at the front of the crowd. Cynthia, the acting as director of ceremonies for today, shot her a thunderous look. She stopped sobbing and sniffled quietly to herself.

"Thank you, Marcus, for your kind words." Cynthia smiled to a young man who had just sat down. Varya recognised him as the last scientist Professor Langford had hired, three years ago. Referred to as her protégée, it was expected that he would now progress through the ranks and, one day, become a professor himself. Varya wondered whether Langford had confided in him about her special research project. She'd been so jarred by Janet's revelation earlier in the day that she hadn't thought to ask who she thought would be her best successor.

"Does anyone else want to say a few words, before we hear from Professor Langford herself?" Cynthia asked, scanning the room, raised on her tiptoes.

Varya stared at the grey-haired woman sitting up the front, facing her colleagues for the last time. Langford caught her eye and stared back. Varya nodded slightly; Langford returned the gesture.

"Sorry," Langford mouthed wordlessly.

Varya shook her head. "No," she mouthed back. "Thank you." Her chest compressed inwards for just a moment before she breathed deeply and managed to compose herself. She quietly brushed away a few tears.

Langford stared for a moment longer as someone else spouted a few platitudes. Then she nodded again and looked away.

"And now, with just ten minutes to go until Rest Time, we'll hear from Professor Langford herself," Cynthia announced, indicating Janet with what she clearly thought was a grand gesture.

Langford opened her mouth and started to speak, but Varya couldn't hear over the ringing in her ears that signalled a rising panic.

Janet Langford sat in a government-issued Rest Time chair. Made from moulded plastic, the deep ocean blue colour made it look more comfortable and peaceful than it really was. The high back supported Langford's head as she leaned against it. It had slight grooves all around so that when Langford slumped into the chair's slight incline, the shallow shelves would catch her head and prevent her neck from lolling around in an undignified fashion. The heavily embroidered cloth that ran the length of her lap and washed over each arm rest—reminding Varya of a table runner—hid the thick band that held Langford to the chair and would prevent her sliding off it altogether. The moulded plastic chair arms were wide enough to hold each of Langford's forearms and help her stay in an upright position for the duration of the ceremony.

The digital clock showed one minute to go. Varya felt like she was going to throw up. She stumbled and Connor caught her elbow to hold her steady.

"Thank you for your sixty-five years and for your sacrifice," Cynthia intoned.

"Thank you for your sixty-five years and for your sacrifice," the crowd responded.

The numbers on the clock turned red.

Ten... nine... Varya knew the programmed chip inserted into Langford's brain stem had activated itself now.

Eight... seven... Langford stared at the clock and tensed.

Six... five... The crowd was silent.

Four... three... Langford's arms began to relax. The first wave of drugs had been released: the calmative.

Two... one... She tensed suddenly again, jerking slightly, and threw her head back. The second wave—the poison—flowed through her system.

And then she was still.

And then she was gone.

Two uniformed figures appeared from behind to drape a white silken bag over the top of Langford and her chair.

"Be at rest forevermore," intoned Cynthia.

"Be at rest forevermore," repeated the crowd.

Varya forced herself to watch as the uniformed officers tipped the chair back and extended the handles which turned the whole structure into a kind of stretcher. They lifted and carried her out of the open door. Varya held her breath until they were out of sight.

"I have to get back to work," Varya muttered to Connor.

CHAPTER SEVEN

Varya relished her time with her mother and son even more than usual that evening. She watched the two from afar as they bent down to inspect a rose bush. Her mother's steely hair glinted in the sunlight. It was always sunny there, no matter how many seasons passed in Varya's life. The air was always cool, with that crisp autumn freshness.

It was as though she looked upon the scene through a glass of water. The boy appeared to shimmer slightly as he reached out to the thorny plant with an open palm; the older woman gently held his wrist and pulled him back, shaking her head with a soft chuckle.

Varya missed her mother with a desperate ache sometimes. She had been used to being able to call her any time of day to ask for her advice. More often than not they ended up arguing—both women stubbornly sure that they were right—but when their conversation ended, Varya always felt clearer in her mind. Calmer, better able to do whatever needed to be done.

In between these now-daily visits, Varya had taken to having conversations with her mother in her mind, playing the role of antagonist herself. But it wasn't the same. She could never quite see things the way her mother did. Instead, her thoughts were muddied by dozens of shades of grey in between the black and the white.

Varya smiled now as she watched her mother. Her son was well cared for there, among the spring flowers. She took a step forward and reached out her hand. The air rippled, like a gentle vertical wave. It felt akin to caressing a cloud and, as always, she felt drawn to the shield between the two worlds. Moving closer, she pressed her face into its shimmering aura and stood on the borderline soaking up the miracle that was this opportunity to see her son each night, as though he were still here. Her son. Varya stepped through and smiled, opened her arms.

"Mummy, Mummy!" The small boy ran to her. He tripped and fell but he didn't cry. There was never blood in here, no grazes, no bruises. Varya strode quickly to meet him as he stood and brushed himself off.

"Kir, my baby boy. Come here." She crouched and picked him up, inhaling the scent of baby shampoo in his eternally freshly-washed hair. She pressed her cheek against his and tried not to cry. No more harm can come to him here. He is safe, she told herself.

Varya peered over his head at her mother, who was straightening up slowly and rubbing her back.

"I can't stay for long," Varya told her.

Elena nodded. "You need your rest. You're tired. You should use this time to sleep." The words echoed strangely, slightly tinny, as they always did.

Varya shook her head. "No. This is more important than rest."

Elena limped over and placed a hand on Varya's cheek.

"And a cure is vital. But you must rest, allow your mind to wander and find a solution."

Varya moved, just slightly, but enough to deflect the older woman's hand.

"My mind must focus to find a solution, Mama. And I can't focus if I'm asleep."

Elena sighed and swatted dismissively at the air between them.

"Bah. You work too hard. Find your peace and what you seek will come to you."

She hobbled past Varya, heading toward a nearby park bench. The sound of her walking stick struck the pavement loudly, echoing in the silence. No joggers passed them in this unearthly park. No parents walking with babies, nor dogs trotting alongside their owners. Even the birds were quiet. Elena sat, resting her hands atop her walking stick, and watched.

"What do you want to do tonight, little one?" Varya asked her son.

"I want a guitar, Mummy. Can I have a guitar? I want to make music. I've seen pictures of guitars, but we can't find a music shop. We've walked and walked but there isn't one. Where can we find one?"

"I'm not sure, baby boy. I'll find out for you, okay?"

Kir nodded vigorously. "Then we can go on a guitar treasure hunt. I like treasure hunts. We went on a puppy dog treasure hunt today and I found five puppy dogs!"

"Is that so?"

"Yep. There was a brown one and a black one and one that is called a Dalmartian."

Varya laughed. "You mean a Dalmatian."

"No, Mummy, a Dalmartian. He came from outer space in his rocket ship I think, or a whizzing round saucer, I'm not sure because he couldn't talk but I did ask him."

The boy peered up at her earnestly. Then he gave her a coy smile.

"But it might just be pretend, but I'm not telling," he whispered.

"Bah, flying dogs. That boy's head is filled with nonsense. It's this place, Varya. It plays tricks with the mind." The old woman stomped her stick on the ground.

"I'd like to meet your Dalmartian one day, baby boy. You say hi, from me, next time you see him, okay?"

"Okay, Mummy."

"I have to go now, sweetheart. I'll be back soon."

The boy pouted. "You always go. You never stay."

"Mummy needs her sleep." Elena appeared behind him and took his hand.

"I want to go, too. I want to sleep, too." Kir snatched his small, smooth hand out of his Nanna's gnarled, wrinkled one.

"Aye. I wish you could, believe me. Following you around all day would exhaust me, if I could still be genuinely exhausted in this place." Elena took his elbow and gently tugged. "I think I saw a possum just before. Shall we check to see if he's still there?"

"Where? Where was he?"

Elena gestured vaguely off into the distance. The boy moved with what seemed like lightning speed.

"'Bye, Mum!" he yelled as he went.

Varya held her hand up in a silent salute. She exchanged a nod with her mother but hesitated.

"He's safe with me," Elena told her. "Go now."

"No pain?" asked Varya, knowing the answer, but still uncertain.

"No pain." Elena shook her head. "It's still a good day, this long, long everlasting day. Always a good day."

Varya nodded and felt the tears gather in her chest.

"Thank you, Mama. Thank you."

Elena smiled slowly. She picked up a small black box from the park bench and slipped in into her dress pocket. "I'll move this back into the apartment for your next visit. I don't think we'll be out here tomorrow." She waved her walking stick at Varya. "Now, shoo. Go back to where you came from and take your rest."

Varya inched her way back through the shimmering air. She watched the little boy becoming smaller and smaller. She closed her eyes and the vista dissolved. She closed her mind and slipped into a deep and peaceful sleep.

CHAPTER EIGHT

"Okay, I'm heading off. You're all right to take Daniel to school today?" Zoe swung her handbag up onto her shoulder and picked up her medical bag. Before Varya had left the night before they'd hastily worked out a schedule of drop-offs and pick-ups so Daniel wouldn't have to walk to and from school by himself. They were leaving nothing to chance—Ben Williams still hadn't shown up. After two days and no word, it was clear he wasn't going to come home of his own accord.

Varya looked up from where she sat on the couch next to Daniel. The boy watched spaceships fly around the wall screen, shooting at each other, while Varya scanned medical journals on the screen on her lap.

"Yes. Yes, that's fine," she answered. "I'm starting late and finishing late. You'll pick him up from school?"

Zoe nodded. "Yes, I'll get him. I'll do a short shift." She held her hand up to Daniel, trying to get her son's attention. "See you later, hon'. Be good for Varya."

Daniel raised his left hand in salute, without taking his eyes off the screen. Zoe rolled her eyes, nodded to Varya, and headed down the hallway. Varya heard the door shut behind her friend as she headed out for the day shift at the city's palliative care unit. A good death, a painless death, that's what the goal was. But always death. The children who Zoe cared for were beyond the point of recovery. There were no extra treatments to try or experimental programs to get them into. There was no cure, no hope. Only waiting, good-byes, and a good and painless death.

That's what they'd told her about Kir five years ago. The tumour was too advanced, it had wrapped itself around his tiny heart. Do a transplant, she'd said. Not possible, the surgeons had shaken their heads. Too close to an artery. Too rare. Too many unknown variables. Too young. No hope.

Prepare for a good and painless death.

That was the point at which she'd met Zoe, in that room with the animals and rainbows printed on white walls. The tubes and beeping monitors decorated with brightly coloured circles.

"How are his pain levels today?" she'd ask as she popped in to say 'hi' at the start or end of her rounds. In the early days they were good, not bad at all. Maybe they could just take him home? Maybe Zoe could talk to their paediatrician? Zoe had hesitated, suggested she and Varya grab a drink in the hospital cafeteria while Kir slept.

Yes, Varya could take her son home, Zoe explained as she stirred her sweetener into a strong, black tea—it was quickly becoming the new national drink since the coffee supplies had started to dry up—but things could turn very quickly and he would be more comfortable at the hospital. Varya could stay beside him. But that tumour, wrapped around the artery. It could choke it at any time. It would cause pain to Kir that couldn't be treated at home. Or the tumour in his brain could rupture, causing seizures. Which, again, could only be treated at hospital.

A rare cancer, they'd been told. Aggressive, sudden, but silent until it had grabbed her son in a chokehold. No cure. Too fast.

Eventually, Zoe explained, when the pain became too much for Kir's tiny body—when, not if, she said—Varya could ask her paediatrician to slowly increase the morphine in his drip, keeping him out of pain. He would become drowsy and calm. Varya would probably have the chance to say a final goodbye before they increased the dose a final time and allowed him to slip into his forever rest.

This was all before Varya decided to take Kir home, despite the medical advice. Before Sebastian said his own goodbyes and left them.

Varya clenched her fists and glanced across at Daniel, willing her heartbeat to slow, her breath to even out. She tried to bring herself back to the present, to connect with the people who were still here.

She breathed in one final time and exhaled slowly and audibly. Daniel looked up at her.

"Hungry?" she asked.

"Always," he answered, stretching his skinny arms above his head.

Varya smiled. This kid, Zoe's kid, kept her anchored. His long-limbed loping ways were at times painfully reminiscent of an awkward age that her own son had never reached but comforting to have around.

She stood now, placing her screen on the low table, and heading out of the small living room to their even smaller kitchen. Rummaging around in the fridge and pantry, she came up with a simple breakfast platter of cheese, crackers, and dried fruit. Daniel glanced at it with a frown as she laid it down on the coffee table between. He paused the space-ships on the big screen, leapt over the arm of the sofa, thun-dered into the kitchen, opened and shut a few cupboards, then stalked back into the living room with a hunk of dried sausage and a stack of rye bread.

Varya smiled and went back to her screen, perched on a bar stool, chewing on a dried apricot. They sat in compan-ionable silence for several minutes.

"Varya..."

Varya looked up from the medical journal she was poring over, surprised to hear Daniel speak her name. Normally she was lucky to get a grunt or a 'hey'.

"Daniel," she responded in kind.

"What was it like, back when people got old? Like, you know, older than sixty-five?"

Varya was glad he was still looking at the wall screen as she tried to arrange her face into something approaching a suitable adult expression. She cleared her throat but failed to start. She took a deep breath. Daniel twisted around to face her, bringing his knees up and resting his elbow on the back cushion.

"You know, before Rest Time?" he pressed.

"Yes, Daniel, I knew what you meant," she said, more curtly than she'd intended. She paused. Images of her grand-mother's disapproving face flashed through her mind, skin cool and smooth in the valleys between the wrinkled peaks.

Tell him the truth, her grandmother's ghost seemed to whisper to her. Varya shook her head.

"It was... terrible," she said brightly. Daniel's face fell slightly, and Nanna shook her head in disgust. Varya swallowed and pressed on with the official version. "Once people reached their eighties, sometimes as early as their seventies, their minds and bodies would start to deteriorate. An entire aged care industry sprung up to care for them, often abusing them behind closed doors. Many lost their minds to dementia, they stopped recognising their own children." She told the story with all the enthusiasm of a spooky ghost tale on Halloween. It rang false even to her own ears.

Daniel had that faraway look in his eyes. He'd stopped listening.

"But surely not everyone was like that?" he interjected. "A kid at school says that he heard somewhere that lots of old people used to be fine, that they even kept working into their nineties." His eyes lit up now. "He said he found a story about an old lady who went out every day to feed her sheep with hay bales from the back of her pick-up truck in the drought of 2018. She was eighty-nine. That's twenty-four extra years on top of what we get." Daniel stopped and looked at Varya expectantly. Imaginary Nanna crossed her arms, leaned against her bright, yellow Laminex bench, and raised both eyebrows questioningly.

"Daniel," she started, in her best imitation of what she understood to be a 'teacher voice'. The challenging look on Daniel's face told her she'd got the tone right. "Daniel... yes, you're right. There were certainly some people who lived well into their nineties independently. They kept working, earning money, stayed healthy, and needed little help." Daniel regarded her triumphantly. "But..." She held a finger up in the air. He glowered at her. "But most of those who were over sixty-five started to decline almost immediately. Their health fell apart, with multiple and complex issues, they stopped working and became a drain on the economy. The healthy, younger people had to pay higher taxes to fund the infirm for decades after they'd stopped contributing to society. The droughts and the storms, the earthquakes, and the bushfires, they kept coming. Resources were scarce and, as a society, we simply couldn't afford to support a massive section of the population who couldn't support themselves. The birth rate continued to decline, and people realised that this was actually a good thing for the planet, for the environment. And so, we went about transitioning to a new economic system and looked at other ways to reduce our population gradually and sustainably. This—the Rest Time Chips—was one of them."

Varya had been a teenager when Rest Time was introduced in Australia. They'd still been behind the early adopters—China and Russia—but ahead of many others, including most African and Pacific Nations. For a while, these countries hadn't needed Rest Time, or the Time Chips—the brutal effects of climate change had taken care of their overpopulation problems. Western Europe and the United Kingdom were still arguing amongst themselves about exceptions and enforcement protocols. But it was coming, even there.

At first it had been voluntary in Australia, with lethal injections provided to those good citizens who were selfless enough to want to ease the burden on their children and grandchildren. But then the food and fuel shortages worsened, the recession turned into a depression and dragged on. The government reduced medical support to over-sixty-fives. Then they reduced the pension at the same time the price of food sky-rocketed. Wealthier elderly, and those who had wealthy children, were taken care of. The lower and middle classes suffered the most. Emaciated bodies were more and more commonly being removed from private aged care homes. Mysterious outbreaks of influenza in government-funded aged care facilities took care of large numbers of the elderly. Research into illnesses which commonly affected the elderly, such as dementia and arthritis, ceased due to their strategic funding cuts.

The slow squeeze was successful. Octogenarians started to show up at their local doctor requesting a lethal injection kit. Septuagenarians looked around and began to see they were the next to go. Retirement wasn't something anyone spoke about or looked forward to anymore. People held onto their jobs, literally for dear life, fearful of being labelled unproductive and being tapped on the shoulder. The meaningful glances, the unsolicited information: "Did you hear they've started selling those injection kits over the counter, if you've got I.D. that shows you're over sixty-five?"

The government ensured the time evangelists were given an ever-increasingly large platform. A program was launched to send these productivity advocates into schools to talk about the innate satisfaction of working hard and living life to the fullest while you were young and healthy. They preached that a life of idleness was detrimental to your health and wellbeing and that those who idled were a drain on society.

The invention of the Rest Time Chips by a joint Australia-China eminent research facility simply breathed permanency into the new end-of-life ritual.

"But before Rest Time Chips, kids weren't taken away so people could steal their years," said Daniel quietly. His expression was reproachful and mournful at the same time.

Varya's heart caught. Imaginary Nanna wiped a tear from her eye and sniffed.

"People have always fought over scarce resources," Varya began, gentler this time. "Oil, gold, land, water. And time has always been a scarce resource. It's just that, in the past, nobody really knew how much of that particular commodity they had, until they ran out of it."

"But now we do know."

Varya nodded. "Yes. Now we know. And now some people fight because the Rest Time Chips have turned time into a commodity that can be bought and sold. And, of course, stolen."

Daniel thought for a moment. "Maybe sixty-five years is enough."

"Maybe." Varya shrugged and turned away, suddenly exhausted.

"I hope Ben comes back soon," Daniel mumbled.

Varya closed her eyes, wishing she could pretend she hadn't heard him. But she was the only one here for Daniel right now. She ran her finger around the edge of the medical journal article on her screen: *The interaction of Rest Time Chips with the nervous system and their effects on the body during life.* She wondered if she should leave Zoe and Daniel, whether her dependence on them for emotional contact had delayed the achievement of her goal by soaking up precious time. Perhaps focusing on another child had dulled her sense of urgency. As her fingertip traced the edge of the screen once more, she pressed gently just after the curve. The screen went black as she pushed herself off the bar stool. Her feet felt heavy as she found her way around the back of the couch and sat down next to this child that wasn't hers but was hers to care for right now. She gently pulled him into her, resting his head on her chest.

"I hope so, too," she whispered into his hair.

CHAPTER NINE

Varya's car lurched forward as it prepared to swing into the kerb in front of Daniel's school finally, after waiting nearly fifteen minutes in a queue that backed up all the way to the end of the narrow street. Traffic was stopped up at the main road thanks to worried parents all insisting on dropping their kids right at the school gate.

The music on the car radio faded as they pulled to a stop. The announcer calmly informed them that, "*Police still have no leads in the case of the disappearance of nine-year-old Ben Williams. Relatives and friends have all been questioned but evidence is pointing towards an abduction. A spokesperson for Rest Time Corps has dismissed rumours that the time thieves may be active again and has asked for patience from the public in what they're calling an 'isolated incident.' A search of the forest surrounding his house commenced at sunrise today, with dozens of volunteers...*"

Varya pushed a button to silence the woman's voice. She scanned the road before unlocking the car doors and nodding to Daniel. Daniel didn't move. He sat, gazing out the window, both hands on the schoolbag at his feet. A car horn sounded behind them.

"Hey, Dan. Come on, kid. Time to go," she said gently.

Daniel took an enormously long breath in and blew it slowly and noisily out of his flared nostrils. He nodded. Without looking at Varya he pushed the car door so hard it swung out and bounced back slightly.

"Sorry," he mumbled, eyes still cast to the floor.

"It's okay."

But it wasn't okay, thought Varya, as she watched him walk through the school gate to safety, before driving away. Ben Williams was out there somewhere. With someone. They were all just stumbling about in the fog, trying to make sense of this new world until everything returned to normal.

If, she chastised herself. *If* everything returned to normal.

"Send message to Zoe. Daniel safe at school. End message." She spoke clearly and confidently to her car.

"Message sent," it replied serenely.

Varya had a sudden urge to swing the car around, call to Daniel and tell him to get back in, and to drive as fast and as far away as possible. But when she looked in the rear-view mirror another car had already taken her place.

Varya swallowed her foreboding and joined the stream of vehicles heading away from the school and towards workplaces. She needed to focus on finding cures, to keep other children safe. Potential kidnappers were not the only threat to a child's safety. And besides, she admitted to herself, she found it was far easier to think of many, faceless, needy children than one familiar, vulnerable child.

CHAPTER TEN

Zoe

Ben Williams walked into Gillard Memorial Hospital at 9.43 a.m. that same day. News items would later describe how his mother walked by his side, her hand at his back, her face pale. His father walked behind him, bringing up the rear, as though he could shut the gate after the horse had bolted. Ben walked like a robot, almost gliding along the floor.

Dr Zoe Parker would tell reporters that she didn't see them come in, but she heard the commotion outside. She'd been doing her rounds, checking up on Annie, a six-year-old girl suffering from a rare form of brain cancer. She always left Annie until last. A year ago, the diagnosis would have been terminal. Zoe would have been prescribing anti-seizure drugs and pain relief. Palliative care only. Rare forms of cancer didn't warrant research investment from the government.

Annie was lucky, Zoe would tell the journalist who later wrote a twelve-hundred-word feature article on the incident. The Minor Miracles Foundation facility had been working on a cure for years. And they'd found one, just in time for Annie to receive it.

Zoe had smiled at the young girl just before Ben walked down that corridor, the article would begin: "Another week and we'll have to send you home, Annie."

Annie's mother had beamed. "Really?"

Dr Parker heard a muffled roar of noise from the corridor. She left Annie's room in time to see the ward doors burst open and Ben Williams appear, flanked by his parents and a team of medical staff.

"I recognised him from the news articles. He goes to my son's school, but I'd never met him," said Dr Parker.

Mrs Williams howled in grief as the doors swung closed behind them, muffling the noise of the media, shutting out the bright lights of their cameras.

A colleague of Dr Parker's pushed them forward gently.

"We need to get him to the scanner, to check his date," Dr Martin told her.

A hush fell over the group then, Dr Parker remembers. That was the point at which she believed the authorities shed the pretence that they thought the abduction had no connection to the horrific time thefts the country endured a decade ago.

Dr Martin opened the door to the treatment room and ushered Ben and his parents in, closing the door to allow them some privacy. Dr Parker described the procedure:

"Dr Martin would have taken the scanner out from its cupboard and plugged it in to charge it a little. It's so rarely used these days, since… He would have asked Ben to sit sideways on the chair, to present the back of his neck to him. There would have been a soft beep as he held the scanner above Ben's Rest Time Chip."

Dr Parker confirmed she had not heard the beep from outside the room, but everyone standing in the corridor that day heard Ms William's cry of anguish as Dr Martin explained to her that her son would be dead before nightfall.

With tears streaming down her face, Dr Parker described how her own legs buckled temporarily. She then ran down three flights of stairs to the car park, found her car, and drove to her son's school. She needed to feel her arms around him, to keep him safe.

CHAPTER ELEVEN

Varya

Varya went back to her own apartment after leaving Daniel at school that morning. She'd rescheduled her meeting with Marisa but there were time tab orders that needed to be filled.

When Zoe's call came through, she was sitting on the sofa in her living room, staring at a picture of her own son and mother, while Marisa counted the packages in the kitchen. In the photograph, her mother was smiling; Kir was pouting. He was so adorable when he sulked. It never lasted long. How could she help keep someone else's child safe when she'd failed her own child so badly?

Zoe's name flashed on the screen. She picked it up immediately. "Zoe? Is Daniel okay?"

"Yes, he's fine," came Zoe's voice. "I mean, I think he's fine. I haven't heard anything. Why, have you heard something?"

"No, I haven't. Where are you? Has something happened?" Varya recognised the note of anxiety in her friend's voice.

"I... I'm outside Daniel's school. I just... I had to be near him."

Varya pictured Zoe sitting at the school's front gate in her car, just as she had earlier that morning. Beyond the wire fence was a strip of green, a concrete path and a flat-roofed building, its walls still stained orange. A fashionable colour for 1976.

Varya heard Zoe tap her fingers frenetically on the steering wheel. She felt the strong urge along with her, while she also tried to resist it: the desperate need to leap out of the car and bang on the classroom windows, shouting for her son. She picked up the photograph of Kir and her mother and placed it on her lap.

"Zo'?" Varya prompted.

"It's Ben Williams. They found him." Zoe sniffed and her breath came in irregular gasps. "I saw him at the hospital, he came in this morning. He looked fine, not hurt, but... Varya, they scanned his date."

Varya swallowed and pinched the edge of the photo frame, feeling the sting from the rough metal against her skin, trying to anchor herself to the present. She felt like she might just float away, her head was spinning.

"It didn't sound good," Zoe blurted out, before she started sobbing.

"I'm so sorry. Oh, Zoe, I'm so sorry." It wasn't her fault, she knew it wasn't her fault, not really. But she felt so responsible. Her hand shook as she replaced Kir's photo on the side table, not trusting her trembling hands to hold it. She stood and began to walk, as though forward motion could somehow help.

"It's happening again, Varya, it's time thieves, it must be. I don't know what to do. How can I keep Daniel safe?"

Varya wanted to tell her to run into the school and hold onto Daniel and never let him out of her sight. But it made no sense to pull him out of school now. Enmeshed in the day-to-day routines, he probably wasn't even thinking of his absent friend. They should leave him there to enjoy the bliss of ignorance for a few more hours.

"Just keep doing what you're doing," she told Zoe instead. "Make sure you're there to pick him up. Let me know if you need me to step in."

"Can't you do something, though? For Ben, even? You know about these things. You know, from before, from last time. You can help." It was an accusation disguised as a plea.

Varya stopped walking and sat down heavily on a kitchen chair, opposite Marisa. She dug her fingers into the thin seat cushion and felt her jaw clench.

"Zoe, I..."

"I'm sorry. I shouldn't have said anything. It's just... I'm sorry. I have to go."

The call ended abruptly. Varya put the phone on the table and laid both her hands over it. She stared across her kitchen into nothingness. Eventually her eyes focused on the small black box perched on a high shelf. Her body shook involuntarily for a moment.

CHAPTER TWELVE

Marisa

Marisa looked at her expectantly, having heard the one-sided conversation and drawn her own conclusions. Varya met her gaze and shook her head.

"I need to get back to work," was all she said.

Marisa knew Varya would be thinking that maybe if she immersed herself in the research this would all blow over soon. It was how her employer and friend operated. Work herself into the ground until the problem had magically been resolved. Marisa had to grant that it had worked well so far for most of Varya's problems—as long as those problems were related to finding treatments for illnesses for which research had previously been underfunded.

Marisa forced herself to breathe evenly. She would need to tread lightly if she were to persuade Varya to get involved in something her instincts were telling her to run from.

"They found the kid? Ben Williams?" she started.

"Yes."

"Bad news, huh?"

"Looks that way, yes." Varya looked down at the packages scattered on the table in front of Marisa. "That's all of them for tonight's drop, yes?"

Marisa shuffled a couple around and nodded.

"Okay. Then we're done here." Varya stood up. Marisa didn't.

It infuriated Marisa that she even had to bring this up. She was quite sure that Varya would have thought of it herself already but dismissed it as too risky. Varya was very good at doing what was necessary for herself and her family. But when it came to helping others, she could be extremely reticent. Marisa shrugged off her indignation. She couldn't fault her for looking out for her family first. It was just human instinct. And the Minor Miracles Foundation had helped dozens of people and their families, which seemed to suit Varya just fine, as long as she didn't have to actually meet any of them.

"The kid, the one that was taken," said Marisa. "He's a friend of your friend's kid, right?"

"Sort of. They're in the same class. I don't think they're close though."

"You could help him, then. If you think they'd stay quiet."

"Help him?" Varya bristled. "I can't tamper with Rest Time Chips. Nobody can."

Marisa snorted. "Well, clearly somebody's figured out how to. Least you could do is give the kid a few time tabs on the house. Just 'til one of the good guys figures out how to tamper his Chip back for him."

Varya leaned over and began putting the packages back into the waiting box.

"Not much point in delaying the inevitable if he's only got a short time left," she said, her tone dull.

Marisa bit her tongue. If this were a time thief copycat, a few days would be the most that Ben Williams could hope to have with his family. She may not have a PhD but the mere fact that the kid's family had time to bring him to the hospital and scan his Chip suggested these new thieves were either more compassionate or less accurate in judgement.

"Not sure his family would agree with you there." Marisa took the box that Varya held out. "I'm just saying, it seems like the kind of thing we could help with."

"We sell a product to fundraise for a medical research facility. We don't get involved in police matters," said Varya flatly.

Marisa held up her free hand. "Alright, alright. I'm just saying."

"Save your talking for our clients."

"Yes, boss." Her tone held a little more sarcasm than she'd intended.

Varya stood, bent forward, hands pressed into the edge of the table, eyes gazing into the mid-distance. She frowned.

"I guess I'll see myself out then," muttered Marisa. She should have known better than to get involved. Maybe it was just a one-off abduction. Just one kid. But she knew from hard experience that if that 'just one kid' happened to be your one kid, the relative global scale of the catastrophe bore little weight on the cataclysmic effect it had on your life. She blinked rapidly and stood.

"What? Yes. Thanks." Varya picked up the empty coffee mugs from the table and turned toward the sink, her mind elsewhere.

Marisa took her cue and left.

CHAPTER THIRTEEN

"Fifteen. I ordered fifteen four-hour strips. There are only ten in here."

Marisa frowned as she peered into the matchbox and shuffled the time tabs around.

"Ah, sorry." She delved back into her bag and pulled out another small box. She opened it and tipped the contents onto her palm. One tab escaped and fluttered onto the side table, coming to rest next to her coffee cup.

"Careful with that." The large woman in the bed har-rumphed and pushed ruby-rimmed glasses up her nose with a swollen-knuckled finger. "Don't want it contaminated with your hideous poison."

Marisa glanced down at her cooling coffee and raised a questioning eyebrow. "Whole lot more natural than dosing yourself with time-altering chemicals," she muttered.

"What? Speak up, girl, I can't hear you."

Marisa slid the matchbox closed. "Fifteen now, all there." She held out the correct tally and presented an empty palm for payment. The woman obediently placed her defective box into Marisa's palm and snatched the new one, holding it to her chest and closing her eyes. She began to hum. Marisa cleared her throat. The woman hummed more loudly.

"Mrs Denisovitch?"

The woman cracked her eyelids open wide enough to be able to narrow them at Marisa.

"Really know how to spoil a moment, don't you, girl?"

Marisa shrugged and waggled her screen at Mrs Denisovitch, head cocked slightly. It had been several decades since she could reasonably be described as a 'girl' and she was taking none of this woman's sass now. Truth be told, Mrs Denisovitch was barely more than fifteen years her senior.

The woman sighed and sat up a little straighter, reaching around the pillows for her own screen. Never letting go of the matchbox, she placed her palm on the screen and then tapped it a few times before dumping it back on the side table.

"There. Done. Now leave me in peace to be able to enjoy my few extra hours of glorious music before they take me out of this hell-hole and put me to rest permanently."

Marisa refreshed her screen to confirm the payment had been received. 'Donation to med resrch', it read. She put her screen in her coat pocket and picked up her coffee cup. Mrs Denisovitch might want her gone quickly, but she wasn't about to pass up the opportunity to finish her free liquid gold. Besides, this was the one place she could safely conduct business all day without having to worry about being questioned. Palliative care for the wealthy. Ironic, really, that euthanasia was still illegal in most countries, but once you hit the magic sixty-five-year mark you'd be put out of your misery, whether you liked it or not. Marisa's clients in palliative care used the tabs as soon as their next round of pain relief kicked in, to extend the agony-free hours they had remaining. Marisa drained her cup and placed it back on the saucer. She straightened her badge—'Volunteer'—and stood up.

Mrs Denisovitch opened both eyes and pushed herself up off the pillows.

"That kiddie that got snatched. Your lot have anything to do with that?"

"What kid?" Marisa feigned ignorance, picking at her nail, and wondering whether her own knuckles would start to swell with arthritis soon. A warm climate to retire to, that's what she needed. Sometimes when she looked at the pamphlets, she could just about the feel the warm rays beating out of them.

"Good grief girl, don't you pay attention to the world around you?"

She shrugged. "Not if I can help it."

"Got snatched outside school a couple days ago. Dropped back today. Expired just a few minutes ago. Just like all those other kids, all those years ago." Mrs Denisovitch looked Marisa up and down and sneered. "Not that you'd remember. You can't be more than, what, twelve?"

"Forty-seven, actually, but thanks." Marisa shuddered, remembering. Varya had been right, then. That poor kid hadn't stood a chance.

"So, it wasn't your lot, then."

Marisa gave a small smile. She wondered if Mrs Denisovitch lay awake imagining a whole network of time-giving angels wandering around the country selling time tabs to the dying wealthy. She didn't realise just how lucky she was to live within a five-mile radius of one of the few remaining time engineers.

"Nope, not us."

"Mmph." Mrs Denisovitch sank back and closed her eyes again. With a flick of her wrist, she dismissed Marisa. "Go, then. Come back next week."

Marisa grinned and gave a three-finger salute before she turned on her heel and moved onto her next client.

Three rooms down the hallway, she nodded and smiled faintly while Mr Keats recounted how he had secretly read half of Shakespeare's complete works in four-hour blocks while under the influence of time tabs.

"Secretly?"

Mr Keats tapped the side of his nose and leered towards her.

"You never know what they'll hold against you next," he told her in a stage whisper. "Might ban the bard sometime soon. Literature like that can be terribly inflammatory."

"Mmm." Marisa twisted her mouth and turned back to the screen on the wall, sipping her next cup of coffee.

"*Nine-year-old boy returned to parents dies. Community fears time thieves.*"

Video footage showed Ben Williams' grief-stricken parents shielded from the media as they were ushered from their home into a waiting police car.

Mr Keats finally exhausted his point and focussed in on Marisa's gaze. He swiped at his personal screen until the sound on the wall screen rose.

"*Nine-year-old Ben Williams was taken two days ago from his home in Waterdown. This morning we brought you the good news that he had been reunited with his family.*"

Cue scenes of a stunned boy being hugged by his parents and photographed by dozens.

"*Tragically, this happy family reunion was shattered just hours later when the child's Rest Time Chip malfunctioned and triggered his death, some fifty-six years early. Police say it's too early in their investigation to speculate as to what could have caused the malfunction.*"

More video footage, this time of a haggard-looking man peering around his front door.

"*Rest Time chips don't malfunction. There's no precedent. This has to be the time thief gangs again,*" he said.

"*Can you tell us why you think that, sir?*" A faceless voice demanded as a microphone inched closer to him.

"*Because I've seen it before. Ten years ago, I lost my nine-year-old son, too.*" His next words were lost to a choked sob. He sniffed and wiped his sleeve across his nose and reddened eyes in one movement. "*I'm sorry, I can't.*" He slammed the door and the screen flicked back to the in-studio presenter. Marisa jerked her head around, lips pursed, as the volume went silent. She opened her mouth to speak but Mr Keats shook his head.

"I'd rather not re-live it, if you don't mind, love. I don't have many days left. I just want to use my time tabs to disappear into my bubble of sonnets." He gave a flourish of his hand, as though the performance was at an end.

Marisa nodded. "Fair enough. I'll leave you to it."

"Thank you."

She stood and paused for a moment, watching the strapline change.

"*Too few similarities to time thief gangs, say police.*"

Marisa snorted softly. A ninety-five per cent match was enough, surely. The fact that they'd left a few hours on the Chip for the family to say goodbye, didn't change the general

pattern of events. Somebody out there had clearly resur-
rected the technology to transfer time between Rest Time
Chips.

"Close the door on the way out, if you wouldn't mind, love,"
said Mr Keats, sitting up in bed and clutching a thick volume
of plays. His outstretched palm held a single blue time tab.

Marisa held his gaze for a moment then left, gently letting
the door click shut after her.

CHAPTER FOURTEEN

Varya

Much later that night—after she'd spent enough hours sitting in her lab, unable to concentrate—Varya was with her son again. It was always happy where he was, always calm. Nothing could hurt Kir here. She felt enveloped by the same safety as she held him close.

"Mummy, how many sick kids are there?" he asked with wide eyes.

Varya pressed her tired cheek against his soft, squishy one.

"You don't need to worry about the sick kids, little one."

Kir pulled away and looked at her, then cuddled up again, squishing his cheek back against hers. He giggled.

"But you'll make them better, won't you?"

"It's Aunty Zoe's job to make them better. I just try to find the medicine for her."

"Did it get lost?"

Varya let go of Kir and ran the palm of her hand over the blades of grass. The idea of discovering medicine that was simply lost was very appealing. It held the otherwise elusive

69

certainty of hope. That a cure existed out there for every illness.

"Mummy?" Kir put a tiny hand on each of her cheeks and gently forced her to face him, pressing the tip of his nose against hers.

"Yes, sweetheart?" she whispered, cupping her hands over the top of his and inhaling his sweet childish breath.

"Mummy, when will you find the medicine to make me better?"

Varya let out a sob and roughly pulled his hands away. Kir began to cry. Starting softly, he worked his way up to a siren wail.

Varya wanted to put her hands over her ears, her hands over her eyes. She wanted to wake up from this nightmare. She felt a hand on her shoulder.

"I think it might be time for you to go," her mother told her. Varya nodded.

In the morning she woke with a gasp, as though someone had been standing on her windpipe. She put her hand to her throat and took desperate, shallow breaths.

CHAPTER FIFTEEN

The state-of-the-art security systems at the Minor Miracles Foundation had been custom-built to keep biohazards in and thieves out. Individual offices, which usually housed simple furniture and password-protected screens, sometimes required a swipe card to enter but were often left unlocked.

Professor Janet Langford's former office was different.

Varya pushed the manual override button and waited, silently crossing her fingers. A keypad slid out just below the palm scanner. She checked the numbers written on a small piece of paper and typed in the code she'd found in her staff locker several hours after Professor Langford's Rest Time ceremony. Glancing around nervously, she waited for the green light to appear and listened for the quiet click of the lock. She pushed the door and went in, just as she thought she saw a figure in her peripheral vision turn the corner. She quickly shut the door behind her and leant against it, her heart thumping as a drop of sweat tickled at the back of her neck.

While she waited for footsteps to approach, she ground her teeth at the irritation of needing to slink around like a thief in her own facility.

"You don't need to be here on-site, you know," Langford had pointed out more than once. "You've hired some of the best scientists this country has to offer and equipped them with everything they could possibly need to do their job. Why not leave them to it?"

"What else would I do with my time? I may as well contribute something." The lack of substance in her statement was laid bare in the silence that Langford allowed to grow. Varya had tried again: "I need to be here. It makes me feel closer to him."

Langford would always sigh then, defeated in the face of parental grief.

"Maybe you need to take a more visibly managerial role, then. It may help give a sense of purpose and place to you. This subterfuge, it can't be healthy."

That had been one of her last suggestions, before her time was up. Langford was right, the subterfuge and creeping around was eating away at Varya. It was directly opposed to what she most wanted, which was to openly declare her credentials and mission to ensure that research into curing rare childhood diseases received the funding it truly deserved. She would do it in the name of her son. She used to believe in the generally accepted communal ideology, right up until it was her own son who was diagnosed with a rare and incurable disease.

"You think I don't want to?" Varya had seethed. "You think I don't want the world to know that it's me who's behind all this, who has made it happen? Funded and driven research to find cures for six diseases, saving the lives of children."

She swallowed, her eyes burning. "How many families have we helped to avoid the sort of grief you and I have both suffered?"

"Dozens," Langford agreed. "But Varya, it's been nearly ten years since your unit was disbanded. People have moved on. The world has moved on."

Her eyes flashed. "They may have moved on, but they haven't forgotten."

"No. I hope we'll never forget something as heinous as the time thieves, lest history repeat itself." Langford reached out and placed her hand gently on Varya's arm. Varya tensed, her flight instinct kicking in. "But I think your track record here will speak for itself. I think it's time to come out of hiding and reveal yourself. Kir has been gone for five years now, Varya. When are you going to stop hiding and start living?"

Standing in Langford's dark, silent office now, Varya wiped at her eyes, which had started to fill at the sensation that, without Langford, she was truly alone again. There was nobody left who knew all the pieces, who could fit them together to see the whole that was Varya.

"Pull yourself together, woman," she hissed at herself, and moved forward to retrieve the files she'd come for.

A click and whoosh of new air and light made her cry out. She turned around and blinked, trying to adjust her eyes to focus on the figure in the office doorway with the bright light at his back.

"Thought it might be you," said Connor. Now that Varya was studying him properly, she realised she didn't even remember hiring him. Was he in the list Langford had sent her for final vetting?

"What are you doing in here?" he asked—a little too casually, Varya thought. But of course, she reminded herself, he saw her as just another one of the lab staff.

"Clearing out the professor's things." She decided to continue with her self-appointed task despite his intrusion. Sometimes the best way to disguise illicit actions was by putting them on open display. Marisa had taught her that.

"In the dark?" Connor flicked on the light. Varya blinked rapidly, frowned, and ground her teeth. She glared at him momentarily. He raised his eyebrows.

Varya slipped her hand into her pocket and pulled out a small, brass key. Deceptively simple, it looked like it might open an old roll-top desk. A perfect circle at one end, a hollow tip and jagged square at the other. Hidden from the sight of the human eye were tiny indentations scratched into the circumference of the barrelled end. She inserted the key into the professor's cabinet and turned it. The top drawer slid open. Varya reached behind the cabinet and pulled out a flat packed box. She held out the cardboard to Connor.

"Here. Make yourself useful."

While Connor constructed the box, Varya used the time to start pulling out files. She piled a handful on the desk and flicked through a few more. These were confidential research files, containing results from experiments that were too sensitive or too uncertain to place on the digital network yet. Secure as it was, any network was vulnerable to cyberattack. Or surveillance. Varya was keen to ensure they were all safely locked away. But today, she was searching for one in particular.

"*Kir*," it was labelled. She found it tucked away in the bottom drawer, right at the back. Three buff-coloured manila folders bound together by two large elastic bands which had worn away the top lips of the cardboard. Varya ran her fingers over the soft edges before she slipped them into the middle of the growing pile on the desk.

"There's more boxes over there, in the corner," she told Connor.

He followed the trajectory of her finger and nodded. Varya ripped out a length of tape from a roll she'd brought with her and lashed it to the top of the box to secure it.

"So, how long have you worked here for?" Connor asked, his voice bright with energy.

Varya eyed him suspiciously. "Since the institute opened."

"You like it?" He watched her, waiting for an answer. Varya stared at him for just a moment too long, until he looked suitably alarmed. Then she nodded.

He got the message and continued to work, silently.

Varya sighed. Maybe the task at hand was making her paranoid. Maybe he really was just trying to get to know her. But why?

"What made you decide to come and work here?" Varya threw him a conversational olive branch.

"I wanted to be a hero, save a kid or two," he grinned.

"Why save a couple of kids with rare diseases here when you could work to save thousands of children from more common ones at the government labs?" she asked, genuinely curious now.

He shrugged and patted the sides of a newly constructed box, checking its integrity before placing more files in. Varya tensed as she watched him pick up the pile with Kir's file in and place it carefully in the box.

"I liked the idea of knowing who I was saving. It's a self-indulgent thing. I'm not motivated by reducing disease numbers. I'm motivated by helping sick people."

"You won't meet many sick people here in the labs. Maybe you should have been a doctor," she retorted.

"I was," he said quietly.

She studied his face. Maybe she'd pegged his age wrong, he must have been older if he'd had the time to have a medical career before switching to a research career.

"I got sick of telling parents their kids were going to die because we couldn't be bothered to spend the resources on finding a way to save them."

That, she understood.

"So, you need some help getting these somewhere?" Connor unfolded himself and stretched to his full height. His back cracked loudly. He grinned; Varya winced. "Sorry."

"They can stay here for now." As much as she would have loved a hand to get the boxes into her car, she couldn't think of a story quickly enough to explain why she might be taking Foundation files home.

He shrugged. "Sure."

They both stood, looking around; eyes meeting briefly as they flitted.

"Do you want to..."

"You can go back to..."

They spoke at once, then fell silent.

"You can go back to work now. I'll finish this up," said Varya.

"You want to go for a drink some time?" Connor asked, leaning against the door frame. Varya only barely restrained herself from rolling her eyes.

"No. Thank you, but no."

Connor didn't seem surprised or disappointed. He just gave her a small smile. Varya thought his eyes looked a little sad. Was that pity? Feeling flushed, she bent down to pick up a box and stack it on top of another. When she straightened, the doorway was empty.

CHAPTER SIXTEEN

Varya sat at one of the long benches in the kitchen. Designed to encourage collaborative discussions at break times, the lab staff collectively conspired to space themselves as far away from each other as possible and to sit in silence. An empty chair separated each person as they contemplated their lunch. Nobody felt like eating in the days following a Rest Time ceremony. It brought their own limited mortality a little too close for comfort.

The screen in the corner flashed up news items on a continuous loop. War in the Middle East. Failed trade talks with China. Celebrations of a unified Korea, finally. The fact that most of North Korea was now dust and rubble... well, it was the price you paid for peace, wasn't it? Rumours were being reported in western news services that Korea was considering following Japan, China, and India with the introduction of compulsory Time Chip technology. Countries with large or ageing populations, or scarce resources, had been the first to follow suit. The United States had introduced a forced roll-out just twelve months after the final phase of implementation in China. India and Singapore followed in the year after that. Many nations offered a voluntary program. The Australian and Chinese governments had made a small fortune selling the technology.

Varya brought a carrot stick to her mouth and bit down. The crunch was too loud. She looked around her to see if anyone responded. They didn't. Still, she concentrated on pushing her molars through the stick in her mouth as slowly as possible to avoid the crunch. A familiar scene flashed up on the screen.

"Ow!" she cried out, as she bit through her cheek instead of the carrot stick.

The woman two seats away from her looked up, eyebrows raised questioningly. Varya frowned and rubbed her cheek. The woman gave her a sympathetic look and went back to prodding at her own meal. Varya's eyes snapped back to the communal screen. A ubiquitous brick building, but that tree in the forecourt, the one that was three stories high and dropped all its leaves in the autumn, leaving the kids to crunch along the path to school. That tree belonged to Daniel's school. She patched her personal screen into the same channel and quickly inserted her earphones.

"*Ben Williams, a nine-year-old student at Ryebald Primary School, was returned to his parents early yesterday morning. Witnesses say he seemed confused and slightly drowsy as he knocked on his own door.*"

The footage cut to a rotund man with glasses, still in his activewear and sweating profusely.

"He stumbled a little, but I couldn't see any physical injuries. He just seemed tired and confused."

The camera cut again, this time to a stretcher carrying a long, white package out to a black van. No face was visible. Varya clutched the edge of the table and bit down on her lip.

"Ben's reunion with his family was brief before devastation followed. He died in hospital just a few short hours after walking back through his own front door."

Varya felt the world spinning. Ben. Daniel. It was all too close. She willed her hand to move, to turn off the feed, but she was transfixed. The story would be replayed repeatedly on every media outlet across the country. What was it about horror and tragedy that held their collective imagination so tightly?

"The sequence of events seems to suggest that the child's Rest Time initiator was triggered decades earlier than expected. Rest Time Corps, the manufacturer of the initiators, denies the possibility that the unit could have been faulty. Police have confirmed that there have been no other cases of faulty initiators in the past ten years."

It wasn't supposed to be possible. The initiator units were buried deep into the spinal cord and could not be removed or tampered with. Each person received their Rest Time date at insertion, which couldn't be altered without killing the host. Varya knew, she had helped design the technology. Before she'd left Rest Time Corps forever.

The Chief Commissioner was being interviewed; multiple microphones were held in front of her like a bunch of pushy tech flowers.

"It's early days and we will, of course, be fully investigating this horrendous crime. But I can now reveal that, based on certain marks discovered at the back of the victim's neck..." A photograph of the back of Ben's neck seemed to show several small burn marks arranged in a neat circle. "...we do believe his initiator unit may have been tampered with."

"Shit," muttered Varya. "Shit, shit, shit."

The lab tech looked up at her again in concern. Varya considered reassuring her that she was okay.

"I have to go." Varya stood, leaving her unfinished meal on the table. Pacing out the door and into the empty hallway, she pushed a button on her personal screen to call Zoe. Zoe picked up immediately.

"Zoe?" For a long minute Varya wondered if the line had connected at all. She was met with only silence.

"Zoe, are you there?"

Varya waited, getting ready to hang up and try again.

"I'm here," whispered Zoe.

"Are you... okay?"

"Daniel's gone."

Varya fell against the wall, just managing to keep her legs from collapsing beneath her.

"What?"

"Daniel. The school called. The police are on their way here now. He's not there. They don't know where he is. I'm at home. We had journalists calling the hospital all morning about Ben, so I left. I came home. I'm home now." Zoe was babbling.

"I'm so sorry. Could he have just... Maybe he..."

"The journalist I talked to... he said the police said the people who took Ben are probably the same time thieves that have taken Daniel. It's on the news. That's what the doctors thought yesterday... that it was time thieves, when Ben came in. They called the Rest Time Authority. But they said the technology simply doesn't exist anymore. They said it couldn't be time thieves. They promised. I don't understand."

Varya pressed her fingernails into her palm.

"I'm so sorry," she said again.

"Is that true? That the technology doesn't exist?" The up-lift at the end of the word, the slight break in her friend's voice. Varya couldn't quite tell if it was hope or an accusation.

"Varya?"

"It's true. It was all destroyed, completely wiped, the last time."

"But if it's time thieves, if they've rebuilt it, we'll need it to help Daniel when he comes back. Can't Rest Time Corps build it, just in case? Can't they do something?"

A janitor rolled his bucket and mop around the corner and headed towards where Varya stood. She turned and shielded the screen with her hand, lowering her voice. "Zoe, I think we should save this conversation for another..."

"A child is dead, Varya! Ben is dead. And Daniel is... he's gone. He's not safe anymore. My little boy isn't safe."

Varya's stomach churned with nausea.

"He's only nine years old. He's barely even lived."

"I'm so sorry," she repeated. "But I can't talk now. I'll come around soon and..."

"Not now. I don't want you here. I want you to find something that will help Daniel. Please."

"Okay. Okay, I'll try."

Varya went back to her lunch and sat down heavily on the seat. The screen in the corner continued to buzz its stream of bad news in the world. Staff continued to walk to and fro up and down the hallway, visible through the full-length glass panels installed all down one side of the lunchroom. Food smells—fruit salad, raisin toast—merged until the room started to spin and close in on Varya.

"Hey."

The light dimmed as she blinked furiously.

"Hey, you okay?"

She took a shallow breath and held it tentatively, then let it out again. She nodded but didn't feel brave enough to turn to greet Connor yet.

He opened his lunch bag and started to unpack the contents. A cheese sandwich and an apple. The bread and the fruit smelled delightfully fresh. Varya inhaled deeply and caught the scent of Connor's sweat in her nostrils as well. It was not unpleasant.

"Just feeling a bit off." She wrapped up the remnants of her own meal and tucked them back into their box. She stood up, too quickly, and leaned forward onto the table, her palms flat, her eyes closed, as a wave of dizziness enveloped her.

Connor watched her, chewing on his sandwich. He swallowed and packed the rest of it away.

"I'll drive you home."

"No, I'm..." She was going to tell him she was fine. She was going to tell him she could look after herself, like she had done for years. But she looked into his eyes and saw genuine concern. She tried it on for a moment, savouring what it felt like to be the one who relied upon others, rather than the one who was leant on. It felt good.

"Actually, thank you, that would be great."

Connor nodded. "Meet me in the car park in ten minutes, then. At your car. We'll move that box of files from your car to mine. I'm guessing you'll be wanting it tonight." He looked up at the screen in the corner pointedly. It was showing a picture of a serious-looking government official, a thumbnail of Ben's smiling face permanently floating in the corner.

Varya looked at the screen and then back at Connor, frowning.

"Ten minutes," he said. Then he left.

CHAPTER SEVENTEEN

Marisa

On the next floor up, an apartment door swung open. Marisa braced herself from her seated position outside Varya's door. She heard the door swing shut, the click echoing down the painted concrete stairwell. Stomp, stomp, stomp. Marisa looked up.

"Afternoon." She held one hand up to the white-haired woman who stood, left foot still hovering uncertainly over the last step. The woman pursed her lips and fingered the ruffle that rippled down the centre of her shirt, neatly hiding the buttons. Apparently deciding that Marisa wasn't an immediate threat, she continued her journey across the landing and down the next flight of stairs.

Marisa chewed her fingernail and listened hopefully for any familiar ascending footsteps.

"Ah, stuff it," she muttered, jumping up and pulling her screen from her back pocket. She tapped and swiped at it a few times, then held the device up to Varya's door. After a moment, the lock clicked. Marisa grinned and pushed the door open gently.

Inside, she moved quietly through the entrance hall, touching the hall stand absentmindedly as she went. There were no pictures on the wall. The carpet was dark grey, the only warmth. Everything else was white. Not for the first time, Marisa mused that her employer had managed to recreate something like a home laboratory. A few more steps through the living room and she turned left to the small kitchen.

"Hello, old friend," she greeted the coffee machine. She took a moment to breathe in the ground coffee before she scooped it out and packed it into the filter. A little jolt of pleasure shot down through the pit of her belly as she wrenched the handle into place and pushed the button. A mechanical whir started up and she waited, mesmerised, for the dark, hot liquid to stream out of the filter and into the waiting cup.

Marisa shrugged her jacket off and sat on a kitchen chair, never taking her eyes off that stream. Even with the hefty commission Varya paid her for selling the time tabs to the entitled wealthy, she couldn't afford to buy more than a single cup of coffee for herself each week. Besides, she preferred to save her own money for her early retirement. She wouldn't need time tabs. She'd work hard now and then have more time than she knew what to do with by the time she turned fifty-five. That was her plan, anyway. She didn't intend to ever have a Rest Time Ceremony. She planned to throw away the calendar in her final months and, with a bit of luck, keel over while sipping a martini on a tropical beach somewhere. As she removed the cup of steaming coffee from the grille, she noticed the way the skin on the back of her hand creased more readily now. Not quite crêpey yet, but almost like soft scales.

"Best hurry up with those savings, woman," she chided herself.

By the time the apartment's front door opened again, Marisa was on to her second cup and starting to feel a little jittery.

The duo that padded down the hallway was silent and tense. Marisa poked her head out of the kitchen and watched in fascination as Varya led a stranger through the door. She'd never seen Varya let anyone other than herself in this apartment before.

Varya paced into the kitchen, dumped her bag, and sat, staring at Marisa's coffee. She chewed her lip and fidgeted. Marisa turned to see the man hovering in the doorway, holding a large box. He raised his knee and hunched over the box to shift it.

"Just over here, maybe?" he asked nobody in particular.

Marisa shrugged and turned back to Varya, frowning. She ignored the dull thump of the box hitting the floor and reached out to touch Varya's hand with a single finger.

"Hey, you've got coffee," said Connor, his excitement overcoming his reticence.

"Specially imported on the black market all the way from Java, just for me." Marisa held her empty cup aloft. The corner of Varya's mouth twitched slightly and she raised an eyebrow.

"Oh." Connor was already running his hands over the machine lightly, inhaling the aroma from the spent granules. "Do you mind if I...?"

"Knock yourself out, kid," said Marisa generously. She watched as Connor gripped the handle and tapped out the spent coffee grinds. She caught the heady whiff of the new granules as he opened the packet and scooped out more. Marisa dipped her head to face Varya's.

"Bit young for you, isn't he?" she muttered.

Varya stood and made to walk past her. She placed a heavy hand on Marisa's shoulder and squeezed. "Be nice. He's from work. He's here to help."

Marisa paused, then continued in a low voice. "I saw the news about Ben. How are you holding up?"

Varya looked directly into her eyes then, fear the main message. She shook her head and pulled her hand away.

"Hey, is this...?" Connor started to say.

Varya moved with lightning speed and snatched the black square out of Connor's hands. She placed it carefully on the table and bent her knees as she lowered herself slowly back into the chair. She cupped her hands protectively over the device. No more than an inch thick, the surface was smooth apart from a tiny green light which blinked at regular intervals.

Connor stared at the device. Marisa stared at Connor.

"A guy from work? Who the hell is he really, Var'?"

"My name's Connor," Connor clarified.

"He's Professor Langford's nephew," explained Varya. She'd asked him the same question herself in the car on the way over. "He used to be a doctor."

Marisa nodded. "Ah, so he knows..."

Varya turned to face Connor, keeping her hands around the device.

"I don't know what he knows," she said.

Marisa cocked her head to the side and flared her eyes.

"So, Connor, nephew of Langford, what do you know? Enlighten us."

The stream of liquid coffee emitting from the machine ended with a faint hiss. Connor turned and picked up the cup, cradling it in both hands before taking a small sip.

"I know that's a Time Lock stabiliser. And I know that it's active. Which means there's a Time Lock somewhere nearby."

Marisa squirmed and sat up, frowning at Varya. Varya moved slowly, apparently engrossed in inspecting the Time Lock stabiliser.

"Janet said you would need help with some research you're doing, something about the Time Chips. She didn't say exactly what, just asked me to..." He trailed off and looked sharply between them.

"She asked you to look out for Varya, didn't she?" said Marisa.

Connor nodded.

"I don't need looking out for," said Varya.

"Okay."

Varya held the device flat in the palm of her hand and carried it over to the shelf above the coffee machine. She placed it carefully next to a small cactus, then stood back to gaze at the montage.

"Don't ever touch it again."

"Okay."

Marisa cocked her head to one side. "So, doctor boy. How can you help us? You good at sales or manufacturing?"

Connor blanched and shook his head slightly.

"I..."

"Marisa," Varya warned.

Marisa put her cup down and opened her hands wide, leaning back in her chair.

"What? He said Langford sent him to help. What else is he going to help with?"

They both turned to Connor expectantly.

"I'm not sure. Without knowing what it is you need, what that stabiliser is for..."

He indicated the device with a flick of his head.

"Nah-ah," Marisa laughed, a slight menace in her tone. "You first. What kind of a doctor were you?"

He paused and lifted his cup to his mouth again. "This is very good coffee. Where did you say it was imported from?"

Varya rubbed at a knot in her shoulder.

"I'm guessing you didn't diagnose coughs and colds," she said.

Connor put the cup down on the stone bench with a clink and sighed softly.

"I was attached to the Rest Time Corps. I worked with the kids who were returned by the time thieves." He paused. "And their families, afterwards."

Marisa gave a low whistle.

"Bullshit," said Varya. "I would remember you. That section of the Corps wasn't that big."

Connor snorted. "I had a Y chromosome, and my name wasn't Sebastian. Of course, you didn't notice me."

Marisa laughed loudly, slapping her palm on the table. "Oh, that's brilliant. I'm going to remember that one."

Varya glared at her. Marisa gave one last hoot, then cleared her throat and fell silent again.

"I was out in the field, mostly. You were in the labs." Connor paused. "Sebastian would remember me."

"Sebastian's not here," said Varya.

Marisa leaned forward. "So, Connor, tell me more about Sebastian." She waved her hand in the air at Varya. "Lover-girl here won't say a word. I figure he must be gorgeous."

Connor opened his mouth to laugh but stopped when he saw Varya's thunderous expression. He cleared his throat.

"Maybe some other time."

"We don't have time for gossip," Varya snapped. "Daniel has been abducted." She looked from Connor to Marisa and back again. Marisa was opening and closing her mouth. That wasn't information that had been shared on any news bulletin she'd seen.

"Marisa can fill you in on the Time Lock." She paused, holding her left hand with her right, trying to stop the shaking.

"You're sure?" said Marisa finally.

"Yes. We may need his help." Satisfied, Varya walked out of the room, turning left down the hallway.

Marisa stared into her cup, trying to get the story straight in her head. Where to begin? She'd kept Varya's secrets for five years but had never had to explain them to someone else.

"Who's Daniel?" Connor lowered himself into a chair opposite her.

She nodded, thankful for the direction. "Good idea. Let's start with something simple. Daniel is the son of Varya's friend, Zoe."

"Okay. And we think he's probably been abducted by the same person who took that other kid?"

Marisa nodded. "Ben Williams."

Connor glanced up at the flashing black box above the coffee machine. The pace of the blinking increased momentarily, then dropped back to its previous rhythm.

"I've read about Time Locks," he said, "I've seen pictures of the prototype stabilisers. They were developed by the Corps during the time thief abductions years ago, to buy time. Scientists hoped they could be used to hold the children in a sort of stasis for as long as it took to develop a method of reversing the drain of their years."

Marisa nodded. She'd never really given the genesis of the Time Locks a lot of thought, but it made sense. Back then, cryogenics was only used on dead bodies by the mega wealthy who believed they would be brought back to life at some point in the future. Marisa rolled her eyes. Why they thought anyone would bother bringing them back to life was beyond her. But massive wealth did strange things to people's perceptions. Somewhere out there was a freezer still full of bodies waiting to be regenerated at some point in the future.

"The Time Lock stabiliser development was abandoned after the time thieves were apprehended. The the research project was shut down. And yet, here it is, what appears to be a fully functioning model." His gaze shifted from the black box to Marisa. "So, who's in the Time Lock?"

Marisa's eyes snapped up. She pursed her lips, then sighed.

"Varya's son, Kir. And her mother, Elena."

"But he's dead." Connor blinked fast, stunned. "Kir... he died. Years ago, didn't he? I mean, that's why she and Sebastian split up, soon after their division of the Rest Time Corps was disbanded."

Marisa just stared at him.

"He's not dead," he said slowly.

Marisa shook her head. "Nope. Alive and chasing birds like any self-respecting four-year-old." She frowned. "Except he's kind of closer to nine years old now. But he looks four. It's complicated."

"Yes, yes, of course. He's in stasis so he doesn't age but he still lives so his mind develops. But..." He looked up at Marisa. "Does his mind develop? Physically?"

Marisa shot him a look of pure irritation. "How should I know? I haven't sliced his brain open recently. I just bring the food."

"You've been inside the Time Lock? Wow, what's it like?" He stood up and went to the kitchen door. Marisa jumped up and grabbed his arm.

"Don't even think about it. Nobody goes in there except me and Varya."

Connor shook his arm free and made as if to move back into the kitchen. "I'm sorry, I just... it's so incredible. They'd tried to get the Time Locks working but never could. And then the technology was destroyed along with everything else."

Marisa flicked her head towards the table. He sat down. She leaned against the bench and crossed her arms.

"Kir's illness was very advanced. Varya was told there was nothing left to do for him. Sebastian wanted her to just let him go, but she couldn't. She wanted to make sure they'd tried everything. Sebastian and Varya had an awful fight. Sebastian said his goodbyes—to both Varya and Kir. Then he left."

"So, the kid's still sick? Inside the Time Lock?"

Marisa shook her head. "Yes and no. Varya told the doctors she wanted to take him home and allow him to die there. They gave her drugs that would keep him comfortable and sent him home. She waited for a point in time when he was feeling well. You know that sweet spot just a half hour or so after you've taken your next dose of medicine? Then she set Elena—that's her mother—and Kir up in the Time Lock. They've been there ever since."

Connor gave a low whistle. "Wow."

Marisa gave him space to process all this while she moved to the sink and started to fill it with warm, soapy water to wash the coffee cups.

"Why hasn't anyone come looking for Kir?" Connor asked finally.

Marisa dried her hands on a small towel hanging from the oven. She shrugged before turning to face him.

"Guess they figured he'd died."

"But wouldn't the hospital expect a body? Wouldn't Sebastian come back for the funeral?"

Marisa laughed. "Doctors and morgues are fairly separate entities. You should know that. Why would the hospital staff follow up? Zoe—she's a doctor—told them she was checking in on Kir. And Sebastian... he was gone. He'd already said his farewell."

The silence stretched between them. Marisa and Connor both waited for Varya to return and tell them what the next step was.

Marisa gazed at Connor. Connor looked away first. Marisa tapped her purple index fingernail on the table between them. Quietly, steadily. Tap, tap, tap. He looked up. She smiled sweetly.

"You work at the Cure Factory, then?"

He nodded slowly, frowning. "Cure Factory?" He tipped his head, lifted one side of his mouth. His eyes sparkled. "I guess that could work."

They both looked up to see Varya gripping the doorframe tightly with one hand. She seemed surprised to see them.

"Var'?" said Marisa softly. "You okay?"

Varya frowned, focusing on a point just over Marisa's head.

"I have to go and see Zoe." Then she looked directly at Connor. "You need to leave now."

"But..." he started.

She shook her head once, decisively. "We'll talk later. Go back to work."

And with that, she left.

Marisa watched the space she'd vacated, her brow lined with concern. She looked back at Connor.

"Off you go then, minion. Back to work."

"What will you do now?" he asked, standing up from his chair.

"I'm going to stay here and have another coffee," she told him.

She waited until she heard the door locks click shut after him, then sighed and stood, stretching her stiff back, and grumbling to herself. She rolled her shoulders to get the kinks out and then wandered out to the hallway and turned left, padding up the carpet to the end room. She laid her palm against the panel next to the door and waited. The square beeped and lit up a soft green. The door whooshed and opened slightly. Marisa pushed it wide but didn't go in. Beyond the single bed was a mirror-fronted built in robe. At least, she knew there was a robe there, though she couldn't see it. A shimmering oval obscured her view of two of the doors. Suspended in mid-air, she could just see the silver edge of the closet door beneath the oval's lowest point. She checked the digital clock on the dresser. Another hour before she was scheduled to take the next food delivery through.

"Hope you're hungry, kid. It's burgers for you tonight," she said softly to the shimmering portal.

CHAPTER EIGHTEEN

Elena

I'm never quite sure if it's the sound or the smell of the portal that alerts me first. We don't have real time here so it's not like I can arrange a time for visits. Sometimes we're here in the house when my Varya appears. Other times she just shows up when we're strumming guitars at the music shop—which we found only a week or so ago thanks to a printed map Varya brought us—poring over books at the book shop or just sitting on the grass watching the clouds roll by. Actually no, that's me romanticising again. The clouds don't roll by anymore. They're still... fixed in placed. I'm quite glad there were a few clouds around on day zero. Otherwise I would miss them. Blue skies are all very well but, somehow, they feel more transient than cloudy ones. Like an empty function room before the people arrive.

Today it's definitely the smell. It's mostly burning plastic, like when you leave an ice cream bucket too close to the stove and it starts—ever so slowly—to melt. But it's also slightly sweet, as though someone tried to stop the melting by drizzling honey over it.

Our Kir smells it too. He twitches his nose and frowns as his little jaw continues to work at breaking up his breakfast. It's not until he hears the static sounds sparking in the next room that he slams down his spoon and jumps up, cereal flying from his open mouth.

"Mummy!" He breathes the word out in a rush of air and bounces out of the kitchen door.

I smile and move to the sink to retrieve a sponge. I start mopping up the flecks left on the table, pushing down the slight pang of irritation that has started to surface with my daughter's visits. By my calculations I've now been parenting this boy far longer than she did. Does that make me his parent, too? Doesn't that give me the right to have him throw down everything at the merest hint of my arrival?

Of course, my jealousy is ridiculous, I know that. I'm always here for our Kir. I have the privilege of spending every moment with him. Something that Varya would kill for, I'm sure. Except that sometimes I'm not so sure. Sometimes, now, I feel the time stretch between her visits and I wonder if more days than usual are passing outside before she steps back through the portal. The way she runs her hand over Kir's head seems more cursory, the nod and initial glance she sends my way have less warmth, more guilt. But perhaps I am simply feeling worn out by living in this endless loop. I'm a patient person but even the patience of a saint would be tried by living through one single never-ending day, over and over again. Even if it is the best of days. Even if it means I get to spend years with my grandson that I otherwise wouldn't. I miss people. I miss their faces.

I wipe up the spill and toss the sponge back in the sink, resume my seat at the table and sip my tea.

After a minute Kir returns, this time attached to Varya like a back-to-front rucksack. Kir is grinning. Varya is not. Her face is a blank canvas, though her hand rubs circles around her son's back. It leaves impressions against his jumper. He wriggles. She is rubbing too hard, she is tense.

"Varya," I say. It is both a question and an acknowledgement.

Her eyes slide over me, but I catch the way she's biting the junction between the corner of her mouth and her cheek. Most people wouldn't notice, but I do. I am her mother. I've been watching this action since she was a tiny toddler: Varya is worried.

"Kir, your mother is not a tree. Please climb down and finish your breakfast," I tell our monkey boy. Varya gently removes him and places him on the seat in front of his half-empty bowl.

"I'm not hungry!" he shouts gleefully, scrambling up to his mother again. It fascinates me, this habit of his. The way he seems to have imprinted on her so strongly in his earlier years that even though he sees her for only a few minutes of each of his days, she still holds such a significant place in his heart.

Varya sits at the chair next to him, opposite me, and lays her hands carefully on her legs.

"Eat, Kir," she tells him.

He pauses and watches her, hoping she'll change her mind. She turns away and his face crumples slightly, though he picks up his spoon, as instructed, and starts to poke at his cereal.

"Varya?" I say again.

"It's Daniel," she mutters, staring at the table.

"Is he sick?" I ask, though in the pit of my stomach I think I already know.

She nods and starts picking at her cuticles. It's a dreadful habit. I tried using that foul-tasting paint you're supposed to use, when she was little, which stopped her from biting them. But ever since then, she picks at them instead. I suppose that's better than biting. There's nothing to say, really. I wait for her to speak. I sip my tea.

"He's... we don't know how much time he'll have left," she says, finally looking me in the eye. I see desperation, guilt, and pain all mixed up. In my heart, all I want to do is comfort my child. She is hurting. But I don't comfort her because she will not thank me for it. She must be allowed her strength. I know this from long experience of being snarled at when I've tried to comfort her. I stomp on my heart and tell it to shut up and take a back seat.

"Bring Daniel to me and Kir. He can stay with us until you work it out." My mouth speaks without consulting my brain. It's the mother-conditioning. I know that Varya has taken on Daniel as a substitute son. I know that Kir's little fists clench every time Varya mentions him, though he doesn't understand why. But it's not Daniel's fault. He's only a child, too. He deserves to be safe until my Varya can find a cure for him as well.

I reach across the table now and touch my daughter's fingertips with my own fingers.

"He'll be safe here."

Varya sheds tears then, rubbing at them quickly with her bony shoulder.

"Thank you," she whispers. Then: "I have to go, I'm sorry."

She stands and Kir almost falls from his chair in his hurried alarm.

"Mama!" he shouts, attaching himself to her leg.

"I'm sorry, baby, I have to go now. I'll be back again very soon." She tries to peel him off, but he's stuck fast. "And I'll be bringing a playmate for you," she says brightly.

This news surprises him enough that he relaxes his grip. I scoop him up and hold him close on my lap. I nod to Varya. Go now. She nods back.

"I'll be back as soon as I can. I have to... explain some things to Zoe first."

Varya hesitates for only a moment before she turns and walks through the doorway. We hear a door open and close, more static as the portal opens again, and then she is gone.

CHAPTER NINETEEN

Marisa

"Dinner time!" Marisa called as she emerged from the portal. She'd started announcing her arrival after being greeted several times by a devastated Kir who had heard and smelled the portal open up with the expectation of his mother arriving. He would still come to greet Marisa—the bringer of food was also very much welcome in Kir's small world—but no longer teared up due to mistaken identity.

Today she stood alone for several moments in the hallway, holding a dinner plate in each hand, waiting for the meaty smell of his favourite burgers to bring Kir to her. Eventually she shrugged and walked the several paces to the kitchen and meals area alone.

Elena stood next to the table, staring down at the cutlery set for two, water glasses neatly aligned above the knives, ketchup bottle in the centre.

"Where's Kir?" Marisa placed the plates gently down on the table in their allocated places.

Elena sat and raised her voice, "Kir! Dinner time!" To Marisa she said, "He's in his room."

Marisa sat opposite Elena and waited. "Is he okay?"

Before Elena could answer, Kir appeared at the doorway, paused, glared at them, then trudged to his seat and sat down heavily.

"It's your favourite," said Marisa, pushing the plate a half-inch closer to him.

Kir sighed dramatically, propped his right elbow on the table and rested his head on his upturned hand. "I'm not hungry," he declared, pushing the plate away and knocking the sauce bottle over.

Marisa caught it before it rolled off the table. Elena slid the plate back towards Kir.

"You'll get nothing else except sandwiches and cereal until tomorrow night, so make the best of it now," said Elena.

Kir pouted and picked up a chip. After using it to push several other chips around, he poked one end into his mouth and started to chew. With his free hand he stacked chips on top of each other to form a small fort.

"They've taken another one," said Marisa. She watched Elena slice a chunk off her own burger and put it in her mouth.

"They say it tastes the same as real meat," said Elena, pushing the food into her cheek and grimacing. "But I remember what real meat tastes like, and this is not it."

Marisa tried again. "This one's the kid of a friend of Varya's."

"Who took one?" asked Kir. "One what?"

"Kir, eat your food. Don't interrupt when adults are talking." Elena's tone held the authority of a bygone era when children were expected to be seen and not heard. Kir huffed softly and started to deconstruct his burger, carefully removing the lettuce and tomato and putting them on the side of his plate before replacing the bun and biting into it.

"Daniel, yes?" said Elena.

"Yes. That's two now," said Marisa. "Ben and Daniel." Her hands fidgeted and her jaw clenched.

"Are they sure it's... them?" she asked, with hopeful doubt.

"The police don't know. Daniel hasn't been returned yet. But the other kid, Ben Williams... it was the same M.O., so..."

"But not confirmed. Not the same people."

"No," said Marisa through clenched teeth. "They haven't arrested anyone, but it's pretty bloody obvious..."

"Nanna, Nanna! She did cursing!"

"Kir! Eat your dinner!" Elena shouted.

Kir shrank down into his seat, confused. His grandmother never raised her voice at him. He sat silently, his hands in his lap. Seeming to remember his Nanna's command, he poked one small hand above the table, plucked a chip off the plate and slipped it into his mouth. He chewed slowly.

"It's not our concern," said Elena to Marisa.

"You think it's just, what, a coincidence? The..." Marisa glanced at Kir. "The timing?"

"I think it's a tragedy. But do I think... he was involved? No, I don't."

"No, of course not..." Marisa paused, looked at Kir again. "He would never do anything to hurt anyone, but..."

"But you think that by dredging up the past, we've somehow awoken a great demon who has started to terrorise the city again."

Marisa sighed. "I just..."

"You feel guilty."

"Yeah, I guess I do."

"Because you think that by helping me, it's somehow your fault. Even if you didn't directly cause it, if your action started a chain reaction of evil, you think that you might be to blame."

Marisa nodded and exhaled slowly. "Yes."

Elena put down her knife and fork and pressed her hands together, elbows on the table.

"We did what we believed was right, to help a mother and her little boy. Nothing evil can possibly come out of such a selfless act. If someone else has chosen to intervene in that process and create evil, then that is their choice and they will pay for it when the time comes and they have to answer to the Lord Almighty." She picked up her cutlery again and stabbed at the chips. "But, for what it's worth, I don't think it is related at all."

Marisa tapped her fingers on the table noiselessly. Kir picked up his fork and stabbed at his own chips, missing and clattering against the plate more often than not.

"Did she tell you about the other kid? When she spoke to you about Daniel this afternoon?"

Elena shook her head and swallowed. "She told me that Daniel is sick. I think she wanted me to infer that he is sick like Kir is sick. No more and no less."

"And you didn't question her."

"No. I will do whatever I can to help my daughter. At the moment, she is on the right course. So, I will believe what I am told to believe and leave the rest to her. Daniel is sick, he needs to be cared for. That's all I care to know."

Marisa stood. "Fine, you stick your head in the sand. I just hope this doesn't all come back to bite you on the arse."

"Nanna, Nanna, she...!" Kir was stopped by his grand-mother's raised hand. He wriggled in his seat, looking about fit to burst. "But! But!"

Marisa turned to Kir. "Kir, I am sorry for cursing." To Elena she said, "I have to go now. I'll collect the plates when I next come."

As Marisa made her way back through the portal, the chiming of Varya's apartment doorbell became louder and more insistent. She strode over and frowned at the screen showing the live feed of the other side of the door. She peered closely. He was a dead ringer for the photographs she'd seen, but surely...

"Identify yourself," she demanded.

He held up his identification to the camera, placing it next to his face for easy comparison.

"Well, bugger me," said Marisa under her breath, smiling as she imagined Kir's excited face at her cussing.

CHAPTER TWENTY

Varya

The police had been and gone, leaving an unmarked car stationed a few houses away, watching out for Daniel. Varya sat in the armchair opposite Zoe and cycled through useless platitudes in her head.

"I'm so sorry," was what she finally settled on.

Zoe's normally blush skin was a sickly shade of white. She held her palms over her kneecaps and rocked herself gently.

"I'm sure he's fine. He's probably just gone to a friend's house," said Zoe, her face blank.

Varya stood tentatively and crept the three steps from her chair to the couch Zoe sat on, watching for signs of rejection. There were none. There was no reaction at all. Varya covered Zoe's hand with her own.

"I can help."

Zoe stopped rocking and looked up at Varya.

"If it's... what we fear. I can help."

"You can reverse the time drain?" asked Zoe hopefully. She became suddenly animated and snatched her hand back.

"If you can do that, then why didn't you tell me, why didn't you help the other child before he..."

"No, Zoe," said Varya quickly, shaking her head firmly. "I can't do that."

Zoe slumped back into the cushions and closed her eyes.

"Then, what?" she whispered. "What can you possibly do to help my baby?"

Varya frowned and dug her own fingers against her knee-caps, trying to decide how to begin.

Zoe's eyes flew open. "Of course! The time tabs. You can give him time tabs. But he would need an awful lot. But I suppose we could keep giving them to him until we can figure out a way to reverse the drain. Do you think it would hurt him at all? Wouldn't he be confused?"

Varya put her hand on Zoe's arm and shook gently.

"Zoe, slow down. What are you talking about?"

Zoe stopped and stared. "The time tabs. The ones you use."

Varya pulled back. "How do you know about them?"

Zoe laughed. "There have been so many times you've walked in here looking half-dead, then disappeared up the hallway for five minutes, only to come back looking perky and refreshed. At first, I thought you might be into drugs, but then I realised... Well, you know." She shrugged. "Your background, and I'd heard rumours. It was obvious."

Zoe laughed again at the expression of alarm on Varya's face. It was her turn to comfort Varya with a hand over hers.

"It was obvious to me. Because I know you. And, naturally, I'm a genius." She grinned. "I'm sure nobody else knows." She searched Varya's face then. "Do they?"

She took a deep breath. "Zoe, there are some things I have to tell you."

Zoe's face fell again, as though she'd just remembered that Daniel was missing. She started to babble. "You know, I've often wanted to ask you for a few tabs, just to help me get some rest after a night shift, so I can do mornings with Daniel instead of..." Varya watched as realisation and shock closed Zoe's face down again.

"Yes, I could give Daniel time tabs. But that wouldn't be enough. I still don't know how to reverse the time drain. That will take longer, and he needs to be looked after. If we used time tabs, he'd need to come out of stasis to eat, talk to others. He's too young to be in stasis by himself. He needs someone to look after him."

"I could look after him," said Zoe. "I'll go in with him."

Varya shook her head. "No, it doesn't work like that. You can't go into a time tab stasis with another person. They're not that sophisticated. And besides, time tabs are illegal." She smiled slightly. "It would be far too obvious if you both kept glitching every couple of minutes."

"Glitching?"

Varya waved her arm. "Sorry, time science lingo."

They both fell silent.

"Maybe he just ran away. Maybe he's just hit that age where he wants a day or two to himself. Kids do that sometimes, you know." Zoe pressed each fingernail into her thumb, one by one, as though playing piano on her own hands to a song only she could hear. By the time she pressed her pinkie fingernails in there was a large red welt on each thumb. She started back at the pointer finger again, harder this time.

"I don't have the technology to reverse a time drain," Varya started quietly. "But I can keep him safe until I figure out how to develop it."

"Okay," said Zoe.

Varya put her hands over both of Zoe's, to stop her causing herself any more pain.

"I'll figure it out, I promise."

Zoe stilled but continued to stare at her hands. "Okay."

"You want me to stay?"

Zoe nodded once.

"Cup of tea?"

She nodded again.

Varya stood and stretched. She moved into the kitchen and started to gather cups and a box of tea, then pulled out her device and sent a message to Marisa.

"We need to find Sebastian. Can you start looking?"

While she waited for the reply, she put a green teabag in the first mug.

"He's literally just arrived at your place. I can totally take the credit still, right?"

Varya swallowed hard while she added water to the tea. Just one mug. She left the other empty.

"Tell him I'm coming."

She carried her device and the steaming mug over to Zoe and put it on the table on top of a coaster. She didn't sit down. Zoe looked up at her.

"I have to go now. To prepare for when Daniel returns."

Zoe nodded. "What if he doesn't come back? What if it's not... them? What if some garden-variety murderer has taken him and we never get him back?"

"He's coming back, Zoe. And when he does, we'll be ready." Crouching down in front of her friend she looked at her intently. Zoe's eyes flicked up, then away. They were bright with barely contained moisture. "Daniel is going to be okay."

Zoe nodded silently, swallowing furiously. "Okay," she whispered.

CHAPTER TWENTY-ONE

Varya stood at her own apartment door and stared at it. White paint covered the steel structure. The bolts were obvious if you knew where to look, though the paintwork was such high gloss it mostly shined to cover the truth of the door. It couldn't be broken down. It had no lock that could be picked, not even by Marisa. This door had kept her safe, or so she told herself.

She held her breath and pressed her hand against the cool plate, felt it tingle with static as she waited for the scanner to do its work, waited for the click and the whoosh.

She glided down the hallway to stand at the kitchen door. She blinked quickly. The sight of her ex-husband felt like a physical blow. Not a bad one, not wounded. But winded, certainly—a breathless blow.

Sebastian turned to face her, and she thought she heard her name come from his moving lips. She thought maybe she said his name as well, but later she realised there was just silence. Was it his hair? Blonde, reaching just below his ears, in need of a good brush but clean. His height? He seemed to take up the whole kitchen with his body. Middle age had been kind to him, she saw. A few lines around his eyes, a softer belly. But he was still strong, still stood tall. He gave her a slight smile, then he did say her name.

"Varya."

She wondered if the others heard him. There was a ringing in her ears, she felt a little dizzy.

"Varya? Are you okay?" After a moment she realised Marisa was talking to her, a worried expression on her face. She sat down suddenly.

"I... yes. Yes, I'm fine. I think I'm just a little tired."

Marisa held her gaze for a moment. It seemed to Varya as though she was transferring her own confidence and strength through that look. She breathed in and drank in her friend's gift. The star-struck schoolgirl was gone in that instant. She nodded her thank you imperceptibly to Marisa. Marisa drew back slightly.

"Sebastian," said Varya. "To what do we owe this pleasure?"

Sebastian seemed to feel the shift in the room and cleared his throat.

"I need to talk to you," Sebastian started, glancing at Marisa questioningly. "Alone."

"Marisa can stay," said Varya.

"I know everything." Marisa waved her hands in circles and spoke the last word with a breathy quality.

"You've seen the news I assume."

"The time theft? Yes," Varya replied simply.

"I'm here in an official capacity." He shifted his weight from one leg to another and crossed his arms.

"Am I a suspect?"

"No, of course not. But you could be in danger."

Varya frowned. "Isn't everyone in danger? Besides, I'm not a child. They won't be interested in me."

"We have reason to believe the transference of time from the abducted child didn't work as expected. They may take more children and they'll need someone with the expertise to assist them."

Varya laughed. "Sounds like you're in more danger than me. As far as most of the world is concerned, I'm just a lab assistant at a medical research facility."

Sebastian glared at her. "And Marisa here? What's her role in all this? Confidante, accomplice in your little illicit time tabs distribution business?" He paused, looking from one to the other, waiting for a reaction. "Lover?"

"Employee," Marisa clarified coldly. She stared hard at Varya. "I guess we haven't flown under the radar as well as we hoped. And yes, there are some members of the community, at all levels, who would associate me with time manipulation skills and abilities."

"Which makes you a target for the thieves as well," said Sebastian.

"Not as well. Instead." Varya slumped visibly, guilt suddenly pressing in on her. "Marisa doesn't have any public association with me. I just manufacture, she... delivers."

Sebastian inhaled slowly, clearly angered. "We'll deal with that later. The profile of your clients has assured your protection from the Rest Time Authority. I don't see that changing. But right now, it sounds like you're both potential targets for the time thieves." Varya started to protest but Sebastian raised his hand to silence her. "Marisa visits here regularly, yes?" Both women nodded. "So, anyone could have been watching. You're both at risk."

"Sebastian, seriously, we're fine. If that's the only reason you're here, to try to play the role of grand protector, you can leave now. We can look after ourselves."

"I think... the Authority has recommended... that you should relocate until the perpetrators are apprehended." He placed a hand on each hip, relying on his official capacity to hold sway. It didn't work.

"Yeah, we're not leaving, but thanks," said Marisa firmly.

"I can't force you." He pulled his device out of his pocket and tapped briefly on the screen. He held it up to Varya. "But take my contact details, in case you change your mind."

Varya stared at him. For five years she had successfully walked in the shadows, avoided confrontation, dealt with only the people she wanted to. Now she felt assaulted by the sheer number of people who seemed to be flooding in across her moat. She pressed her finger on her own device for a second then held it up and nodded.

Sebastian tapped again and slipped it back in his pocket. "I'll show myself out."

Marisa and Varya were left alone, each releasing a sigh of relief.

"Five years, right? You haven't seen him in five years?"

"That's right."

"And that's all he has to say to you? Doesn't ask after your welfare, what you've been doing all this time?"

"To be fair, the whole purpose of his visit was specifically to enquire after our welfare."

Marisa stood and moved over to the stove. "That's not what I meant."

"No, I know," Varya admitted.

"Have you told Elena?"

Varya nodded.

"Yes, it was Mum's idea, to take in Daniel."

Marisa raised an eyebrow.

Varya batted her doubt away with her hand. "She offered, anyway."

"Now what? We just wait?"

She nodded. "We wait."

"You'll need to figure out how to reverse the drain."

"It's less a matter of figuring it out and more a matter of finding the technology."

"It exists?"

"Yes, it exists."

"But I thought it was destroyed years ago? Didn't you all have to destroy it? It should be gone." Marisa sounded uncharacteristically panicked.

"The time transfer tech was supposed to be destroyed as well," said Varya quietly. "It wasn't. It's a lot to ask of a person to destroy a major scientific breakthrough simply because a few people decided to use it for evil."

"Yes, and dozens of children died because of it," said Marisa angrily.

"Hundreds of people die each year on the roads, but we don't decide to destroy all the cars."

"The roads aren't deliberately trying to kill them, though."

"Okay, I'll give you that one. Guns. People kill each other in the thousands, usually for their own benefit. Firearms technology has continued to be developed. They haven't all been destroyed."

"No, but we need that technology for defence as well. It keeps us safe."

Varya smiled. "Yes, it does. And how are the Rest Time Chips any different?"

"Ugh, let's argue about this later, I know I'm right. I've got a ladies' soirée this afternoon that I need to get ready for. I can't stand those high and mighty rich people and their first world problems."

Varya watched as Marisa disappeared through the kitchen archway and returned a moment later with a bottle of Sapphiric Gin. The sun caught the purple glass as she moved towards the cabinet and flashed a colourful shadow across Varya's hand. She turned her hand over as the light played on it and smirked while Marisa's back was turned. The 'high and mighty rich' set were the only reason she had access to spirits at all. It was a non-essential luxury, which meant only the mega wealthy had the money or influence to obtain it.

Varya moved over to the bottle and stroked it absentmindedly before pouring herself a glass. Just a small one. A quarter-inch. Just to take the edge off. She inhaled the fumes and made a face.

"You're meant to drink it, not snort it," said Marisa.

Varya stared into her glass for a moment longer, then tipped her head back and downed the contents. She cherished the mild burn that spread down her throat and through her belly.

"Have you got the case ready for this afternoon?" asked Marisa.

Varya nodded and unlocked the cabinet behind her. She reached down and pulled out the sleek red briefcase they used to lend some class to these soirées. The usual tin box that Marisa took to the palliative care wards would never do for this set. They needed to believe they were special. They paid a premium for the perception.

Marisa picked it up and nodded. "What did you want to find Sebastian for, anyway? You never said."

Varya shook her head and held up her device. "Not now. I'll contact him later."

Marisa paused and wrinkled her nose but headed towards the door anyway.

"Alright. I'll be back tomorrow unless you need me sooner."

Varya nodded and watched her leave.

CHAPTER TWENTY-TWO

Marisa

It was a strange sort of employment she'd found herself in, Marisa reflected, selling time to those who had seemingly limitless supplies. The woollen plush pile gave way beneath the spiked heels of her shoes. She felt a sudden urge to rip them off and snuggle her feet into the depths of the carpet. Regular people didn't have carpet like this. Wool was expensive. It came from sheep, which required grass to graze, which required land and water to grow, which was in shorter and shorter supply since the rivers started to dry up.

In fact, everything in this vast cavern of a mansion was one big "screw you" to the restrictions of modern life. A giant water fountain trickled away in the reception area, greeting visitors and warning them by its very presence: 'Normal rules do not apply to us'.

Marisa knelt in front of the marble table at the front of the drawing room and unlocked her briefcase. One coiffed head turned away from its conversation to inspect the new noises. Marisa locked eyes with the woman briefly, staring just long enough to be impertinent, then dropped her gaze.

In her peripheral vision she watched the red lips purse, the matching fingernails transfer the champagne glass into the other hand and pause. Then the head turned away, back to the clipped chatter of the other heads.

That's all these women were to Marisa – heads and bank accounts. Do the presentation, take the payments, hand over the time tabs, and get out. Just like selling Tupperware. Which, it occurred to her, these women took it as casually as.

The super wealthy didn't work, you see. It was the ultimate status symbol in a society where most people worked sixty-hour weeks to afford the luxury of living an extra twenty-five years—to the age of sixty-five—these women idled away all one hundred and sixty-eight hours available to them. They had maids and gardeners, cooks and chauffeurs. And, though they each had at least one child, they had several nannies to care for them. It was ironic, really. Poor women wanted time tabs to add hours to their day, so they had the energy to care for their children after working twelve hours to earn their basic entitlements. Wealthy women didn't seem to want to see their children at all.

Marisa laid out the tiny glittering boxes which contained various quotas of hours. Purple with a shimmering stripe for ten four-hour strips, jade with a mother-of-pearl stripe for twenty four-hour strips. And isolated at one end of the table was a single faux-diamond encrusted box. It contained thirty, eight-hour strips: enough to eschew sleep for an entire month. This was the box no woman would order today, but for which all eight women would contact Marisa slyly afterwards, thinking they were the only one. The diamond box allowed the socialites to be present at parties until the small hours of the morning and still be on time for their personal trainer session at six o'clock sharp. All while looking fresh as a daisy thanks to the eight hours of solid rest they slipped in between.

The diamond box cost four times the price of the next package down and was Marisa's brainchild after listening carefully to conversations at these soirées for some months.

"Why wouldn't they just buy sixty four-hour slips for less?" Varya had been sceptical.

"Prestige. And purpose," Marisa had replied. "To show they can afford to control their lives as closely as they choose."

The diamond boxes had quickly become their best seller.

Marisa pushed the glittering cube gently on the golden silk cloth so that it sat slightly out of alignment with the row of lesser boxes. Then she stood and waited. It was a dance of status, this waiting. The host would eventually look up and nod to her, indicating that she had seen that Marisa was ready to begin. This bestowed upon her a respect not given to the ordinary servants.

Marisa would then have to wait a while longer. It was usually between five and ten minutes. Long enough to put her in her place, short enough to avoid angering her. After all, the women in this room needed her. She was the only dealer of time tabs. If they lost her, they would lose their connection to a status symbol that had become integral to their social existence.

And they might have to start leaving parties before midnight.

The host had installed new chandeliers, Marisa noticed, since she'd last been here, perhaps six months ago. Six electric candles and twenty crystal teardrop pendants. Twenty-one if you counted the central ball which hung a couple of inches below the rest. It lit the moulded plaster ceiling beautifully, with soft roses intertwined and reflected across the room. The same old painting hung from the back wall; a mass of coloured flecks from orange and brown rising upwards to merge with blues and greys and eventually ending in white. Marisa could never quite decide whether it was actually the work of a famous artist or simply a framed version of something one of their kids had brought home from kindergarten.

Eventually the host started to tap her guests on the shoulder, one by one, and murmured their approval for them to approach the marble table and select their products. In low voices they asked Marisa the same questions they'd asked last time and she gave them the same answers. It was a ritual to fill their days, this hushed presenting and purchasing. In truth, they could have placed their orders electronically and she would have left them at the door. But how else were idle, wealthy women to fill their days?

"Do you ever sample the wares yourself?" asked one woman, a short, mousey thing, probably around twenty-five, though it was hard to tell underneath all that make-up and plastic surgery.

Marisa shook her head slightly. "No."

The woman wrinkled her nose, offended to feel she'd been rebuffed in a moment of attempted comradery.

"Well. Perhaps you should," she said tersely. "You look like you could do with a little more sleep." She ordered two purple boxes. Marisa held up the invoice on her screen—donation to the Minor Miracles Foundation. The woman nodded and hovered her screen close to Marisa's until it buzzed.

"May your time be plentiful," she said, bowing almost imperceptibly. It was a phrase and gesture she'd added to the ritual early on.

It worked. The woman's icy demeanour melted, and she bobbed a little in return, then giggled and turned away to re-join her coterie. Marisa struggled to avoid an eye roll, blinking slowly instead. When she opened her eyes again, she was confronted by a sharp-faced woman wearing a long, scarlet duster jacket. Marisa frowned slightly. She didn't remember seeing this particular customer before. The woman pointed to the jade boxes.

"Three of them," she ordered.

Marisa bit her tongue and bent down to pick and pack the stock. She felt, rather than saw, the woman attempt to peer over the table at her.

"How do they work, anyway?"

"I'm afraid I can't divulge that, ma'am," said Marisa, staring off towards a side window as she held out the bag in one hand and her screen in the other.

The woman hesitated. "I don't particularly fancy putting anything in my body when I don't know what it'll do."

"It's very complicated technology, but it's perfectly safe. I'm sure your friends would tell you, if you care to ask them."

"As it happens, I have a PhD in complicated technology. Maybe you could give me a basic rundown? Will it interfere with my Time Chip, for starters?"

Marisa regarded her directly. The woman's eyes were almost the same jade as the time tab boxes, maybe a shade or two further towards blue.

"They speed up your bodily functions, including your brain's perception of time. You'll feel normal, but everything around you will appear as though it's in slow motion. Anyone watching you will see mostly just a blur. It's why we recommend you partake of your time tabs in a secluded, secure area."

The woman narrowed her eyes. "But it won't deduct extra time from my Time Chip?"

Marisa shook her head slightly. "No, you'll move through time itself at the same pace."

The woman tapped Marisa's screen with her own and took the bag.

"I had to be sure. Marguerite over there was trying to tell me that they slow down time. They thought maybe it put you in a bubble."

It was Marisa's turn to peer around the stranger at the gaggle of women behind her.

"Yes. They don't have PhDs in complicated technology though, do they?" she murmured.

The woman snorted, gave her a half-smile, and stalked away.

Half an hour later Marisa had packed up her wares, walked briskly down the terraced front stairs, and sank into the front seat of her car. She deposited her briefcase onto the floor of the passenger side. Then she called Varya.

"All done. Made enough to keep the Cure Factory running for another couple of months. Tomorrow morning I'm going to the shelter to hand out a few tabs to cleanse my psyche."

"Okay. Thanks."

Marisa noticed that Varya didn't laugh, as she usually did at this point in their monthly soirée ritual.

Marisa's finger wavered over the 'call end' icon. "How're you travelling?"

Silence.

"Need me to do anything to prepare for Daniel?"

"No, thanks," said Varya. "It's under control. Just waiting now."

CHAPTER TWENTY-THREE

Varya

Time seemed to slow exponentially as Varya paced back and forth in Zoe's apartment. Her friend sat and sobbed while they both waited.

It took thirty-six hours for Daniel to reappear. They spent the first hour waiting for the police to arrive. The second and third hours consisted of answering the detective's questions. Yes, he went to school this morning. No, they hadn't noticed anything out of the ordinary. No, there had been no troubles at home. Yes, he was in good health and of sound mind.

Then came thirty-three hours of trying not to check the news media, pretending there weren't journalists waiting outside the apartment block, preparing food only to pick at it rather than eat it. Thirty-three hours of waiting for the police to call. Thirty-three hours of waiting for Daniel to come home, to tell them he'd just gone to a friend's house and forgotten to tell them.

During those long hours, Varya and Zoe made plans. Zoe called her most trusted colleagues at the hospital and asked for their cooperation and silence. Varya ensured ongoing access to discreet transport for Daniel between Zoe's home, the hospital, and her own apartment.

Daniel knocked on the door of his home at five minutes past four o'clock in the morning. The street was quiet, the journalists had gone home or were sleeping in their cars on the street.

Varya shook Zoe awake when she saw his face on the building's front door monitor. She opened the apartment door before he could knock and stepped aside so Zoe could wrap her arms around him. The pale colour of his face, the haunted look in his eyes, and the nature of his return told them everything they needed to know.

"We're taking you to the hospital," Varya whispered.

Daniel stared blankly at her over his mother's shoulder.

Thirteen minutes later they walked through the hospital's staff entry and were greeted by Dr Falk, a short, dark man who was naturally inclined to silence and seriousness. He ushered them through to the same examination room Ben Williams had sat in only a few days earlier. They all held their breath as he scanned Daniel's Chip.

Zoe turned her face from the machine to Dr Falk, her expression a question mark.

"Seven hours," he proclaimed softly. "He has seven hours left. I'm so sorry."

Varya nodded. "We'll take him with us now. You'll sort out the paperwork for us, as we discussed?"

Dr Falk had already turned away to tap at the screen receiving data from the scanner.

"Yes, of course." He turned and looked directly at Varya. "I wish you all the best. I don't want to have to use this again any time soon," he said, weighing the scanner in his hand before placing it back in the drawer.

"And you'll call me if there are any other children. Anyone else who is returned and needs help?"

He nodded. "I have your number."

They bundled Daniel back into Zoe's car and drove straight to Varya's apartment. With six hours and twenty-three minutes of life left, he stood at the shimmering threshold into the Time Lock.

Varya had explained as best she could as she drove the quiet, dark roads that led from the hospital to her home. Daniel would step through a portal into a world where time was frozen in a single moment five years ago. Inside that world was Varya's mother, Elena. She would look after him and Kir—Varya's son, who was already there—until the technology to reverse the time drain was found.

"I'm not going to die?" he asked in a small voice.

Zoe squeezed his hand and started to cry. "No, sweetheart, you're not going to die. I promise."

Varya glanced in the rear-view mirror as Daniel buried his head in his mother's chest and sobbed against her. She fought the urge to release her own tears. Tears of anger and frustration. This shouldn't be happening again. The time transfer technology, though it wasn't destroyed, was well secured. She'd watched with her own eyes as it was placed in a vault deep underground. Could somebody really have re-invented it? Only a person with access to the complete body of time engineering knowledge and a few strokes of good luck could possibly have achieved such a feat. After all, that was how they'd developed the technology in the first place.

The aim of the research project had been to develop a new, more reliable calibration test for the Time Chips, to make sure they would only fire as programmed. There had been a small but problematic number of Chips which had misfired, causing the death of the host a few months earlier than their allocated sixty-five years. During trials of the calibration tests, one of the lab techs had fiddled with some of the specs, mostly out of pure boredom, and discovered the Chip could be rewound, sort of like putting an old car in reverse to make the odometer tick backwards. The problem was, once rewound, it wouldn't go forward any further than it had previously been programmed to and seemed to then lose more time. If you took a twenty-minute Chip that had already run ten minutes, and rewound it back to five minutes, it would trigger five minutes later. It made no sense—it simply didn't add up.

The trials were paused while the mechanism that enabled the rewinding was encrypted more securely.

But, of course, scientists being the insatiably curious creatures that they are, Varya and a few others set about trying to find out where the time went. They hypothesised that the Chip hadn't actually been rewound, but drained of time, which was why the twenty-minute Chip didn't give the host extra time after being 'rewound'. The time had to go somewhere. They eventually figured out that the time could be syphoned and captured in a partially full Chip using a transfer device. A neat trick, but not one they thought would ever be particularly useful. After all, nobody would ever want to lose time. They filed a report, locked away the transfer device prototypes and forgot about it.

When one of the more troublesome lab techs left the project a few months later, everybody breathed a sigh of relief. Lance was the kind of guy who argued the point with people who had years more experience than he did and whined when his breaks were three minutes shorter than the statutory minimum. He was also caught taking chocolate from the charity box without paying, on more than one occasion.

What nobody realised was that Lance was also the kind of guy to take the time transfer technology and Time Chip encryption codes and sell them on the black market to the kinds of people who could definitely benefit from the ability to take time. Especially if those years could be transferred to somebody else for profit.

Varya and Zoe sat on the bed in Varya's spare room with Daniel between them. Varya caught a glimpse of herself in the mirrored wardrobe doors. Guilt seemed etched into her tired face. Was history repeating itself? Was this all her fault, again? She looked away quickly. There would be time for self-flagellation and blame allocation later.

"When I press this button, the portal to the Time Lock will appear. Once you step through it your Time Chip will pause. It won't re-start until you come back through." Varya held up the black box to show Daniel.

"Does it hurt?"

"No. It feels a little like walking through a cool, gentle waterfall, except you won't get wet."

"Why can't Mum come with me?"

The corners of Zoe's mouth twitched again.

Varya touched Daniel's shoulder and she steered him back to meet her eyes.

"The Time Lock is not legal," she said plainly. "It's not that it's illegal, technically, but it exists outside of the law. I'm afraid that if it's discovered the authorities will shut it down. It's possible they would eventually decide it's not dangerous and allow it to be in use again, but that would take a lot longer than six hours and..." She paused to consult her screen, on which she'd set a countdown timer. "... sixteen minutes."

Zoe recovered herself enough to take back the narrative. "I have to stay here and pretend that everything has happened as the authorities expect."

Daniel frowned. "You have to stay here and pretend I'm dead."

Zoe bit her lip and nodded sadly. "Yes."

"But you're going to figure out how to reverse the drain and you'll come and get me when you have?"

"Yes," said Varya.

"But I'll visit you," said Zoe. "Every day."

Daniel stood up. "Alright. What do I do now? Just walk into it?"

"I'll go first, just follow me," said Varya, standing up and taking Daniel's hand to lead him through. She braced herself for the sudden, brief plunge in temperature, and then felt Daniel shudder as he failed to brace for the same.

CHAPTER TWENTY-FOUR

Elena

It was my idea, you must understand, to come in here with Kir. Four years of age, he was, so full of life and then to be told there's nothing more they can do. It just wasn't true.

"You go. Go and find out what more can be done," I told my Varya. She held our little boy's hand and looked into his face. His eyes were dark smudges above his pale little cheeks.

"I can't, Mama. I don't know what else to do, either."

"You're a scientist," I told her. "You will find the answers."

"Mama, shush. Enough." She said it so gently, my Varya, though I heard the catch in her voice. She had given up all hope, you see. That monstrous excuse of a husband and father had left and taken it all with him. I'll never forgive him for that. I sat down on the bed then, on the same side as her, jolting Kir slightly as I came to rest. I took her hand. I made her look at me.

"You are a magician scientist who discovered how to bend the laws of time itself and alter the course of a person's life. This..." I waved my hand theatrically at the bed, the boy and

129

everything that was attached to him. "This is easy. All you need is time and money."

She looked at me then. I wanted to make her angry, I wanted to fire up the girl I had fought with for so long. But I saw only despair, incredulity. And pity.

"Mama, I'm a physicist. Was a physicist. I don't know anything about medical science. All the money in the world is useless without time and expertise. I don't have the expertise and Kir..." She trailed off and her eyes drifted back to her little boy. It seemed as though the minutes were draining out of him as we watched.

"You know how to make time." My Varya, she didn't move. She didn't look at me, but she didn't dismiss me. I knew, then, that I would win the day. I chose my words carefully. "So, go now - make the time. For Kir, and for me. Then I will care for him while you find a way to make the money and the expertise happen."

"I don't know how long it will take," she whispered, not moving.

"I will care for our little boy. For however long it takes," I told her firmly. "Go. Find a way to make him live."

My Varya reached out her hand to that pale little boy and brushed the fragile strands back from his forehead. Then she bent her forefinger and ran the soft skin of the middle section down his soft, cool cheek.

My Varya nodded. "Okay. Okay, I will go and make the time." She looked up at me with dry eyes then, and stood. She kissed me lightly on the cheek and almost floated out the door. I sat down and took her place on the chair, warmed by her. I took our Kir's cool, unmoving hand. And I waited.

I chose the place, that was my one condition. If I was going to be spending months—and we had thought it would only be months when we first started—I wanted to make sure it was in a place that I knew and loved. It's the place where I grew up, and where I would have moved back to had I had the chance. It was never an option though, not really. I would follow that little boy to the ends of the earth.

I was happy to let Varya go, back when she was a baby-faced university graduate and she decided she needed to move cities to do her studies. To learn about time and how to bend it. Children need time away from their parent, to grow and find out that they really can stand on their own two feet. And so, she went, flying on an airplane, north to Sydney, to the University of New South Wales, where they teach them these things of national importance. Of course, back then it was all so new, just an idea thought of by the National Committee that the scientists were scratching their heads to see if they could make a reality. That took priority for the whole faculty, creating the Time Chips. Her bending-of-time research project would have to wait. Policy before pleasure.

And what a pleasure it was to my Varya to learn all there was about time and how it worked. When I called her each week, she was full of news. Did I know that the Time Chips were based on technology which could actually sense time? There was no clock inside them, nothing you could just wind forward or backwards. They could literally sense how many seconds, minutes or years had passed. Sixty-five exactly, for each person. And embedded right into the brain stem, so that they couldn't be tampered with at all. Perfectly safe, nothing to worry about.

My heart sang for her, the joy I felt at her excitement—it was wondrous. Though all the while it was mixed with my foreboding of what might come. Because too much joy cannot exist within one person without finding somewhere to leak out eventually. And once that hole has been punctured it can grow and grow until all the joy has ebbed away and left nothing but a hollow shell. I didn't want my Varya to become a hollow shell.

At first it was just fine because the hole was just tiny, the size of a pin head, just enough to release the built-up pressure of all her happiness. It leaked out onto a young man named Sebastian who was also in her class. An extra that he was taking, it was, an 'elective', I think they called it. He was a police officer. A student of policing, whatever it is they teach there. I can't imagine it's much. You either have the intellect to solve problems and deal with people or you don't, I think. Sebastian had the one but not so much of the other. Perhaps it was simply that they didn't teach the people part well enough.

Varya didn't seem to mind. They spent all their hours talking about time and its infinite possibilities. Her joy leaked out onto him, seeped into his pores, and made his mouth twitch upwards. Uncharacteristically, that upwards mouth corner trend continued for some time. Long enough for him to marry my Varya.

But that joy, it just kept leaking right out of her. I still hold that Sebastian responsible for not even trying to plug the hole.

It dripped and it dripped the deeper he got her involved in the cases of the time thieves. Invaluable knowledge, he said she had. 'Help save the children', was the carrot he dangled in front of her. Nobody could maintain their joy in the face of all those stolen babies returned to their parents, only to wilt forever soon after.

She never did figure out how to do it; turn back the hands of time. It broke her in the end.

Sebastian and his policing friends saved the day by shooting a few of the thieves and capturing another few. Importantly, they captured the impossible technology that the thieves had somehow made possible. It was turned over to Varya and her colleagues to study and understand. But the public, they were heartbroken, and they were angry. Mostly, they were scared. They wanted the technology destroyed. They wanted to never have to fear for the minutes and hours and days they planned to spend with their babies before they left home to find their joy, like my Varya had. It is a wicked thing to have parenting hours stolen from you.

And yet here I am, being given back more hours than I could ever possibly imagine, or perhaps even want, with my grandson Kir. Now a new child is to be placed under my care as well. Daniel, a nine-year-old boy. What do I know about nine-year-old boys? Not much, that's what.

CHAPTER TWENTY-FIVE

Varya

Varya and Daniel were greeted by Kir at the Time Lock portal, the smaller boy bouncing up and down, ready to greet his mother. Varya braced herself as Kir flung himself at her legs, but she kept on walking. Kir giggled as he rose up and down on Varya's leg, her right foot dug into his bottom. His laughter drowned out the sounds of adult murmuring until they arrived in the kitchen. He peered around and noticed more legs. His gaze travelled upwards to Daniel's face and his eyes opened wide.

"Mama!" he exclaimed.

Daniel gave him an awkward smile and held up his palm in greeting.

"Mama, Nanna! A moving person! It's a moving person!" He stood up and raced around to the far side of the round table where Elena sat, a steaming cup of tea in a saucer in front of her. She chuckled as she picked him up and held him close.

"Yes, Kir, it's a moving person." To Daniel she explained, "We don't get moving people around here much, as you'll soon find out."

"Mama, this is Daniel." Varya touched Daniel's shoulder. "And this is his mother, Zoe." Varya tried to catch Zoe's eye but she was too busy staring at Kir.

"He's really alive. All this time," she said. She inched towards the chair nearest to Elena and the boy and sat, to get a closer look. "How do you feel?"

"I'm hungry!" shouted Kir, very loudly, in her face, then leaned back against his grandmother and roared with laughter.

"Oh hush, child, you are not hungry. You've just finished eating your breakfast." Elena shook her head.

"But you're not in any pain?" asked Zoe, lifting one of his arms and then the other, turning them over and searching for signs of... what? She addressed Elena then. "He's been well?"

"Fit as a fiddle," Elena retorted. "Runs me off my feet." Kir bounced up and down in her lap to demonstrate. "Ouch! You've got a bony bottom, Kir. Get off me now, you'll have me as bruised as a mango dropped from a hot air balloon."

Kir leaped off her lap and went to run out of the room. He stopped short at Daniel's feet and looked directly up into his face.

"Who are you?" he asked.

"I'm Daniel," said Daniel, taking a small step backwards. Varya watched them closely. She thought he seemed sort of glad to see his former playmate, whom he must have really only remembered from photographs, stories and snippets of his own memories. Mostly, though, he seemed thoroughly overwhelmed and confused.

Varya crouched down beside Kir so their eyes were level. "You two used to be great friends when Daniel was younger. You were four years old together."

"I've been four years old for five years!" said Kir proudly, holding up the correct number of fingers, splayed widely. "But Nanna lets me put an extra candle on my cake every year anyway. Ssh, it's a secret." He looked from his mother to Daniel and back again. "Can I show him my room now? I've been learning how to play Jingle Bells on my guitar so I can play it at Christmas for everyone!"

"How about you show Daniel the Blue Room first?" suggested Varya.

"Why?"

"Because he's going to be staying with you and Nanna for a while and that's where he'll be sleeping," she explained. "He'll probably want to put his bag down in there. It's pretty heavy." She whispered this last part conspiratorially to Kir. Kir looked at the bag.

"Why? Why is he staying here? He's a moving person. Moving people don't stay here, only the frozen-in-time ones. Moving people come and then they go. Like you and Marisa and... and..." He trailed off, throwing a quick glance to his grandmother.

"You ask a lot of questions," said Daniel, finally smiling.

"Go show him the Blue Room and Daniel might answer some of the questions for you," Varya suggested.

Kir gazed up at the moving boy with new respect. "Okay, it's down here!" He pushed past Daniel and ran down the hallway.

Daniel looked at his mother hesitantly, who nodded. He hefted his bag higher on his shoulder and followed Kir.

"Is he cured?" Zoe asked, after the children were out of ear shot.

Varya shook her head. "No."

"But he seems so well."

Varya smiled. "He does, doesn't he?"

"How long can he stay this way for?" Zoe turned to Elena. "And Elena, you must be nearly..."

"... nearly seventy, dear, though I don't look a day over sixty-four, yes?" She laughed, a deep-throated—yet somehow tired—sound. "I feel it in my bones, don't you worry."

"Nothing wrong with your bones, Mama. You're as fit as a fiddle." Varya stood up and moved over to the sink. "He's safe for now, Zoe. How about you stop here for a few minutes and have a coffee and something to eat? It's not going to be easy out there." She jerked her head over her shoulder towards the portal and shuddered slightly.

There was something about the Time Lock which always made Varya feel like she'd come home. If you didn't look outside the window and you didn't stay for too long, it was almost as if Kir had just gone to stay with his grandmother for the weekend. If you discounted the passing of time and the lack of growth on Kir's part, it almost felt normal. This was the life they should have lived. At times she'd been tempted to simply stay in the Time Lock. To live this frozen existence for as long as the three of them could stand it. But it wasn't practical. Who would work to provide the food? Who would maintain the portal itself? Varya shuddered at the idea of being trapped in the Time Lock to waste away.

Zoe took the proffered ham and cheese sandwich gratefully and swallowed a few bites. She had barely eaten in days. While she chewed and waited for the coffee to percolate, Varya filled in the gaps for Elena.

"Kir hasn't aged at all," Zoe interjected, still trapped in the same cycle of wonder.

Varya delivered the steaming mugs to the table and sat down opposite her friend. She shook her head. "No, he hasn't."

"Not at the cellular level nor the developmental. He's still very much a four-year-old child. It's incredible."

"It is," Varya agreed, though with much less enthusiasm. "It's halted the progression of the cancer as well. The breadth of what he knows is astonishing, as he's built it up over the past five years. But it's all still within the bounds of what you'd expect from an above-average four-year-old. He can write, but he still gets his 'b's and 'd's mixed up. He can read, but anything beyond two syllables he needs to sound out.'

"It's fascinating. I'd love to..."

"... do some tests?" Varya shot her a wry smile and a raised eyebrow. "Take some blood, maybe, do a full brain scan, submit him to a biopsy or two?"

Zoe grimaced and shook her head slightly. "Sorry."

Elena clattered her empty cup against her saucer. "Nobody's doing tests on my grandson. He's not a guinea pig. Where's my fresh tea, Varya? Why don't I get any, hmm?"

Varya rolled her eyes but took her mother's freshly empty teacup and refilled it from the old-fashioned tea pot, complete with crocheted tea cosy to keep the brew warm.

"It's okay, it's a natural curiosity for a doctor. I've had the same thoughts myself. Why doesn't the passing of time seem to affect him? What is it doing to him on a cellular level, if anything?"

Elena took a sip and muttered into her teacup. "Yes, very worried about Kir. Nobody worries about Elena. The passing of time means nothing to an old woman."

Varya ignored her. "Any changes would be most notice-able in Kir rather than Mum, given he's at a stage where he would normally experience rapid growth."

"Unlike me who would normally be experiencing rapid deterioration."

"Ma! You'd normally be experiencing decomposition if it weren't for the Time Lock."

Zoe startled. "Of course. You would have been…"

"Yes, yes." Elena waved her hand as though it was the most natural thing in the world to live past her official expiration date. Though her coy smile gave away her true pride. "I've cheated the Rest Time Authority. I'm living proof that you can live past sixty-five and still be useful to society."

"I don't think they'd accept you as a case study, given your body is still sixty-four," said Varya dismissively, though she smiled after saying it. She turned back to Zoe. "Kir is not a good test subject."

"No, no, of course not. I mean, he's your son," said Zoe quickly. "I'm sorry."

"That's not what I meant. From an objective point of view, he's not a good test subject because he came in with a termi-nal illness. He came into the Time Lock pumped full of drugs to keep him stable for a few minutes longer. And it's worked. But any tests would be corrupted by the drugs." She paused. "And his illness." She stared at the hallway entry, down which they heard a plucked guitar float from time to time. "Besides, I've had other scientific priorities over the past few years. The effects of time stasis in motion on the human body is a study that will have to wait."

CHAPTER TWENTY-SIX

Elena

I never finished telling you about my Varya's joy. We'll let these two scientific women chat while I explain it to you, shall we?

As I said, Varya's joy leaked out of her thanks to her involvement in those terrible time thief cases. But not all of it was gone just yet. The hole was still small enough to plug and that plug came along when she needed it, right towards the end of the period of horror. The plug was just the size of a pea at first. She told me and nobody else, not even Sebastian. She just kept on working. He would have made her stop, you see, but she didn't want to. She was still trying to save those poor children, though her confidence was being shattered with each new failure. I can't imagine what she was going through. I was a primary school teacher, little kids, you see. When I failed, a few kids might be less able to read and write and count in tens than they otherwise might have been. But they never died because of it. Not like Varya's work.

That pea-sized joy plug grew into a peach-sized plug and kept right on growing. It made the corners of her mouth twitch upwards ever so slightly, even though fear and failure conspired to regularly drag them down again.

By the time the police caught the thieves and stopped the horror, that plug was the size of a melon and could be hidden no longer. Her joy was watertight by the time she shared it with Sebastian. He was mystified. I watched him touch her as though confused. She no longer leaked joy that he could soak up. Her reserve of happiness was being held tight inside herself by a Kir-shaped plug. Kir fed off her and grew, and her joy fed off him and grew alongside him.

For a while after he was born, my Varya floated in joy. That child had unlimited bottles of happiness to rain over anyone in his presence.

And then, a few short years later, the diagnosis came that changed everything. I watched the hole open again. I tried to plug it for her, with hope and possibilities of cures.

But then, the news that there would be no hope. No cure for our Kir, no plug for my Varya. The day we heard the words 'rare form of aggressive childhood cancer' and 'no research funding' I watched the joy flow out faster.

A few weeks later came the words 'palliative care' and I realised all the joy had gone. My Varya was empty, there was nothing left to plug.

CHAPTER TWENTY-SEVEN

Marisa

The morning light retained a chilled, watery quality to it as Marisa pulled her jacket tightly around her and buttoned it at the front. She wore a very different outfit to the one she'd paraded at the mansion soirée the previous afternoon. Worn boots, faded jeans, and an old jacket were her choices of disguise today. Rest Time Chips had done nothing to change the desperation experienced by women with children escaping from violent partners. If anything, the pressure to work longer hours to extend their life from forty to sixty-five had pushed them right to the edge.

It was a noble idea, incentivising work like that. But, unfortunately, the definition of 'work' didn't include raising the next generation of children. Well, unless those children weren't your own. Day-care centres still operated with twelve children to a room. Job prospects had boomed for childcare attendants, with mothers pushed into the workforce in droves and needing somewhere to leave their offspring. Having a child automatically added fifteen years to your life span, taking it up to fifty-five. This ensured children were cared for by their parents until they could look after themselves. But for a parent who wanted more than that, a mother who wanted as much time as possible with her child, to see them grow and perhaps have their own children? Those parents had to join the ranks of sixty-hour-a-week workers to earn enough credits for the right to live to the maximum age allowed of sixty-five. It was a cruel choice to have to make. Less time with your young children at the start of their lives, more time with your adult children – and maybe even your grandchildren - towards the end of your own life.

Then, of course, there was the problem of simply affording to feed, house, and care for the children. Wages were kept low by the number of low-skilled workers competing for a finite number of menial jobs. Automation had taken over most of the mid-wage jobs. That meant that most of the poor worked for long hours performing meaningless tasks for a pittance in pay.

Marisa shook herself slightly. Caring for her own child wasn't a problem she had to face, nor was poverty. Not anymore, not since Varya and her mad schemes came into her life. She looked up at the nondescript apartment block in front of her. It differed from the apartment blocks either side only by the extra locks on the door and the bars on the windows. And even then, it was only one or two extra locks compared to the apartment block to the left, and the bars extended to one extra storey compared to the apartment block on the right.

She raised her hand to press the bell and announced herself and her intention when Tina's disembodied voice sounded over the intercom.

Tina was a thin woman in her sixties with a grim face but sparkling eyes. She let Marisa in, then disappeared through an internal door and reappeared behind a reception desk.

"Marisa."

"Tina."

"What do you have for us today?"

Marisa pulled her screen out of her pocket, tapped at it, and held it up so Tina could see. In exchange for her success with the soirée set, Marisa had requested five per cent of the profits be diverted to support this women's shelter. It was a small gesture but one that helped Marisa keep her focus. Her experience of rare childhood diseases was very different to Varya's. Her son died in a tiny room with bare cupboards and bars on the windows, not dissimilar to the ones laid out above her head now. There was no expensive medicine sent home with him, they had to make do with paracetamol. It provided little comfort in the face of the wracking coughs which shook his tiny frame.

This wasn't a story Marisa had chosen to share with Varya. In fact, she'd shared no story at all, just a request to do this one thing, plus one-hundred four-hour time tabs to distribute each month to the women who lived here with their children. Marisa hadn't expected her employer to understand and was glad she'd asked for no explanation.

"Every month?" she'd asked.

Marisa had nodded. "Yes, every month. To be available on the first of the month and to be distributed when I get around to it."

"Okay." And they'd moved on to the next order. The time tabs had been ready on the first of every month since then, without fail. Varya never mentioned them, just handed them over with the latest order. She never asked where they went.

Marisa was never entirely sure whether it was because she was being discreet, or because she simply didn't care.

Maybe that wasn't fair. We all had a limited supply of care factor, Marisa knew. Maybe Varya's quota was fully allocated to the Kir Problem. She could forgive that. If she'd had a chance to save her son, she would have thrown her own care factor quota—plus anyone else's that she could beg, borrow or steal—at his problem. Marisa's son's problem had been simple, though. Not a rare or complicated disease. Just asthma. Exacerbated by poor health, poor food, and a cold apartment when the heat turned off because the money ran out. Rationed medicine because that, too, ran out when the money did, which it seemed to do all too often. The night of his final asthma attack, she'd called the ambulance when his lips turned blue. By the time they came his breath had stopped, his warmth starting to fade in the cold, cold room. And still they sent her a bill for the ambulance.

Marisa knew what life was like for the women in this apartment block. After working twelve-hour days, five days a week, they would come home to feed and care for their child—bathing them, putting them to bed, washing their clothes and preparing for the next day. It was hard to find any time to spend with them that wasn't overshadowed by complete exhaustion.

The time tabs helped a little. For some it meant being able to have a four-hour nap as soon as they got home and waking up more refreshed and able to actually enjoy spending time with their child. For others it meant four hours of time on the weekend to spend studying for a new qualification, one that would lead to a higher-paying job and allow them to leave the shelter and rent a better home, one far away from the perpetrator who sent them running for shelter in the first place. A home without bars on the windows.

Tina peered over her glasses at the numbers on the screen and picked up a screen from behind the desk to hold it up in front of Marisa's. It buzzed: transaction completed. Tina nodded towards an empty space over Marisa's shoulder.

"Rec room's cleared if you want to use that today. They know you're coming."

Marisa put her screen away and headed into the room behind her. The bare walls and bright orange plastic moulded chairs made a stark contrast to her sales platform the day prior. In one corner sat smaller chairs and tables, faded reds and blues with assorted cups full of pencils, worn down inconsistently. Someone had tried to cheer up the room by tacking children's drawings to the wall. Sunshine and aliens seemed to be the main themes. Marisa smiled and sat down in one of the less cracked adult chairs. They were clean, at least. Shelters like this used to receive government funding, before, when gender equality was a focus. Now everybody assumed gender inequity was a thing of the past. The flavour of the month had moved on. Age equality was the new focus. And yet still it was often the women who kept their child close when relationships broke down, even when violence played no part.

Her customers drifted in one by one. Some brought their son or daughter with them; some left them under the erratically watchful eye of older children upstairs. Marisa mused that 'customers' wasn't quite the right word. No payment was made, though goods were passed over.

Rosa used her time tabs to get some extra sleep after working four extra hours online while her child slept. The money paid for hearing aids for her daughter.

Maggie came with a gurgling baby on her hip. She used her tabs to get a solid four hours of sleep in between night feeds.

Lenny used hers to simply get some time to herself after putting her twins to bed. She told Marisa she'd started reading her way through a full set of Georgette Heyer's classic romance novels that she'd found at a second-hand shop.

Marisa snorted.

"A girl can dream, can't she?" laughed Lenny.

"You've not been a girl for a good couple of decades, Lenny," Marisa observed as she handed over the plain matchbox of tabs. "Just as long as you know they're fiction."

Lenny took the matchbox and opened it immediately to stare greedily at the smooth, transparent slips. "No chance of me looking for my own real-life version, love. I've already got two kids sleeping in bunks in the room next door. I've got no desire to share my own room with any breathing body, whether it's man-shaped or baby-shaped."

Lenny closed the box and tapped it against her palm twice before she stood up.

"Thank you. Hope to see you again next month. May your time be plentiful."

A grin creased the corners of Marisa's mouth. It was her own brand of social sabotage to implant the same phrase here, at the other end of town, when the idle socialites twenty blocks away thought it was their own specially coded greeting.

She smiled warmly at her. "You're welcome. May your time be plentiful too."

Her screen buzzed on the table next to her. A message from Varya: "*Daniel safely returned and enclosed. Food package for three tonight, please.*"

"Oh, good. Wonderful." Marisa pushed a breath out of her lungs that she seemed to have been holding since Daniel was taken. She peered into her tin box. Only two matchboxes left.

"*Nearly done here. Let me know what you need next,*" she tapped back.

"*Meet me at apartment,*" came the swift reply.

Marisa held up her palm in farewell to Tina in reception as she walked the same path she had an hour earlier.

"Hey, before you go, love..." Tina started, leaning forward onto the counter, and looking down the hallway and back to Marisa.

Marisa stopped and lowered her hand.

"I was just wondering whether you knew anything about these time thieves." The last two words were spoken in a stage whisper.

"Only as much as anyone who watches the news."

Tina rubbed her thumbnail against the pen she held, making grating noises as she passed the raised brand letters each time.

"It's just that, I mean, I don't know if it means anything, but I was thinking." She stopped and slotted the pen back in its stand so hard that the little strand of silver balls connecting the two rattled against the desk. "Nah, don't worry. I'm wasting your time on gossip."

Marisa inched closer to the desk and put her palm down, a single finger reaching out to hold the strand still.

"I'm listening."

"Well, these past few weeks we've had two kids go missing, about four days apart. Violent dads, drug-addicted mothers. A six-year-old girl and an eight-year-old boy. Figured they'd done a runner, or the dad took 'em. But now, I wonder if it isn't tied up with this other stuff that's been going on."

Marisa frowned. "You reported it to the police?"

"'Course I did. They didn't do much, took a statement from me, couldn't rouse the mums. Not much to go on. Can't blame them really."

"And they never came back?"

"Nup. Haven't seen nor heard from neither of them since." She paused, expectantly. "So? What do you think?"

Marisa shook her head. "Sounds like what you said—runaways or fathers."

Tina shrugged and sighed. "Ah well. I hope they're okay."

"Yeah. Me too."

CHAPTER TWENTY-EIGHT

"Why Ben?" Marisa stepped into the apartment past Varya and turned to face her.

"Hello to you, too," said Varya, closing the door gently.

"Why Daniel?"

"I don't understand. What do you mean?"

"Why would they take older kids who can fend for themselves, from a middle-class district, rather than younger kids with more years on their Chips from poorer neighbourhoods where it's less likely to make headlines? It doesn't make sense."

"I don't think anyone has ever accused those monsters of being sensible, Marisa. Maybe they're just not very bright."

"Or maybe they're trying to make a point."

"What point? That dying young is awful?"

Marisa looked away in frustration, annoyed at Varya for not being receptive to the idea and annoyed at herself for not having thought it out more.

Babies and toddlers were the logical children to take to maximise the number of years left to drain from the Chips.

But they were harder to snatch, rarely left unattended. They were also harder to return unnoticed. The returning was smart, she'd always thought, in a macabre kind of way. It left no pile of bodies, but everyone was so focused on the trauma of the dying child, they didn't have a chance to ask for details of the kidnappers. Not that the returned children could have told them much anyway, apart from vague memories of a drugged haze.

Varya waited for Marisa to say something more. When she didn't, she turned on her heel and returned to the kitchen, not waiting for her employee to follow. Marisa took her time to collect herself. She could hear murmuring in the kitchen and strained to identify the other voice. It wasn't Zoe's voice, as she'd expected. Too low. She dared to hope that, after all these years, Varya had finally agreed to ask Sebastian for help.

It was the rational thing to do. Other cures had been pushed through the labs at a satisfactory rate. Kir's cure was still languishing in the unsolved mysteries bucket after more than four long years. There was no guarantee that Sebastian could provide the breakthrough that Varya needed, but it was the next logical step. Marisa continued listening to the voices, calm and in control, and wondered if Varya had become a little too comfortable with having her son and mother preserved in a living museum. She pushed herself off the wall where she had slumped and trudged up the apartment's short hallway.

The small, round dining table held a sea of papers and clips which Connor and Varya pushed around, turned, and exchanged at regular intervals. Varya looked up briefly but returned her eyes to the papers before she spoke.

"I shopped for ingredients, they're in the fridge. Recipes for the week are in the folder."

Marisa pursed her lips and wriggled her nose. Varya was an easy boss and some-time friend, as long as you didn't second guess her. Question her judgement and she would shut down, just like this. Marisa resolved to try to keep any further thoughts about the time thefts to herself, focus on stashing away money for her retirement and getting out of here.

She flicked through the recipes Varya had bookmarked. Pizza with tomato sauce and pepperoni but no herbs, just as Kir liked it. Spaghetti with expensive meat sauce, but with added pureed vegetables – enough to provide extra nutrients but not enough so that Kir would notice it. Kir didn't like vegetables, which was kind of fine when you were only four years old for one year, but not so great when your fussiness was artificially extended beyond the usual age thresholds. And for sweets: freshly baked donuts with jam in the middle. The exact same strawberry and raspberry jam that you could only find at one particular monthly market just outside of the city. The market that Varya made time to go to every single month.

"Have you called Sebastian yet?" Marisa ventured, with more confidence in her tone than she felt.

"No. Why would I need to call Sebastian?" Varya asked in a slightly strained voice, still shuffling and arranging papers. "Do *you* feel, in any way, in imminent danger?"

Connor stopped his shuffling and looked up, alerted to the tension between the two women. Marisa slapped a wooden board down on the counter and started to assemble the dough in a bowl next to it.

"Oh, you know. I just thought maybe he might know something about that time transfer technology thing you mentioned before. Not that I'd know anything about that, of course, just making conversation." She measured and poured the water and started to fold in the flour, her back to Varya.

"I'm sure I don't need his help with that," Varya retorted stiffly. "If he knew anything about it, he would have already offered it up."

"Varya!" Marisa was done with being diplomatic. It was never her strong suit.

"What?"

Marisa spun to face her, floury hands still poised over the glass bowl. "Yesterday you finally agreed to let me try to find Sebastian to ask for his help. Then he just waltzes into your apartment, and now you've changed your mind?"

Varya avoided Marisa's glare, staring at the kickboards of the cabinets. She took a breath. Her fingers rubbed at the paper she was holding.

"I don't need his... advice, as such. I just need his access."

Marisa frowned. "His access? You mean like passwords or something?" She looked to Connor for help. He shrugged.

"He doesn't know the time transfer technology still exists. But he does have access to where it was stored."

"So, tell him to go and get it!" Marisa shouted.

She shook her head sadly. "It's not that simple."

"Yes, actually, it is." Marisa picked up Varya's phone from the counter and stomped over to hand it to her, shedding flour on her clean pants. "Call him."

Varya took the phone with her fingertips and laid it down carefully on the table, then started to brush at the flour dust on her lap. "I don't need to," she said. "I've already arranged to meet him this afternoon."

The fury drained from Marisa. She leaned against the bench and watched Varya. She felt tired.

"You're not going to tell him, are you?"

Varya shook her head slightly. "There's no need to."

Marisa closed her eyes. "How many more secrets are you going to keep from him?"

"As many as necessary."

CHAPTER TWENTY-NINE

Daniel

"And this is Yappy Dog, and this is Teresa the Wonder Sheep, and this is Rooster." Kir patted each one of his stuffed friends on the head. "Say hello to Daniel!" He turned and grinned.

"That's not a rooster. It's a hen." Daniel pointed to the rotund fluffy ball with a chewed-up bit of orange material hanging from its beak. "It doesn't have a comb."

Kir blinked, crestfallen.

"You know, the bit that goes on the rooster's head?" Daniel planted his hand against the centre of his skull and waggled his fingers in the air, demonstrating. "This one is a girl chicken."

"Well, her name is still Rooster." Kir picked up the gender-fluid poultry and wrapped his arms around it defensively. He sat on his bed and watched his new moving friend, still undecided about whether he was happy about his arrival. When he had imagined one of the frozen children coming to life, they had always been far more agreeable than the one that stood in front of him. The frozen children just laughed when

155

he told his joke about the knock knocks and the interrupting ghost. And they always nodded when he told them things and they stood exactly where he wanted them to stand when they played statues. Daniel was standing a little bit too close for Kir's liking, hands in pockets and a sad look on his face. Daniel was also very tall.

"Your mum says we used to play together when I was little," said Daniel.

Kir continued to stare. The tour of his bedroom was now complete, and he didn't quite know what to say to Daniel that wouldn't be wrong again. He wasn't sure if he liked him yet, but he didn't want to make him leave before he'd decided.

"Do you remember me?" asked Daniel. "From when I was little?" It was becoming clear to him that, although this might be the same boy he'd played Matchbox cars with at age four, they were no longer equal. Kir was still just a little boy. Daniel realised that he was perhaps intimidating the small boy with his height, and sat down, cross-legged on the carpet, in a swift drop-collapse manoeuvre. Kir started to swing his legs, low at first but then higher and then just a little bit higher. He reached out his big toe. It nearly touched Daniel's nose. He giggled.

"Hey!" said Daniel, catching the boy's foot in his hand gently.

"Are you staying?"

"For a while, yes, I guess. Not too long." Daniel thought for a moment. "I have to get back to school. I've got a basketball quarter-final next week."

"Oh," said Kir. "So not long."

Daniel shook his head. "I don't think so."

Kir sat up straight, excited to have thought of something else to talk about.

"What sickness do you have? I have cancer."

Daniel laughed. "Oh, I'm not sick."

Kir frowned. "Then why are you here? My Mum brought me here 'cause I'm sick and she has to find a cure before I can come out again. Why did your mum bring you here?"

Daniel leaned forward and flicked Rooster's orange beard. Kir snatched the toy away, out of his reach.

"I guess you could say I'm not sick, but I'll die real soon if Varya can't find a cure to fix me."

Kir eyed him suspiciously, then raised a single eyebrow. "And you think 'Rooster' is a weird name for a chicken? That makes more sense than what you just said."

"Hey, Dan." Zoe appeared at the doorway, smiling hopefully at the two of them. "Making friends?"

"We were already friends," Kir announced. "When Daniel was little." He nodded sagely at Daniel, who looked back at him in mild surprise.

"Well, that's wonderful. You look after Dan for me, then, won't you, Kir? I have to go away for a while, but I'll be back to visit again soon."

Daniel winced at his mother's attempt at casualness

"Don't worry, she'll come back again. Mums always come back." Kir reached out to pat the older boy awkwardly on the shoulder, almost toppling himself off the bed.

"That's right, Kir. Mums always come back," Zoe agreed quietly. To Daniel, she said, "Hug?"

He paused, sneaking a look at Kir to see what he thought of hugs. Kir sat and watched Zoe with excitement approaching deification. Daniel got up slowly and presented himself for a reluctant hug. It felt better than he'd expected. When she let go it was too soon. He swallowed what threatened to become a whimper.

"I know it's been confusing and scary but you're going to be okay." Daniel wasn't sure if she was talking to him or herself. Maybe both. She nodded. He nodded back. "Okay. I'll see you soon."

CHAPTER THIRTY

Varya

Varya tried her best to avoid shuddering as she followed Sebastian down the corridor at Rest Time Corps. Her eyes focused on the hairs on her ex-husband's neck, just above his jacket collar. He needed a haircut. The black hairs were peppered with grey now, where they curled in short, wispy clumps below the intended hairline. In her peripheral vision she could see signs marked 'Lab 1' and 'Lab 3' to her left.

Varya had never gone back to work after Kir was born. She relied on the time credit she'd received for birthing him, and the credits she'd earned in overtime before he was born, to extend her life span closer to the sixty-five year maximum. She'd planned to only take a couple of years off, then go back and work longer hours again. It would only mean a month or two of missed time credits, if any. At the time she'd been happy to trade earning thirty extra days in the future to spend a whole year of time with her baby son. But then two years turned into three years, which soon crept into four. And then Kir got sick, so there was no question of returning.

She didn't miss these cold, sterile halls. Her own medical research facility had artwork on the walls to remind staff who they were working for, really. Collages of sick kids and their families, both before and after diagnosis. And then, the best collage of them all—the kids they'd saved. Healthy kids playing catch, drawing pictures, blowing out candles on their birthday cakes.

Rest Time Corps was a series of grey painted walls adorned with warning signs about potential hazards or security levels.

Varya was concentrating so fiercely on Sebastian's neck that she nearly stepped on his heels as he came to a stop in front of a single elevator. He pushed the button and they waited.

"What are you hoping to find down there?" He glanced sideways at her.

"Research papers, maybe even partial plans," she answered vaguely.

"Weren't they all destroyed, though?"

She shrugged. "People always keep random notes. They might help."

"We could use some help," he muttered.

She looked at him sharply as they stepped into the elevator. "Another child?"

He shook his head. "No, not..."

Yet. That was what he'd meant to say, Varya was sure. He'd seemed frustrated and confused during the brief interview he'd subjected her to. She'd told him she was here to help look for scraps which might lead to the recreation of the time transfer technology, to save the kids. She'd explained how the last kid taken had been her friend's son. He didn't seem convinced of her story. Then again, she hadn't felt in a particularly helpful mood and had refused to answer most of his questions—both those relating to the case and herself.

"How's your friend... Zoe?"

"As you'd expect." Varya was already striding away from him, through the stacks. He stood and watched her go. She slowed and then stopped, scanning the labels. Looking up, she called out to him. "Where's the ladder?"

He picked up a step ladder to his left and brought it over. She climbed up, pulled an archive box down, and handed it to him. He placed it on the floor, and she handed him down the one behind it. Jumping several rungs to the concrete floor, she crouched down and pulled the lid off the second box. Inside was a mess of different sized sheets of paper jumbled together with paper clips, rolled mats of plans, and a couple of small black boxes. She threw him a backward glance and shifted so that her body blocked his view.

"This could take a while," she said, her palm flat on the top of the papers.

"I can wait," he replied, taking a seat on one of the lower rungs of the ladder.

With her back to him, she started pulling out papers and scanning them, placing them on the ground next to her. She opened one black box and closed it, then dropped it heavily on the discard pile. Then another. And another.

"It's not here," she muttered. Her movements became more frantic as she continued to pull the contents of the box out, scattering them in heaps across the floor. She tore the lid off the first box and upended the whole container, pushing the papers into cascades to separate anything caught between. "It's not here." She stood and glared at him, a wild look in her eye. "Move." She scaled the ladder and her upper body disappeared into the shelf as she checked the space vacated by the boxes.

"Have any of the files been moved?" she asked him.

"What? No." He started to pick up discarded papers and place them back in their boxes.

She stopped and turned to face him; a full head taller than him on the ladder.

"Who's had access to these boxes in the past five years? Who had authorisation to remove any contents?"

Sebastian shook his head. "Anyone. Everyone."

"Shit. Don't you lot have security anymore? Isn't this place supposed to be accountable and safe and..." Varya took up Sebastian's former place at the foot of the ladder and put her head in her hands.

"This whole place is a secure facility, Varya. You need top-level clearance just to get through the front door."

When she raised her face to his, anger had given way to fear.

"It's gone," she whispered.

"What's gone?" he asked.

"The time transfer tech. It's gone. It was here."

"Varya, what's going on with you? The time transfer tech was always gone. It was destroyed, along with the plans."

She shook her head, tears rolling down her face.

"Reg and I kept one. Just in case."

He frowned. "In case of what?"

"In case the Rest Time Authority changed their minds. About letting us use it. The discovery was such a fluke, it could have taken decades to re-develop. We thought it might be needed again someday."

She wiped at her face, sniffed, and tried to stand. "Reg. Where is he? I'll ask him. Maybe he moved it."

Sebastian helped her up and then kept hold of her arm. "Reg left not long after you did, Varya. The Corps was pretty much swept clean of anyone who'd been on the original project. Everyone signed non-disclosure agreements and were given severance packages large enough to keep them happy and quiet."

"We have to find him."

"You think he..."

Varya nodded. "Not Reg. He wouldn't, but maybe... Oh god, what have we done?"

Varya realised Sebastian was holding on to both of her upper arms, his grip too tight. She pulled away and stared at the boxes on the floor.

Sebastian cleared his throat. "I'll work on finding Reg. If he's stolen time transfer tech that may have been used by the time thieves, it's part of my case anyway." He paused. "Do you think there's anything else in there that could help to reconstruct the tech?" His gaze flicked down at the messy piles.

"Maybe." She looked up at Sebastian, horror mixed with hope. "Can I take the boxes?"

He picked up one and inspected the label, then gave her a quick once over. "They're not classified, so yes. But you'll have to sign a bunch of forms first."

"Okay."

He hesitated. "That's not a good sign, you know. Whoever assessed the contents clearly thought there wasn't anything particularly useful in these boxes if they're not highly classified."

Varya laughed then, a hollow sound that wasn't full of mirth. "Whoever classified them didn't know what they were looking at."

Sebastian raised an eyebrow.

"They're useful to me," she explained.

"Okay. Let's get you loaded up and out of here then."

"Thank you."

He stared at her a moment, then joined her on the floor to repack the boxes. "Do you really think you can do it?"

"Do what?"

"Reconstruct the time transfer technology."

Varya stopped packing and sat back on her heels. "Yes, I do."

"It's very complicated."

"Yes, it is."

"I can ask for leave from here. You know, to help you out."

Her expression didn't change, though her hand twitched. "You don't have the right qualifications."

Sebastian reached out and touched her upper arm. Varya jerked back and glared at him.

"I don't need qualifications," he said. "I have an excellent understanding of how the tech works and I have more experience in this area than you do."

Varya stood up, the box balanced at her hip. "I invented the time transfer technology. I did it once. I can do it again."

Sebastian closed the lid of his box and stood to face her. He raised himself to his full height and stepped closer, so she was forced to look up.

"This isn't the time to be stubborn, Varya," he said softly. "You need my help, whether you want it or not. By refusing me out of spite you're endangering the lives of children."

Varya spoke slowly and without emotion. "I don't want your help. And I'm not accepting it." She stared up at him, with the full knowledge that her laboratory was also a high security facility and he couldn't enter without the necessary clearance. She was the only one who was authorised to provide clearance and had no intention of doing so. "We're wasting valuable time. Where are the papers I need to sign?"

She waited until the papers were sorted, the boxes locked safely in the car with her, and the car was at least five minutes away from Rest Time Corps. Then she relaxed her clenched jaw and allowed her hands to shake with a heady mixture of relief and rage. If he thought he could use the same tactics against her that had worked five years ago, he was sorely mistaken.

CHAPTER THIRTY-ONE

Marisa

Marisa lifted the lid of the box that Varya had perched on the kitchen counter. She peered inside and thumbed a few dozen pages.

"So, there's no digital back-up for these?"

"Nope," Varya sat at the table reading the top page of an inch-thick stack, a mug of coffee in her hand.

"These are literally the only copies left?"

"Yep."

Marisa let the cardboard lid fall to the side, softly clattering onto the bench. She inhaled the dusty aroma and wafted it towards herself.

"Come to me, great elixir of immortality, fill me with your secrets," she intoned.

Varya put her coffee mug down and looked up.

"What the hell are you doing?" she demanded.

Marisa shrugged. "Thought I'd give it a shot."

"I don't think it works like that," said Zoe, giving her a weary smile.

Varya had tried to send Zoe home, but she'd returned to the apartment first thing that morning, preferring to stay as close to her son and the Time Lock as possible. Varya had argued that she needed to continue life as normal to avoid suspicion. Zoe pointed out that it was perfectly normal for her to want to avoid spending time in a space she had once shared with her son, which would bring back painful memories. After some more reasoning (Varya) and a few tears (Zoe), Zoe had finally gotten her way and taken up residence in the tiny, white apartment.

Marisa patted her cheeks and ran her fingers over her cheekbones. "I'm sure my skin feels smoother already." Her audience was unappreciative. "Seriously, though, it's pretty amazing, don't you think? Within these boxes is literally the secret to eternal life."

"Yes," said Varya flatly. "If you have access to enough people willing to drain their time and transfer it to yourself."

Marisa watched guiltily as Zoe's head jerked briefly in the direction of Kir's old bedroom, where the Time Lock portal was hidden away.

Varya put the papers down and took off her reading glasses. "This is going to take some time, and I need quiet to think, so would you mind...?"

"Sorry," Marisa whispered, turning back to her recipe book and beginning a stock take of ingredients.

Zoe plucked a few sheets of paper from the box at Varya's feet. "There's a lot of material here. I could help out if you like, do some reading, make some summaries."

Varya peered over her glasses, which she'd replaced on her face already.

Zoe tried again. "I mean, there's a fair bit here that's actually pretty close to medical terminology rather than the physics of it. I could take the medical stuff. If you think it might... speed things up, I mean.'"

"Not like you're in any rush at all," muttered Marisa.

Varya glared at her back. To Zoe she said, "It's pretty advanced, but I think most people with a postgrad degree in medical science would be able to follow it. So, yes, if you think you're up for it, that'd be great."

Marisa turned towards them, leaned back against the bench and crossed her arms, eyebrows raised.

"Oh really, Var'? Anyone with, say, a PhD in medical science could help out? And there's a lot of material to get through?" She tipped her head to one side and tapped a finger against her chin. "I wonder where you could possibly get a ready supply of people who have PhDs in medical science? I mean, it's not like you know many people like that, is it?"

"Oh my god, of course, the lab." Zoe was quick to catch on. "Varya, could we borrow your lab staff for a couple of days?"

Varya started to shake her head but Marisa interrupted with a pointed finger.

"Oh, no you don't. You can do this."

"It'll attract too much attention."

"Not if you sell it the right way."

"This isn't a sales transaction, Marisa," she snapped.

"Everything is a sales transaction if you look at it the right way."

"I won't put Kir's Time Lock in jeopardy to..."

"... save Daniel?" Zoe finished quietly.

"That's not what I meant."

Marisa pulled out a kitchen chair, sat on it, and stared hard at Varya.

"You don't need to tell them about the Time Lock, or about Kir. They don't need to have anything to do with this.

You just sell it as a mini project to help the government resurrect a technology which will save the missing kids. Same as anything else those scientists do—find ways to save kids."

"But I'll have to tell them about my involvement in the initial project."

Marisa shrugged. "I've been telling you for years, you should tell them anyway. I don't think the reaction will be as bad as you think. They'll understand the irresistible drive to follow the thread of knowledge, wherever it may take you. They're researchers, after all. In fact, they're probably the best audience to start practising your story on."

Varya nodded once, then a second time, more firmly.

"Okay. Okay, yes, we'll give it a try. I'll read through these today and put a team together at the labs in the morning." She turned to Zoe, who clapped her hands together, eyes bright. "You realise this is only one part of helping Daniel, right? Even if we can put together a time transfer device, we still need the Rest Time Corps to find the person who Daniel's time was transferred to, so we can transfer it back?"

Zoe waved away any doubt. "Yes, but he's safe for now. And, even if we never find the person responsible, he can still receive time transferred from someone else, can't he? Another donor?"

Varya looked at her then and saw past the smile to the desperation behind it. Her first thought was to tell Zoe it was illegal, it was unethical, to transfer time from herself to her son. But then, wouldn't she do the same for Kir? Give him ten of her years, or even twenty, just so that he could live? In the end, she simply nodded and selected a stack of papers for Zoe to start reading through, along with a four-hour time tab to buy them extra time.

CHAPTER THIRTY-TWO

Elena

For a significant portion of my married life, I wished my husband dead. He wasn't a terrible man, you must understand. I didn't even dislike him. Not very much, anyway. It's just that there came a point when living with him became more difficult than the prospect of living without him.

I'd thought about his death at great length. It wouldn't be painful. It would be entirely accidental and I would be utterly devastated, but staunch, in my grief. I would hold it together for the children. We would speak of their father fondly and keep photographs of him around the house and celebrate his memory.

There was no need for me to actively intervene. I knew, in my bones, that he wouldn't live a long life. Call it a premonition, second sight or just plain wishful thinking.

Stan Galanos, that was his name. He was a solicitor who worked in a city office drafting corporate documents and finding loopholes in contracts. Not exactly dangerous work. He was normally home by six o'clock but from time to time his hours would unexpectedly extend.

Come six-thirty on any given night, I'd wonder whether he was simply working late, or perhaps the trains had been delayed. I'd put plastic wrap over his cooling dinner, send young Varya off to have her shower, and daydream. In my daydreams the doorbell would ring. It would be two police officers, there to tell me that they were very sorry, but my husband had been involved in a terrible accident. Was there anybody who could stay with the children while I came to identify the body?

By seven-thirty, when I'd be packing Varya off to bed with a story and a kiss, I'd surreptitiously check my phone to see if perhaps there had been a city shooting? Stan worked near the family courts, so I imagined perhaps an estranged father had run amok with a sawn-off shotgun, maybe he'd travelled into the city to fight for custody of his children. "No, your Honour, I never beat them with a strap. Except when I'd had a few, but that was the alcohol, and I couldn't help it. And yes, of course I beat my wife when she was disobedient. But it was only for her own good. And I said sorry afterwards."

But in this daydream of mine, his pleas had fallen on deaf, unsympathetic ears. Those bastard judges, he would think to himself, always siding with the mothers because the world was against fathers. It had nothing to do with the evidence submitted by their local hospital—of broken bones and testimony that it was the father's hands that snapped them.

And so, the children were denied a father and the father snapped and roared out of the court with the specific intent of denying passers-by their lives.

And I pictured my poor, poor husband getting caught up within the toxic male rage which emanated from this hypothetical man who was just trying to be the best father he could be—in his own opinion.

I would peer at my phone and frown, waiting for it to ring. Instead, just as I was dimming Varya's bedroom light and planning how I was going to get through the next twelve months pretending to be surprised and devastated about my widowhood, my phone would illuminate and vibrate with a message from Stan.

"*So sorry, lost track of time. So much work on right now. Leaving now. Love you. See you soon.*"

And so, it was with great surprise that I woke up one morning to discover my husband cold and stiff in the bed beside me. A heart attack at age fifty-four. So pedestrian, so predictable, so convenient.

We mourned him. I flashed his death certificate at the superannuation company (his retirements savings were not inconsiderable), at the bank (the house was now mine out-right) and Varya's school (to have his name taken off the correspondence that he never bothered to read anyway). And then I slid in between the cool sheets of our marital bed each night and slept, unassailed and deeply.

Like a good widow, I spent nearly a month in that bed before I felt able to return to work. I got up to take Varya to school and then I went back to bed. I got up again in the afternoons to welcome her home.

A few years later, when Varya came home from her not-so-new-anymore job at the Rest Time Corps, rambling something about life spans, I nodded sagely. Her father, rest his soul, would have been fascinated to hear about the scientific basis of this newly discovered innate life force – complete with genetically coded 'use by' date – but I didn't have to work too hard to understand the general gist. I quickly realised that I knew about life spans already. It's just that a couple of generations back we called it things like 'fate' or said, 'her number had just come up'.

The disturbing thing, and what really made me sit up and listen, was that Varya's colleague—Reginald, a quiet-mannered, tall weed of a man—thought he could harness this life force. He wanted to bottle it, basically, though I don't think he ever figured out how. With Varya's help he did, however, figure out how to transfer it from one animal to another. Immortal mice, can you imagine it?

When the time thefts started people were all up in arms about the Time Chips and them being tampered with. But Time Chips are manmade devices, loaded with poison. That's all they are. Encrypted, defended, tamper-proof, whatever. They're no use to anyone else. You can't 'transfer time' from one Chip to another. Why wouldn't you just hack into and re-program the existing Chip if you wanted to live longer?

And yet, that's what the news reports all said. The Time Chips of the kids had been tampered with, the hospital scanners said so. They leaked a couple of clips to prove it. Returned with just a few hours left on the clock. The people who stole the children must have done it to steal their time, that was the conclusion everyone jumped to. These were kidnappers who wanted to live forever.

But of course, delaying your lethal injection isn't going to matter half a damn if your number is up anyway, is it?

I heard Varya and Reginald whispering over their single malt whiskeys one night, after the first few children had been returned. She'd brought him home with her, which I thought strange—she only had eyes for Sebastian by then, you understand—until I realised what they were whispering about, of course.

"It's the time transfer devices that were stolen, I'm sure of it," he trembled, his intonation rising and threatening to push up the volume.

"But it's the Time Chips that have been killing them at precise moments, they've clearly calibrated them specifically." Varya's voice was soft, comforting, but I heard the slight note of panic, that only I could pick up on.

"But why, Varya, why would they do that? Why would anyone go to the trouble of kidnapping a child, rewinding their Time Chip, and returning them to their parents, just so they can watch them die?"

"A psychopath, a serial killer, maybe? Maybe it has nothing to do with profit."

"No, there are too many children, too many places. It's not just a serial killer, this is an organised syndicate. They're taking the life span, I'm sure of it. They're just hacking the Time Chips as well to cover it up. It's all smoke screens and mirrors."

"You're being paranoid," she said, trying to soothe. "There's no way to be certain that the life spans have been drained."

"You're being naïve," he hissed. "Where do you think the missing time transfer prototypes have gone?"

"Keep your voice down. They were probably confiscated and destroyed. It's not like we were supposed to have them anyway."

"Varya, they were stolen. If they'd been confiscated, you and I would have been marched out of that facility and straight into the nearest prison. That project was stopped by someone high up."

"But... but you said we had approval."

"We did. It was retracted."

There was silence for a good while, then. My own hand shook, and I wished I had a tumbler of that single malt to fortify me, too. I feared for my Varya then, for what she'd gotten herself mixed up in. She was a good girl, you must understand. And goodness knows, she's paid her penance a thousand times over since then.

Then Reginald said this: "I have one left, that I hid apart from the other ones."

"So, use it. Test your theory."

I heard the clink of glass against glass then, as he put his down on the table.

"I'm going to."

He left after that. I listened to the front door close and my Varya go to her bedroom and slam her door. I didn't hear anything after that, but I did watch my daughter become more withdrawn and fearful. I wanted to put it down to it simply being an extension of the fear everyone was feeling. She worked long, long hours trying to help find a way to 'fix' the kids who were returned, before their Time Chips kicked in. But one after another, they dropped dead in front of the nation's eyes. It was horrifying.

And then, Sebastian and his esteemed colleagues caught the bastards and their technology. The technology was destroyed, the bastards sent to jail for life, and we all set about living our allotted years to the fullest again.

By then Varya had married Sebastian and left me for good, and Kir was already rolling around Varya's womb, unbeknownst to us all.

I had a few delightful years to myself, after Varya moved in with Sebastian and before Kir got sick.

I didn't particularly want it to come to an end. But at sixty-four years of age the Rest Time Authority thought I'd had enough time for fun. If only they knew about my retirement bonus in here, with Kir. It does get a little boring at times. I look forward to catching up on some Netflix when I get out. But I'm happy to wait for the right moment.

CHAPTER THIRTY-THREE

Marisa

Marisa brought spaghetti bolognese into the Time Lock for dinner that evening. Enough for three this time. She hadn't had the chance to check what Daniel's favourite meal was, but she figured she couldn't go wrong with spaghetti bolognese. She smiled as she watched Daniel mop up the last of his sauce with a chunk of bread and stuff it in his mouth. Kir watched the newcomer in fascination, stooping to take a bite of his own meal from time to time whenever prompted to by Elena.

Elena glanced at Marisa meaningfully and raised an eyebrow. Marisa nodded and flicked her head at the children, raising her own eyebrows.

"Kir, why don't you show Daniel your game of 3D snakes and ladders?"

"I'm bored of snakes and ladders. I've already played it eleventy billion times," Kir complained, dropping his head onto the table.

"Well maybe it will become even more interesting on the eleventy billion and first time," said Elena.

Kir bumped his head against his arms again. "No."

Daniel tried to stifle a laugh.

"Maybe you'll be able to beat Daniel," said Marisa. "He's probably only played it twenty times. You're an expert compared to him."

Kir's head snapped up as he considered Daniel as a potential new opponent.

Daniel shook his head. "Thirty times, at least. And I've won twenty-seven of them, I reckon."

Kir ran out of the room and down the hallway towards his bedroom, shouting, "I've played eleventy billion times! I'm going to win!"

Daniel took another slice of bread from the table and folded it in his hands before following the small boy with an amused smile on his face.

Elena watched Marisa as she stared after the children. "They're safe for now," Elena reassured her.

"Do you think it's our fault Kir is still here? Maybe if we'd pushed harder, earlier."

Elena shook her head and started to collect the dirty dishes from the table. "My Varya cannot be told. She is stubborn, that girl, always has been." She stood and carried the stack of plates over to the sink and started to fill it. "Our job is to look after the boys and keep them safe while she finds a way to fix them."

Marisa moved over to the sink and plucked a fresh dishcloth from the second drawer down.

"She's agreed to turn the lab over to figuring out how to fix Daniel. And any other kids who might be taken and returned."

Elena nodded and submerged the stack of dishes into the warm soapy water. "And Reginald? Did you ask him?"

"Yes, I did." Marisa paused, fidgeting with the cloth. "He swears it has nothing to do with him, that he kept the time transfer device locked away. Do you trust him?"

She hesitated for a moment and then nodded. "To be truthful, yes, I do."

"I've asked him to check, anyway. To make sure it's still there. He says he will, but he can't get to the location just yet. He won't tell me where it is."

Elena smiled. "That's our Reginald, always trying to protect everyone."

Marisa took a cleaned dish and wiped in slow circles. "He wants to talk to you."

"Oh?"

"Something about making plans for the future."

"Ah, yes. The future." Elena placed the last plate on the draining board, dried her hands and sat back down at the table.

"He wants me to bring him to you tonight."

Elena sighed. "Yes, yes. Bring him in. I'll make sure the children are asleep."

Marisa gathered the clean plates in her arms and bit her lip. "What plans are you making, Elena?"

Elena waved her away. "Nothing you need to worry about now. Just know that, when the time comes, we won't forget about you."

Marisa frowned and opened her mouth to protest but then sighed and closed it again. Elena was every bit as stubborn as her daughter.

"I'll be back with Reg in three hours, then," she finally said.

CHAPTER THIRTY-FOUR

Daniel

"Nanna, Nanna! I won snakes and ladders! And now I'm ready for my Entiac!" Kir came racing around the corner of the living room and crashed into his grandmother's knees. He giggled and placed his head in her lap.

Elena sighed and reached behind her for a large brown bottle which sat on top of the piano.

"Has Yappy Dog cleaned his teeth?" she asked.

"Yes!" shouted Kir.

"And has Teresa the Wonder Sheep gone to the toilet?" Elena poked the boy in the side gently. He collapsed on the floor in a puddle of giggles.

"Yes!" he cried, elated.

Elena took a deep breath but then held it and winked at Daniel. Kir sat up and blinked rapidly at her, expectantly.

"Rooster!" she called out. "Rooster, have you chosen a bedtime story?" She cupped her hand around her ear. Kir listened intently as well. Daniel looked around, unsure what was happening. Elena leaned forward, her chin almost touching her knees. "Rooster says he wants to read *Good-night Moon*. That okay with you?" she whispered.

Kir nodded and held both hands up to his mouth, as though he could stuff his laughter back in. "Yes," he whispered, leaning forward, and touching her forehead.

Elena stood up suddenly, bottle in hand. "Then off to bed we go!" To Daniel she said, "I'll be back in about ten minutes."

Daniel sat and waited, listening to Kir's laughter settle down. Elena's words became progressively softer and then morphed into a lullaby. Eventually, there was silence.

"What's Entiac?" he asked her when she returned to her chair.

She regarded him as though she'd forgotten he was there, then closed her eyes.

"It stands for Night-Time In A Cup."

"Oh."

She opened both eyes again and looked at him curiously. "Do you feel tired?"

"A little," he admitted. It wasn't a huge need for sleep, more a weariness born of confusion and stress.

"I'm sorry, then. You will probably feel a little tired until you leave the Time Lock, if that's how you came in." She sighed and shut her eyes again. "Entiac is a sleeping draught. Kir came into the Time Lock shortly after he'd woken up from a nap, and about an hour after he'd taken medication which stopped the symptoms of his illness. Especially the pain. The downside, for me, is that it means his energy never runs down."

"He's always that bouncy?"

She nodded and sighed softly. "He's always that bouncy."

"But you came in tired?"

Elena shook her head. "No, I came in as well rested as a sixty-four-year-old can be. I don't get particularly tired either. But I do get worn down. I love that little boy like nothing else, but even I can't answer his incessant questions every minute of every hour for years on end." She raised her eyebrows at him pointedly. "Perhaps you'd like a rest too?"

"Oh. Yes, I'm sure a rest would be good." He stood quickly, feeling as though he'd been caught doing something he shouldn't. "I'll, um, go to my room then."

Elena nodded her approval. "I'll let you know when to come out. If you prefer a sleeping draught—some 'Entiac' as Kir calls it—let me know."

He shook his head. He'd had enough of being drugged and losing time these past few days.

"Good night, then," said Daniel, glancing over Elena's shoulder at the bright sunlight streaming through the window.

"Good night."

Sometime later—maybe half an hour, maybe three times that, it was hard to tell—Daniel thought he smelled something odd, like burning plastic. He removed the headphones he was wearing and listened. He heard nothing and the smell seemed to grow fainter the more he breathed it in. He frowned and put the headphones back on, watching episodes on an old DVD player of a kids' cartoon from five years ago. It was enough to keep his mind from straying for the moment, but he hoped his mum or Varya could find him some more age-appropriate viewing when they next came to visit. He had no idea how long he would be stranded here, and no idea how much time had passed outside the Time

Lock either. He chewed his lip again and turned the volume up, determined not to think about it.

They were all treating him like he might shatter at any moment, as though he'd gone through a traumatic experience. There hadn't been a spare moment to explain to them that, actually, he didn't really remember anything. He remembered being at school, hearing the bell ringing but after that it was a blank screen until he showed up at his own front door. At first, when he saw his mother's panicked face, he thought something had gone wrong at the hospital, another kid had died maybe. His mum always told people she dealt with it just fine, it was part of the job, she was glad she could make their passing a little more comfortable, a little more dignified. But he always knew when the strain was becoming too much. He'd stopped asking, though, when he hadn't been able to get proper answers from her. In the end, asking only brought more attention down on his own head, as though it could have been him lying in that hospital bed, the life ebbing out of him.

And now... now, it *was* him.

He didn't feel any different. Nothing hurt, there was no distress. He supposed he should feel fear at his close scrape with death. But it was such an intangible idea, that he could no longer exist in just a few hours if he stepped outside of the Time Lock.

The Time Lock itself was what had him absolutely fascinated. He'd always got the sense there was more to Aunt Varya, tried to pick her brains about what he knew was her specialty, but she'd always pushed him away. In every other subject she was generous with her knowledge, but when it came to Rest Time Chips, she treated him like a kid who was too young to know.

Now it all made sense. She'd had Kir stashed away, in suspended animation, for all this time. His old playmate—who he did kind of vaguely remember. Yappy Dog was what had done it for him. He was sure Kir used to drag the stuffed toy to kindergarten with him every day. He remembered a kid with hair about the same colour as Kir's, and the voice—the voice was the same too. But mostly it was that stuffed dog that he remembered, its droopy ears and chewed up tail.

He tried to focus on the cartoon in front of him, but it was such babyish stuff. Maybe he could ask Elena for some of that Entiac draught that Kir had. He sighed, closed the DVD player, and put it on the bedside table. Whose apartment was this, anyway? He didn't recognise it and thought he probably would have if it was Kir and Aunt Varya's old place. Maybe it was Elena's. The bedroom he'd been allocated definitely had a 'guest room' vibe to it. There were piles of old magazines in one corner, a cream-coloured box with the word 'Singer' on the side, and half a dozen framed pictures pushed against the wall. Apart from the single bed and bedside table, it looked pretty much like the dumping ground for everything else in this otherwise neat home.

Daniel went to the door of the room, pressed his ear against it, and listened. Elena had told him to stay here until she told him it was morning, time to come out. She didn't seem like the kind of person you'd want to cross; an old-fashioned parent-type who would probably actually yell at you if you disobeyed her. Not like the parents he knew, who all wanted to sit down and have discussions about your feelings. Like the old TV shows he'd seen where the parents— usually the father—laid down the rules and everyone had to follow them. Or else. The 'or else' part was always a bit vague, but Varya told him (out of his mother's ear shot) that kids used to get hit if they misbehaved.

He didn't think Elena would hit him, but what if he needed to go to the toilet? That was a legitimate reason to leave his room, surely? Maybe she'd have some other DVDs he could borrow that were a bit more interesting. Even some documentaries, maybe, or he could ask to have a look at the books on the bookshelf in the living room.

There was that smell again, the burning. What if there was a fire? Another legitimate reason to leave the room. He looked down at the gap underneath the door. No smoke. He touched the door. It wasn't hot. He pressed down the long door handle slowly, bracing for a squeak, and pulled at the door. He took a deep breath and peered through the small gap he'd made, his heart thumping. Then he jumped back and slammed the door. Elena was out there, in the hallway.

"Daniel? Are you okay in there?" Her voice came muffled through the door.

He held his breath and listened to the soft fall of her footsteps as they came closer. At the sound of her knock he took a step backwards. The door opened slowly. His eyes were wide.

"Daniel." She smiled at him and his heart started to slow to its normal pace. He was being a stupid kid, jumping at shadows. This was Kir's grandma, she wasn't going to hurt him. "You look like you've seen a ghost, dear. Why don't you come out to the living room and I'll make you some hot cocoa?" She left the door open and beckoned for him to follow her. He hesitated then took slow steps behind her. "I'm sorry, dear, I realise now it was too much to ask of you to simply shut yourself away and wait out the night. You're probably used to constant action where you come from. Kir and I have grown so used to making the hours stretch, amusing ourselves with small things."

Daniel stood in the living room doorway and watched as she bustled about, collecting mugs from this cupboard and chocolate powder from that one.

Elena turned. "Sit, dear, sit."

Daniel did as he was told and sat, placing his hands on the table. It seemed the polite thing to do.

"I haven't even asked you, have I?" she said.

"Asked me?" said Daniel.

"What illness you've been suffering." She looked at him expectantly, teaspoon raised in one hand, powdered chocolate tin in the other. He examined her face and thought he saw pity, but it was always hard to tell with adults, especially older ones.

"I'm not sick."

Elena's face darkened a moment but then she seemed to change her mind. "I'm sorry to pry, I was just looking to make some conversation. Why don't you tell me about your life out there instead?" She waved her spoon in the general direction of the hallway and the Time Lock's portal. "What do you do with your time? What do other kids your age do with their time? Are they still into the same computer games?"

Daniel stared at her as realisation dawned. Varya hadn't told Elena about the time thieves. Elena must think he had cancer or something, like Kir. He opened his mouth to explain to her. Maybe Varya just hadn't had the time. But the moment had passed, and she was now saying something about Sonic the Hedgehog and arcade games, back in her own childhood. He peered over his shoulder and down the hallway, hoping his mum would return soon.

CHAPTER THIRTY-FIVE

Varya

Varya stood at the front of the largest laboratory at the Minor Miracles Foundation, seven scientists seated at scattered benches around the room.

"This is a paper-only project," she said. "No digital note-taking, no emailing, no online databases. We've been entrusted with this material by the Rest Time Corps and we will ensure that nothing related to this leaves this room. Is that clear?"

Connor weaved his way slowly around the room, distributing manila folders of photocopied material. Inside each folder were copies of the notes Varya had obtained from the Rest Time Corps archive alongside a summary of everything she remembered about the time transfer tech.

"In your hands you now have everything that's known about how to create a device which is capable of transferring blocks of time from one Rest Time Chip to another. We're going to use it to recreate the device. Once we have a prototype, we'll turn it over to the Rest Time Corps to enable them to assist any others who fall victim to the time thieves."

Varya's voice wavered slightly as she clasped her hands together.

A scientist shot his hand into the air, eyes on the sheet of paper in front of him. "This is kind of outside of our usual area of expertise. Isn't there someone else who could do this?" Varya saw genuine concern on his face.

Her initial revelation that she was taking on a senior management role at the facility, effective immediately, hadn't seemed to bother anyone very much. It wasn't like she was taking on the CEO role, and she'd been there long enough, working long enough hours, that questions had started to be asked about why her career appeared to have stalled. She'd shrugged off Marisa's urging to tell the entire truth of her background and her role in setting up the charity in the first place. Marisa wanted her to step out from behind the curtain completely. Varya wasn't ready to go that far just yet.

She had, however, agreed that imparting some information about her career path was probably necessary. She dug a fingernail into her palm and forced a smile.

"At heart, you're all scientists. Granted, you don't have doctorates in temporal physics, but that's not what this requires. Think of this as more of a scientific problem-solving exercise. The answers are already there, they've been found before. Your role is to figure out how to put the pieces of the puzzle back together again." She took a deep breath. "My role is to identify, and fill in, the missing pieces." There was some murmuring to her left. She fought the urge to look or try to listen to what they were saying. "You know that I have worked here for the past four-and-a-half years, as a lab tech. You know that I went to UNSW and completed my doctorate there. What you don't know is that I did a stint attached to the Rest Time Corps after I graduated."

"I knew it! I told you so!" A scientist to her left clapped in excitement and nudged the older man next to her. Then she pointed at Varya. "You've cut your hair. And dyed it. But I knew it was you. I watched all the news items back then."

"What news items?" called out another voice.

"She invented the time transfer tech," she said, in an awed, hushed tone.

Varya nodded. "I was on the team that invented the time transfer tech, yes."

"Hey, something I never really understood. We can add bonus years to Time Chips, yeah? So, how come they couldn't just add years back to the kids' Chips when they returned?" The woman leaned forward eagerly, as though Varya was an oracle who was about to provide an answer to her most burning question.

"We did think of trying that on the first few kids that were returned, but the tech doesn't work like that." She turned and started to draw on the whiteboard behind her. "Each person gets a limit of sixty-five years programmed into their Chip at birth." She wrote '65' at the end of the straight line she'd drawn. "It's not a quota so much as a limitation. There's no guarantee you'll make it to sixty-five. That's up to your life span, which might be fifty-five, thirty or even two." She spoke slowly and emphasised the keywords. After pausing briefly, she drew a small vertical slash across the line approximately two-thirds from the start. "But there's a blocker artificially programmed in at forty years. If you meet the requirements of the time extension—work extra hours, produce a child, steer clear of trouble with the law—the blocker will be deactivated, and you can push past it." She paused to gather her thoughts. Trying to explain complex temporal concepts to scientists who studied a completely different branch was not easy. Every eye in the room was studying either the notes in front of them or squinting at the board. Connor caught her eye and smiled encouragingly. She'd already practised on him that morning, answering much the same questions then.

Varya turned and started to point at the earlier vertical slashes. "The time transfer tech works on this life span section. The unknown quantity. The returned children had been drained of their life span and it had already been inserted into someone else. The time thieves didn't know whether they were going to be able to extract sixty years, or six, of the children's life span. The time transfer tech can also *measure* a person's life span. It can tell you when you're going to die, barring a catastrophic incident such as car accident or gunshot wound." She started to draw a long arrow from one of the slashes back to the start of the timeline, then pointed to it. "The only way to get this life span back is to either retrieve their original life span or take a life span from somebody else."

"Wouldn't the parents have volunteered to donate life span?" asked a woman in the back row, rubbing her pregnant belly.

Varya nodded and felt her face grow hot. "Yes, they did. Of course, they did. But the Rest Time Authority wouldn't allow it." She left it at that.

The older man at the front frowned. Varya glanced at him and thought she could see his thought processes as his facial expressions changed. Her stomach flipped. This was exactly what she'd feared, exactly why she'd kept a low profile all these years.

"So, it's your fault they're in this mess," he said eventually.

"Simon!" The woman pushed him again, not so gently this time.

Varya looked at him levelly, her old friend, guilt, threatening to drown her. "In a sense, yes. As a scientist yourself, I'm sure you can appreciate the excitement that comes with the discovery of a new technology. Life span isn't something we ever thought we could even quantify, hold on to, let alone transfer from one human being to another."

"But you did," he said.

"Yes, we did. And we have paid for that naïve excitement dearly, I assure you. Which is why the technology and most of the instructions on how to build it were destroyed."

"Except somebody's figured it out again."

"Yes, it appears that way."

Silence filled the room. The man looked smug and satisfied.

"This morning, please read through the folders and have a think about how you want to approach the problem. We'll reconvene in two hours." Varya turned her back on the room, signalling an end to the presentation. She picked up the whiteboard eraser and started to rub at her diagrams. It occurred to her as she rubbed out the final arrow that it might have been helpful to leave it there. Too late now.

"You okay?" Connor murmured at her side. Varya took an involuntary step sideways. He was too close, far too close, and speaking too softly. It was all just too intimate for her, and after her meeting with Sebastian she found her faith in her own perceptions starting to slip again. He'd always had that effect on her, as though he carried some magnetic field around him that messed with her own radar signals. When she was with Sebastian, she always felt as though she was fighting through a constant fog. In the past it had been a happy fog, mostly. But still a fog. She shook her head slightly.

"I'm fine." She looked up, tried to smile a little to give support to the lie. "Little tired, maybe."

"You know, I was thinking. About how I could be useful in all of this. I was wondering if you'd like me to be the liaison between us and Rest Time Corps? I know how they work; I know how we work, and you'd be free to focus on the research. It would also mean you wouldn't have to..." He trailed off deliberately.

"I don't need... I mean, thanks, yes. That would be great, actually." Varya remembered her promise to Marisa, to try to share the burden around, to stop trying to take it all on her own shoulders. She sat down at the presentation bench at the front of the room and shuffled her own papers, trying to gather her thoughts enough to start work herself. She was just wondering whether it might not be a bad idea to find another room, away from people, when the pregnant scientist pulled a chair over and sat down beside her.

"Hi, it's Kayla, isn't it?"

Kayla beamed. "Yes, that's me."

"And... how far along are you?" Varya mentally kicked herself at the inane question. How many times had she been asked the same question herself during her pregnancy, and how annoying had it become?

"Twenty-six weeks. We're so excited."

"You're not worried about still working? I mean, the chemicals in the labs..." Varya projected her own concerns onto Kayla, remembering her complete refusal to give up work before she went into labour. Looking back, she was horrified that she hadn't given any thought to her working conditions. Kayla waved a dismissive hand.

"No, it's fine. I'm on a project where I've already checked out all the substances we're working with and they're all totally safe." There was a brief pause, enough time for Kayla to rearrange her excited expectant-mum face into an altogether more serious one.

"This time transfer tech. It can tell you when you're going to die, can't it?"

"Not quite. It can tell you the maximum amount of time you have left. This could be superseded by either a Rest Time Chip's initiation, or another catastrophic but unforeseen event."

"My friend's sister, when she was thirteen, just passed away in her sleep. Nobody had any idea why, there was no medical reason. Her heart just... stopped."

Varya nodded thoughtfully.

"Do you think it could have been the end of her life span?"

"Maybe," said Varya. "But I don't really know a lot about how it works, I'm sorry. I've told you as much as I know. We were able to discover how to transfer it, but you've seen how that worked out. No further research has been done on life spans and any information about it has been suppressed by the government. You could only imagine the general panic if word got out. Some people would demand the technology to measure their life spans. The repercussions from knowing the date of your premature death were deemed too great."

Kayla snorted. "We already know the date of our premature death," she said bitterly. "It's sixty-five." She rubbed her belly and admired it for a moment. "Then again, if this little one was only meant for a short time in this world, I don't think I'd want to know." Her hand flew to her mouth. "Oh, I'm so sorry, I didn't mean... I didn't think."

Varya closed her eyes, took a quiet breath, and opened them again. "It's okay."

"I'm so sorry for your loss. I read about what happened to your son. It's so unfair."

"Thank you." Varya picked up a sheaf of papers and held them in front of herself.

"I should probably get back to work," said Kayla. "Time is ticking."

"Yes," said Varya. "It certainly is."

CHAPTER THIRTY-SIX

Varya had just managed to get her mind focused on the task at hand and was jotting down notes furiously as she remembered fragments of the solution from the past. She almost didn't hear her screen vibrating. Annoyed, she picked it up and was planning to cancel the call, until she saw the caller ID.

"Connor is supposed to call you." Varya made no effort to hide her irritation. "He's going to be the liaison between our organisations for this project." She frowned into the silence. "Hello?"

A soft laugh. "I was calling to see if you wanted to meet up for lunch," said Sebastian. "I can hear you're well into re-search mode, though, so..."

"I'm sorry, I just..." She wasn't really sorry.

"It's okay. That tone of yours, just brings back the memo-ries, that's all."

Damn him. Damn him and his memories. She bit her tongue and held her breath, willing herself to stay silent.

"How about dinner? I'll leave here around six." She mentally kicked herself. "I could meet you at that Mexican place we used to take Kir to. It's on my way home." It was his voice, that hypnotic voice. Not the law enforcement one. That had never gotten him anywhere with her, which had taken him a while to figure out. It was the perceptive I-can-see-right-through-you warm tone that sent shivers down her spine.

"Done. I'll see you there at six-fifteen," he said.

She tapped the red circle on her screen and tried to regain her focus.

CHAPTER THIRTY-SEVEN

At thirty-seven minutes past six o'clock, Varya pushed open the heavy door to El Nido. She knew immediately that it was a mistake. If she was trying to keep her distance from Sebastian, and her mouth shut, it was exactly the wrong place to be. A small, local eatery, popular with families who had young children who weren't quite ready to be out without being loud and annoying, she and Sebastian had visited here almost weekly. As a baby, Kir would sit in one of the white moulded plastic highchairs and sort refried beans on his tray with immense concentration, popping one in his mouth from time to time. In the months before his diagnosis he had graduated to sitting on a proper chair at the table with them and scribbling over the paper tablecloth, using crayons the wait staff had given him.

The décor had barely changed. There was a new picture of cacti on the back wall and the specials on the chalkboard had rotated. But the polished concrete floor echoed just the same way as Varya made her way over to the small table where Sebastian sat, margarita already in hand. She slid sideways into a seat and picked up the identical drink he'd ordered for her. She took a large gulp, savouring the familiar mixture of cold ice and burning liquor.

Sebastian turned his glass around in his hands, watching her intently. He gave her a smile that wasn't really a smile.

"This is harder than I thought it would be," he said.

"Have you ordered?" she asked, after meeting his eyes briefly and then flicking her own eyes down to study the menu. "I'm starving."

He leaned forward and held out a hand as though to touch her. She moved back and held the menu up higher.

Sebastian spoke quietly but urgently. "What were his last days like? Was he in pain?"

Tears of rage and pain burned at the backs of her eyes. She swallowed them down with another gulp of margarita.

"You wouldn't need to ask me if you'd stayed."

He opened his mouth to respond but she held out her hand to flag down a passing waitress. "Nachos, please, with beef. And a tequila, straight." She handed over her menu and waited for Sebastian to order.

"Have you found Reg?" she asked when the waitress had left.

"No, we haven't." He paused and Varya stiffened, waiting to see if he would try to resume his previous line of questioning. Whether he noticed or not, he clearly thought the better of trying again today. He relaxed back in his chair and straightened his shoulders. Was it her imagination or did he also puff out his chest just a little? "We're pursuing several lines of enquiry, though it seems he more or less went off the grid when he left Rest Time Corps. We're running facial recognition software through the last few months of CCTV footage at the moment. If that doesn't work, we'll move to satellite images."

Varya nodded her approval.

"There have been some other developments, though. Two more kids have disappeared." He let the words slide from his mouth dispassionately, pushed out like a weather report.

"Are they related?" Varya asked, hopefully. She immediately felt guilty. The guilt at hoping these abductions weren't related to the time thefts was overlaid by the guilt of not having recreated the time transfer device yet and the guilt of having assisted in its original invention.

Sebastian shook his head. "We don't know yet. One of them, a girl aged six from across town, has been involved in a custody dispute so it's possible that the non-custodial parent took her. The other one, a girl aged ten, routinely walked herself home from school and let herself into an empty house. So, there's plenty of opportunity for abduction there, or she might have just run away. We have to hope that, if it is related to the other time thefts, we have the tools to treat them when they're returned."

"We're working as fast as we can on the time transfer device."

"I know. And we're doing everything we can to find the perpetrators so the life span can be restored when we find the kids."

"We're making progress."

"So are we."

What if they both progressed more slowly than the time thieves? It was the unasked question that hung thickly between them.

Varya nodded her thanks to the waitress and sipped at her drink, this time burning liquid without the relief of cooling ice. It felt appropriate to the situation.

"It's happening all over again, isn't it?" she said dully.

"Yes, but at least we know the M.O. this time. We have a head start; we know how to prepare."

A thought occurred to her. "Is there any chance this is simply a regular serial killer with a talent for hacking?"

Sebastian frowned. "What do you mean? How is that any better?"

"Have you considered that it might not be a repeat of the previous time thefts? Maybe this isn't about the life span, maybe it has nothing to do with the time transfer device, after all. It could be just some psychopath getting their rocks off by killing kids." She sipped again at her tequila. The official narrative seeded in the public consciousness was that the Chips couldn't be tampered with. The truth was that with enough time, knowledge and talent, any machine could be hacked. Of course, another truth was that it didn't change anything substantively, it just meant that it might not be Varya's fault.

"I suppose that would change the motive, but not the result."

"It would mean that finding Reg might not be your first priority."

Sebastian shrugged. "It's not our first priority now. First priority is finding the missing kids, second is making sure they're safe and third is figuring out who killed Daniel and Ben. At the moment, finding Reg mainly fits in with the third. Though if the motive is life span transference, he shoots up the list a little."

"But why would he want years anyway?"

"Maybe he wants to be immortal, who knows? Maybe he wants money and he's found someone who wants to be immortal *and* has money."

"Or maybe Reg was threatened and forced to help the perps. Or maybe he has nothing to do with it after all and the technology was simply stolen from the Rest Time Corps archive." Varya knew she was clutching at straws now. She knew that Sebastian knew it too, as the tone and volume of her voice rose.

"Only you and Reg knew the technology still existed, and where it was located. That gives rise to a few possibilities. Either he took it, or he enabled someone else to, or you took it, or you enabled someone else to. Or you're lying about its existence." Sebastian spoke in a soft, steely voice that made the hairs on the back of Varya's neck stand up.

"I'm not lying," she said firmly. "And I didn't take it."

Sebastian worked his jaw forward and backward and took a slow breath in. "Well, then. I guess I'll continue investigating the crimes that have been committed and you can continue trying to put together the technology that might stop more kids from dying."

Varya had an overwhelming desire to stand up and leave the restaurant, even though she knew she'd lost the argument. She wasn't quite sure how, and she wasn't even quite sure what they were arguing about. It felt like all too familiar ground. What started as a civilised conversation quickly degenerated into hissing veiled threats and insults through clenched teeth.

"And here are your nachos with beef. And for you, sir, the burritos with chicken. Can I get you anything else? Another drink?" The peppy waitress cut the air with an oblivious shredder and placed their meals in front of them. Varya felt herself relax slightly.

"No, thank you," Sebastian said. "We're fine."

"I guess we'd better eat and get back to it, then," said Varya, who felt very far from fine indeed.

CHAPTER THIRTY-EIGHT

Marisa

Marisa flicked through shows on the screen, the tiles whizzing past faster than she could reasonably focus on them. She pressed one at random and an over-the-top theme song started up, accompanying a middle-aged couple in matching cowboy hats sitting on matching mechanical bulls. She turned it off and tossed the remote to the other end of Varya's sofa, sending a disgusted grunt with it.

Her shift was well and truly over, she mused. She could just go home, to her own apartment, and leave Varya to her angst. This was nothing to do with Marisa, not really. She was just an employee saving up for early retirement. She'd be out of here in a few years if all went to plan, sunning herself on a beach somewhere. Maybe up in Bali, somewhere the beers were cheap and the nasi goreng cheaper.

Marisa sighed and swung her feet up onto the couch, laying her head back on the cushioned arm rest.

"Get a grip, girl. This ain't your problem." She willed her legs to swing back to the floor. She eyed the door and imagined herself walking through it. But then she imagined Varya walking back in from dinner with her ex-husband, all tight-lipped on the outside and distraught on the inside. No, Varya would need someone to talk to or she'd end up pressing the self-destruct button. Marisa felt protective of her, like a mother hen. Except not, she chortled, because she'd never had the desire to peck her to death. Well, peck her a little, maybe, but not to death. She closed her eyes for a few minutes before she heard the click and soft whoosh of the heavy door opening. She opened one eye to watch Varya enter.

"Hey," Marisa said softly.

"Hey," said Varya, her eyes flitting over her once before she continued through to the kitchen. Marisa rolled off the sofa with a sigh, then got to her feet and followed.

Varya pulled a plain, squat glass out of a top cabinet, and a full bottle of amber liquid from another. She poured a glass for herself at the kitchen table and swilled it around, staring at it, bottle still firmly clutched in her other hand. After a moment she tipped her head back, swallowed the full glass and started pouring another. Marisa waited for her to finish, then confiscated the bottle.

"Hey, hey, you need to share that." Eyeing her friend with a worried expression that didn't match her tone, she lifted a matching glass from the top cabinet and sat opposite her. "So? How'd it go?"

"It was a mistake. I shouldn't have gone," she admitted bitterly.

"Well, yeah. True." Marisa started, cautiously. She took a sip of the liquid. It was good, warming liquor. Quality stuff. "Where do you get this shit from? This is amazing, even better than my soirée stash."

"Two more kids are missing," Varya mumbled into her glass. "Two girls."

"Okay."

Varya looked up. "Six and ten years old. They don't know if the abductions are related. The girls haven't been returned yet."

There was a pleading in her eyes that caught Marisa off guard. She took another careful sip before replying.

"So, you'll be ready this time. If it's the time thieves, you'll pop them in the Time Lock with Kir and Daniel, where they can all play happily until you get this time transfer tech sorted and Sebastian and his pals find the thieves to transfer the time back again." She threw back the remainder of her glass and reached for the bottle. "Easy peasy."

Varya shook her head. "No. No, I can't."

Marisa slammed her glass down. "Yes, you can. And you will."

"You don't understand. I can't just start letting anyone into that Time Lock. The Rest Time Authority will find out and shut it down."

"Why would they shut it down when it would kill four kids?"

Varya tapped nervously at her glass, her breathing becoming ragged and uneven. "Maybe not now, maybe they would wait until this mess is sorted and the three other kids are safe." She started turning her glass slowly. "But then what about Kir? They won't just allow the Time Lock to stay open indefinitely."

Marisa felt the full force of Varya's maternal pleading as she looked at her in appeal. "Varya, how long are you going to keep that kid in there for?" It was a question she'd been wanting to ask for a very long time but hadn't dared.

"As long as it takes," Varya whispered, barely audible.

"And what if it takes another ten years? What if it takes your entire lifetime? Or you die, still not having fixed him? What then?"

Varya clenched her glass, the muscles on the backs of her hands popping out until Marisa feared the glass would shatter.

"What kind of a life is that for him?" Marisa ventured.

"I'll find a cure. It has to be out there. I just need to keep trying." It came out like a chant, like a mantra against the darkness that small children use against monsters under their bed.

"But what if you don't?"

"I will!" Varya shouted.

Marisa let the air settle for a minute before she spoke again. "Just to recap, so I've got this straight in my mind. You're willing to let two little girls die. You're willing to sentence your own son to relive his fourth year for the next twenty years, and your mother to care for him, all because..." She looked at Varya, then looked away. "Because you can't let go." Her voice broke on the final two words.

"Get out," said Varya, her voice dangerous and low.

"Varya, you need to think this through. There's still time to change your mind."

"I said, get out!"

Marisa nodded. "Okay. I'll see you tomorrow afternoon, then. I'll be back by five to get the dinners ready." She paused, watching Varya, whose head was now in her hands, as though inhaling the whiskey vapours could cure her pain. "I'll see myself out."

CHAPTER THIRTY-NINE

Elena

It all happened so quickly; you must understand. Not Kir's illness, but what came after. The illness was slow. It had been with him for many months, creeping around his body and ingratiating itself like a greasy new banking executive. Once it took a hold on my grandson it grew cocky and decided to show itself. Of course, when we became aware of its presence, we took him to the doctors and they did everything they could to extract that nasty infestation. But every time we thought they'd driven it away completely, it would rise to the surface again. Until it grew so confident in its new fiefdom that it took a dramatic stand and made it known that it wouldn't let go, that it was here to stay. Illnesses, they're not too bright, you see. They don't have a brain, just instinct. If illnesses had a brain, they'd know never to kill us. They'd learn to live in harmony with our bodies, sharing the fleshy resources and leaving us at least enough to continue our everyday functions. Letting us pump our illness-tainted blood around our veins and exhale our infected breath into the atmosphere. But letting us stay here nonetheless, on this earth. With our loved ones.

The infestation our Kir has is a Terminal Illness. They are the tyrant of the unwellness world and will stop at nothing. Kir's Terminal Illness didn't stop until it completely dominated his whole little body, no matter how hard the doctors fought against it.

The war was lost slowly—skirmish by skirmish—but the final battle still, somehow, caught everyone by surprise. Even though we knew it was coming.

I asked my Varya what she planned to do while myself and our Kir lived our suspended lives. Beat the illness, she said simply. Kill it once and for all so Kir could come out and grow into a bigger boy and then a man and an old man. Or as old as they'll allow us to be these days. Not bent over and shuffling maybe, but at least creased and a little papery.

After a few months in our sunny pastures I asked my Varya, what will you do if you cannot cure the disease? I asked her gently, because my Varya, she is quick to anger, especially when her competency is questioned. She is like a child when that happens, stomping her foot as her face turns red. But when I asked her after those few months, she told me quietly and calmly that she would find a cure. All she needed was time. I nodded and told her that Kir and I would give her all the time she needed.

There was some hope at the two-year mark. We all got terribly excited. But then our hopes were dashed again. Back to the beginning we went.

After three years I asked my Varya again, has there been any progress? How is the research going? She went a little pale and started to tell me about the new picture books she was going to bring to her little boy. I waited while she spoke of the one with the dinosaur on the cover, the one with the lists of music on the back pages and the CDs she would bring so we could play the music. Then I asked her again. I pretended I assumed she hadn't heard me.

"There have been some... unexpected anomalies." She spoke these words after a very long pause and a little preparatory handwringing. My Varya always uses long words she thinks I don't understand to try to scare me away from topics she doesn't wish to discuss.

I folded my hands neatly in my lap and I told her a story that my mother used to tell me.

Once upon a time there was a king. The king wished very much to live forever, for he was frightened of death. His advisers taught him that those who did good deeds and followed the rules of the kingdom could expect eternal comforts. Those who didn't would roast in the flames of the underworld. The king knew to which eternity his bad deeds destined him. And, for that reason, he decided the solution to the problem was to live forever.

To protect his health, he built high walls all around the palace and forbade anyone from entering before they'd served a period of fourteen days in isolation, to prove they carried no illnesses. He employed royal tasters to test each morsel of food to check for poison. He ate only the best foods and exercised every day. The king surrounded himself with the best doctors he could find and did everything to placate his neighbours with diplomacy rather than swords.

The king lived a great many years this way, a great many more than the record-keepers could detect that any king had lived before him.

And then one day, the king was taking his daily walk in the royal walled gardens when he spied a small boy sitting on a small boulder. The boy was whittling away at a piece of bark.

"What are you making, boy?" asked the king, as he sat beside him. The boy grinned at the king and placed the piece of bark in the royal fellow's outstretched palm. The boy hung his head forwards and a great, deep laugh started to rumble its way up out of his shoes, travelled through his body and shot up out of his small mouth. The king could not take his eyes off the piece of bark in his hand. It was fashioned into a great wall of flames and started to heat up and burn into the paper-thin skin of his palm. The boy continued to laugh and laugh as the king opened his own mouth to scream. But nothing came out. As the king was engulfed by flames and reduced to ash, he heard the boy say:

"You cannot escape the inevitable, old man. Time will pass and your time will come when it is your time. And now, it is your time."

My Varya, she did not like this story. She told me she was no longer a child who could be scared by silly old stories. She left in a great hurry that day. But when she came back, she told me her own story. She called it 'science' and spoke of 'life spans'. But, as far as I could tell, it all amounted to what the old king was told. Your time will come when it is your time.

And so, I knew what I had to do.

I had to find out when it would be our Kir's time. Because if I did not, my Varya could spend the rest of her time, and mine too, trying to outrun the inescapable. Do I regret the consequences of my actions? Yes, of course I do. But I did what I thought was right. I did what I had to do for my Varya and Kir.

CHAPTER FORTY

Varya

Varya strode into the small room adjacent to the main laboratory and pressed the door shut behind her. She peered over Connor's shoulder.

"That's Professor Langford's research. Why aren't you working on the transfer device?"

Connor looked up, surprised and blinking. He shook his head a little and went back to the papers before him. Varya stood above him and crossed her arms. Eventually he sighed softly and looked up, his head tipped to one side.

"They're nearly there," he pointed out. "They don't need me." He waited for her to contradict him. When she didn't, he bent his head back over the papers, his finger moving on its journey down to the bottom of the page again.

Varya pulled a chair over and sat, trying to keep her shoulders straight in a seated stance of seniority. Connor was right. She'd just been to visit the room full of talented scientists and was astonished at the speed at which they'd worked through the problems. There was a near-constant buzz of conversation from several self-formed groups, each of which had taken ownership of a particular element of the recreation. Before she left, she'd given authorisation for the first build attempt to begin. At this rate they would have a prototype in the next day or two. Unfortunately, they may not have time to test it out on anything other than a live subject. But Connor was right, he wasn't needed right now.

"Have you heard anything from the investigation?" Varya had kept her distance from Sebastian since last night, ignoring the several calls she'd received from him this morning.

"Yes. Nothing new yet. They're still 'pursuing leads'." Connor kept his head down but raised his eyebrows at the last two words and intonated them in such a way as to suggest that the investigators were doing something other than what they said.

"They haven't found Reg?"

"No. But if we can recreate the time transfer tech, it won't matter."

Varya was silent.

Connor looked up and frowned. "It won't matter, will it?"

"No. No, it won't matter," she said quietly. She nodded towards the papers scattered over the table. "Found anything?"

Connor leaned back and spread his hands over his thighs, surveying the organised chaos. He glanced at his notes and scrolled up a little, then shook his head.

"Janet was a brilliant scientist."

"Yes, I know."

"And she'd been working on this for a long time. Years, in fact." Connor paused for effect. "She was very thorough."

"You're not telling me anything I don't know, Connor." Varya picked up the stack of papers closest to her and shuffled through them to hide her agitation.

"There were projects that were being worked on when I was at Rest Time Corps. They weren't official—strictly off the books and out of the media's eye—but they had their own wing. It was locked down, entirely classified, and only a select few were given clearance to enter. I heard from a friend recently that some of the projects have had great success in finding what they were looking for."

"You're going to tell me that I should talk to Sebastian, aren't you?"

"It's the most direct way, yes. Your other options are to try to poach staff from Rest Time Corps and get them to come and work here on similar projects and hope they'll be... flexible enough to find the answers you're seeking. Or you can resort to non-legal avenues. Of course, both of those options will take much longer and carry greater risk." He tried to catch Varya's eye, but she was studying the papers intently. He noticed she'd read a single page several times. "It's your call."

"The other two options don't involve telling Sebastian."

"Varya, he's going to find out eventually. Once you get Kir out of there, he'll want to see his son. And he'll want to know... everything."

"You're assuming he'll get to see his son again."

"What?" The word escaped Connor's mouth before it had time to consult his brain.

"You heard me."

"Varya, you can't be serious," he said softly. This wasn't the Varya his aunt had told him about. Or maybe it was. Her single goal had become protecting her son. And protecting her son appeared to have morphed into keeping her son away from everyone who might have any interest in anything other than keeping him alive.

"Sebastian would have the best of intentions. But the thirst for knowledge—maybe not his, but Rest Time Corps'— would override everything else. Including Kir's wellbeing. It's just the way it is. It's just the way we are." The wave of her hand encompassed the room of scientists next door, Connor and even herself. "It was the way I was, before I had Kir to think of."

Connor contemplated this for a moment. He didn't think it was the way he was. But perhaps he'd spent too long working with the kids who had died at the hands of the time thieves all those years ago. It had certainly changed him in ways he couldn't articulate. He swallowed and nodded.

"I'll keep looking through these papers, see if there are any gaps, any avenues that could be explored."

Varya stood and returned the chair to its original resting place.

"And that friend of yours? From Rest Time Corps?"

"Yes?"

"Feel free to let them know we're looking for new staff. And we pay generously."

Connor nodded and watched Varya straighten herself and stride back out of the room, shutting the door behind her.

CHAPTER FORTY-ONE

Zoe

It had been a long day and Zoe had been very much looking forward to escaping from the hospital to visit her son. Keeping up the charade of being a grieving mother was almost as traumatic as actually being one. Or so she thought. Actually, that was probably ridiculous. Nothing could be worse than actually losing Daniel. Her mind was exhausted. The days spent pacing around their home or frozen on the couch, staring at her screen, willing it to ring or not ring. Willing the door to open or not open. Fearing the worst. Living the worst through her own dark imaginings.

It was all too much.

In amongst it all, her gratitude towards Varya thoroughly overwhelmed her. Her friend was still living the nightmare, had been for years. And all through that she had managed to save so many other sick children with her charity's research. But was yet to save her own.

Zoe found her mouth forming a smile as she remembered the relieved look on the parents' faces today at the hospital as she'd told them that the surgery had been successful.

Their little girl would be coming home with them as soon as she had recovered. Thanks to the Minor Miracles Foundation they now had the right combination of a surgical procedure and post-surgery treatment that worked for this particular type of rare brain cancer.

Varya greeted her at the door to her apartment and ushered her through to the Time Lock.

"You're not coming in?" Zoe asked, as Varya nodded her towards the portal but remained standing by the door.

Varya shook her head. "It's not my usual visiting time yet. And I have some work I want to get done first."

Zoe shivered as she stepped through the portal. She wondered if a person could ever get used to the strange feeling of passing through a burning waterfall. It wasn't a pleasant experience, but it was a small price to pay to spend time with her son.

"Mum!" said Daniel, peering around the hallway. He seemed suspended in movement, unable to decide whether to act the nonchalant tween or run to his mother as he really wanted to. Zoe bridged the distance between them and flung her arms around him. Clearly relieved, he hugged her back.

"How are you? How do you feel? Do you have enough food?"

"Hi, Aunty Zoe!" Kir shouted, bounding down the hallway and trying to wrap his short arms around both of them at once. Daniel loosened his grip on his mother a little to include the small boy in their embrace. He smiled to see Kir happy again. With the comings and goings of outsiders over the past couple of days he'd come to realise that Kir wasn't this upbeat all the time. In fact, his natural state seemed to be quiet and lethargic. He was happiest when Daniel suggested playing games or going outside, though he had trouble letting someone else be in charge of anything.

It was clear to Daniel that Kir was lonely. It couldn't be easy having only your grandmother as a playmate all day, every day—for either Kir or Elena.

"Aunty Varya says they've nearly finished re-building the time transfer technology," Zoe confided to Daniel as they sat around the kitchen table, her hand fluttering near his, trying to resist gripping it in her hands. He'd made it clear that he was happy to see her and be hugged temporarily, but now he would revert to the slightly reserved nine-year-old that he was.

"They still need to find the person to transfer it back from though, don't they?"

"Yes, but they have some leads. I'm sure they'll find them soon." Zoe tried to exude a confidence she didn't feel. Her face fell slightly as Daniel's shoulders slumped.

"It took them months to find them last time, didn't it?"

"You're safe here for now. If it takes months, it takes months. I'll download some series for you and bring them in, so you don't miss too much." Zoe's forced laughter fell flat. Daniel glanced through the archway to where Elena and Kir sat, playing a card game of memory on a small table placed next to Elena's armchair. Something felt off in here. The frozen world of people and animals outside the apartment, the way Elena seemed to move slowly to pass the time.

It was excruciating. He was used to the fast pace of life outside the Time Lock, where he could hold several conversations at once on his device, while watching a video on the large screen and reading an article on his personal screen. Here there was only one task at a time. Every time the portal closed after someone left it felt like the apartment shrank in around him, and Kir's mood turned darker.

"I got one! I got the boats!" Kir exclaimed, snatching the matching cards from the table and adding them to his small pile. "I need to pee now!" He jumped up and ran past Zoe, nearly crashing into her chair and then into the doorway as he corrected his course to the bathroom.

Zoe laughed. "How has he been? Still no signs of disease progression?"

Elena smiled. "No, he's fit as a fiddle, or so it would seem. No memory loss, no seizures in a long time. It's as though he were never sick."

"No pain? Restricted mobility?"

"None."

Zoe ruffled Kir's hair as he came flying back through the kitchen to take his seat at Elena's feet again. As she placed her palm lightly on his scalp and felt a thin ridge running across his skin, she frowned, the vision suddenly replaced with the memory of another small head, around the same size, on an operating table earlier today. She shook her head slightly to clear the vision and questioned her own memory. There were lots of variations of childhood brain cancer and they all behaved differently.

The rest of the visit seemed to pass quickly. They ate the dinner Marisa delivered, Varya came to spend her daily hour with Kir, and then she and Zoe said their goodbyes and left together.

CHAPTER FORTY-TWO

Varya

Back in the apartment, Zoe turned to Varya. She hesitated, opened her mouth, and then closed it again.

"What?" asked Varya.

"It's probably nothing. It's just..."

Varya's tone was gentle but impatient. "It's been a long day for both of us, Zoe. Just spit it out."

"Kir's tumour, it was a ZhangWei's cyst, wasn't it? I mean, I could check his file, but I just figured you'd remember." She let it hang in the air between them. It felt like time had frozen again. Zoe silently urged her friend to tell her she was wrong, that it was another disease, a much more complicated one for which the cure eluded them.

"Varya?" she said faintly.

Varya avoided her pleading gaze. "Yes, it's a ZhangWei's cyst."

"But I operated on one of those this morning. Using the technique and treatment plan your facility developed."

Varya nodded and moved towards the couch. She sank down, her legs seeming to give way beneath her.

"I don't understand. Varya? Talk to me. What's going on?" She went and sat beside her friend, desperately hoping for a reasonable explanation about why she would keep her own son locked up unnecessarily. Eventually Varya lifted her face and Zoe saw the tears streaming down her cheeks.

"It's my fault. The treatment won't be enough and it's all my fault."

The words tumbled out on top of each other then, like a broken dam wall. Varya told her everything. It was a relief, to be able to talk to someone about it again, properly.

But Zoe understood completely, as a paediatrician and a mother. Varya began to wish she had confided in her friend long before now.

"Oh Varya, I'm so sorry." Zoe's own eyes filled with sympathetic tears. "I know you feel like it's your fault. And I know you think that your mother and Kir are safe for now, so you have time. But living like that, it's no life for them. Connor's right, you have to go to Sebastian and ask for his help."

Varya nodded. "I know. But if Mum leaves the Time Lock, she doesn't have..."

Zoe held her hand and finished the sentence Varya couldn't. "She doesn't have long to live. I know. But you'll get through this, Var'. You need to do it, for Kir's sake."

"I can't lose my mum, Zoe. I don't know what I'd do without her."

Zoe smiled through her own tears. "We all lose our mums, eventually. And it's awful, but it's also normal and inevitable and necessary." She patted Varya's hand. "And I'll be here for you."

"I'm so scared, Zoe." Varya wiped at her tears and took a few deep, shaky breaths. "Let's just get through this first, we'll get Daniel back. Then I'll go to Sebastian, I promise. I just need some time to prepare mentally. And Kir is safe for now."

CHAPTER FORTY-THREE

Elena

The sunshine is soft but warm in this little world of ours. It's a mid-afternoon spring sun, the kind that doesn't burn. There's no frost or dampness left on the grass and the gentle heat releases the wonderful new grass smell into the otherwise odourless air.

I watch Kir chase Mon-Mon, his favourite magpie, around a tree. Mon-Mon squawks at him, waiting for him to come within centimetres of his tail feathers before hopping away. I smile. The bird is in no danger. I know that he will fly up into the branches of the big gum tree if Kir starts to annoy him. Once Mon-Mon misjudged and Kir managed to grab him, pulling a small black feather from amongst his black plumage. Mon-Mon got his revenge by flying up into the gum and defecating into Kir's outstretched hand. Kir refused to play at all for several days after that. Mon-Mon hasn't used that particular punishment again.

"Can we go to the music shop?" Kir is bouncing up and down in front of me. I don't want to go to the music shop, it's a good half hour walk from here. I am tired. But Kir is not.

I glance over at Daniel, who is sitting against the gum tree staring into space and wonder whether nine years old is old enough to be left in charge of an energetic four-year-old.

I check my watch, which tells the true time, and sigh. It is still hours until bedtime. Until I'll tuck Kir into his little bed and close the blackout curtains against the afternoon sun. The same sun he'll wake up to on the morning of the same day. I wonder if Mon-Mon gets tired, if he sleeps. I've never seen him do so, but then I wouldn't. He's a bird.

I brace myself and push up from the park bench. I hold out my hand and paint a smile on my face.

"Yes, baby boy. Let's go to the music shop and see what they have today. Daniel, would you like to come?"

"Yay!" Kir hurls two fistfuls of grass into the air and twirls. I've told him not to pick the grass. I can see bare patches in the distant lawn where he pulled too many in the early days before it occurred to me that they might not grow back. We've moved play areas since then. He's getting better at remembering.

Daniel joins us, a pace or two behind, and as we walk, I watch two white butterflies duel in the flowers. Butterflies or moths? I never could remember. The smaller animals seem to have stayed with us in this world, moving and thriving. After all these years I still can't see a pattern. The dogs stay frozen, next to their owners, out for a never-ending walk. But a few of the birds and the bees, they roam freely. I wonder if Mon-Mon's feather has grown back, or whether that's something else that will never return.

We pass the Green Coat Lady, as we've creatively named her. I'm not sure why she got named after her clothes while a bird gets an entirely new name from Kir. I suppose it's because the bird can be a playmate. I shiver slightly as we pass, as though passing a graveyard. Except that the inhabitant of this body has simply walked on into the future. She's older, Green Coat Lady, even older than me, I think sometimes. Chances are she's walked into her Rest Time by now. I wonder briefly if I could somehow move this figure, stash her where I don't have to look at her any longer. I glance back and notice Daniel gives her a wide berth.

"Slow down, Kir!" I call out, panicked, as I turn back and realise I've lost sight of him. He's only gone around the corner, past the pharmacy, but I worry anyway. He doesn't hear me. His mop of curls reappears as he bounds across the road, giving a high-five to the blue SUV parked right out the front of the music store. It's not like he's going to get run over. That car hasn't moved in years. Kir waves and sticks his tongue out at the toddler in the rear seat. I swear sometimes that little girl moves her eyes when he passes by. I'm not good with ages of children, it's been too long since I was surrounded by them, but if I had to guess I'd say she's about two? Or *was* about two years old. I wonder if she told her mother about the little boy at the window. Her mother's head is bent forward, about to collect her handbag from the passenger footwell of the car. There's another booster seat in the back next to the little girl. I like to think that they were popping into the music store to buy a guitar for the young child that seat belongs to. Maybe for a birthday? A sixth birthday, if he—or she—was at school? Two-thirty-six in the afternoon it is. Two-thirty-six forever and always. Fifty-four minutes for this mum to unclip her toddler, go into the store, select a guitar, and hide it in the trunk before going to pick up her other child from the school gate.

He'd be quite good at guitar by now, I'd imagine. Or she. After a few years of lessons. Or maybe it wasn't for them.

Maybe they passed it onto their little sister. Maybe it's in landfill by now.

This is how I amuse myself; this is how I pass the hours. By telling stories about each of these frozen montages. What they're doing at two-thirty-six in the afternoon on the main street of a small town, surrounded by mountains. What they might be doing now in the unfrozen world. Where they moved on to.

"Nanna, Nanna!"

I can see Kir through the window. He's got 'his' guitar already, a tiny blue model with four nylon strings that are easy for little fingers to strum. Daniel has overtaken me and joined Kir inside. Kir hands him a tiny red guitar. I've showed Kir how to use a pick, but he insists on using his fingers. He likes to listen to the individual notes, moving his fingers up and down the frets to hear them change. Again and again and again, with the obsessive attention to repetition that only a child of his age can muster and appreciate.

I enter the store and take my place on the stool in front of the grand piano.

"What are we playing today, Monsieur Maestro?" I demand grandly, looking down my nose at Kir. Kir giggles.

"Castle on a Cloud!" he shouts.

"Of course, young sir. An excellent selection." I begin to play the classic child's fantasy song from Les Misérables. I avoid looking at Kir while I play, and he sings. Daniel remains silent, withdrawn. Kir loves this song because it speaks of rooms full of toys, and dozens of other kids to play with. I always dread it just a little. My mind has a cruel habit of conflating little Kir with the image I have of a lonely girl dressed in rags on a darkened stage. Cold, starved, abandoned by her mother, and worked near to death by her supposed caregivers. It's not real, of course. Kir is happy enough. I glance at the man behind the counter, leaning on the flat surface, reading the same magazine. The same line, over and over. I smile as I remember Kir escaping my supervision a week or so ago and climbing up onto the chair to tickle him on the back of the neck. I imagine, again, him shivering slightly at two-thirty-six in the afternoon and looking around, perhaps catching the faint strains of light opera played on the grand piano. Perhaps shrugging, shaking his head, and going back to his magazine.

We walk home slowly. Kir's burst of manic energy has finally wound down a little. He has run laps of the toy store, counted all the tins of blue paint in the hardware store and chosen us a new house from the realtor's window. Today it was a rural property outside of town. Five bedrooms, a wrap-around porch, and stables for the horses to sleep in. He was a little crushed when I explained it would take a whole hour to drive there and goodness knows how many hours to walk, given none of the cars started.

Back home I fix him and Daniel peanut butter sandwiches and send them off to prepare for bedtime. Daniel quietly accepts my offer of 'Entiac' to give him a few hours of oblivion. It will take him time to adjust, though I dearly hope he won't need to stay for long. I hope he's out of here and back in the world of the living soon. Kir reads aloud to himself for half an hour or so before the babble stops suddenly, and I know he's fallen into what passes for sleep in here. I climb into bed myself and lay there staring at the ceiling, exhausted but awake, waiting for semi-consciousness to fill a few more hours.

At 3a.m., according to my watch, I am wide awake. I lie in the darkness afforded by curtains velcroed to the walls.

I imagine what the sounds of the night should be. Cicadas causing a ruckus, rubbing their wings together to keep small children awake? No, too early in the year. Not hot enough. An electric car quietly buzzing past on its way home, carrying its passenger to bed from a late shift at the hospital maybe? Voices out on the street, people laughing and chatting, walking home from a friend's party? Only on weekends.

Kir is only four years old in body, but at least twice that in years on earth. I knew it would take time to find the cure, but I never imagined it would be this long. I envisioned months, not years. I regret nothing. I'd do these years all over again if it meant giving our boy a chance to live. But I do begin to worry about what his life will be like when his time comes again. I have started a list in my mind of all the things we will have to re-teach him. How to talk to other people. How to play with children. Don't run on the road. Dogs might bite you, steer clear.

I fear others will think of him as a child prodigy, reading novels and playing guitar. They will expect more of him and he will fail to deliver. He is our wonderful, special Kir. But he is also just a regular, normal boy.

I suppose time will catch up with him eventually. Maybe we can home-school him for a few years while he adjusts. It's not unusual, especially for sick children. And it's not like he'll miss the company of children his own age. He's learned to live without it.

All the muscles in my body tense as I hear a new noise. At first, I think I'm imagining it, so I still and wait for an encore. It's a noise I haven't heard in many years.

There it is again. A wet, choking sound, followed by a thump on the wall.

"Kir!" I wail as I leap out of bed, ignoring my protesting, creaky limbs, and bound into his room.

Kir is having a seizure.

I go into autopilot, clearing the area around him, making sure he won't hurt himself with the jerking and flailing limbs.

It lasts just minutes, but it changes everything.

Afterwards, he is still again, and I have wiped his mouth. His pale, bruised eyelids have closed again, and his breathing is regular. I sit, and I let the tears fall down my cheeks and feel the fear constrict my chest.

Time is moving on for Kir. Maybe it's only a minute, but it's enough. Time is running out.

CHAPTER FORTY-FOUR

Varya

Varya sat on the couch for a long time after Zoe left. She emptied her vodka glass and still she stayed, watching the last of the day's light refracted through the crystal patterns. The light faded altogether and still she stayed, in the near-dark, the only illumination a faint glow from the kitchen light in the next room.

Zoe's words haunted her. She had found a cure to Kir's disease, it was true. It had happened faster than she'd feared, though more slowly than she'd hoped. She'd arranged for the operating theatre at the Minor Miracles Foundation to be opened secretly. Professor Langford had arranged for the surgeon, anaesthetist, and theatre nurses to visit on a Sunday morning. They were told that Kir was the child of a major donor to the charity who didn't want to wait until the treatment passed the myriad waiting periods and evidentiary requirements for new treatments. They were sure this would work.

The day she'd brought Kir out of the Time Lock was magical. So much hope, so much excitement from the little boy who'd spent two years already locked away. He'd wanted to touch everything in the apartment; he'd commented on everything he saw from the car on the way to the research facility. Varya had been too tense to respond to most of it. Marisa answered his questions. Yes, the other cars move too. Yes, it is very dark at night-time, but the lights come on so that everyone can see. No, this isn't the same area he lived in with Nanna. Yes, Nanna was fine back at the apartment.

"Oh no, I have no interest in coming with you to the operation. I am very much looking forward to having myself a nice, long, hot shower here in your apartment, thank you very much. With running water. Lots and lots of running water," Elena had told her. That was another anomaly of the Time Lock—no running water. All the water had to be brought in from the outside in large containers and fed into the plumbing system. The pipes had frozen in time.

Six weeks, Elena and Kir and spent outside of the Time Lock. The operation was difficult. A new procedure, a small mistake resulting in significant blood loss. Kir pulled through though, transfusions of donor blood were close at hand to replace what he lost. A new learning for the research team; a mistake that would not be repeated on the next child. The post-operative treatment was successful. Varya had started to turn her mind to her mother's Rest Time Ceremony. After gaining an extra two years of time, she had just one day left.

Kir was home in his own bedroom in the apartment when he'd had the first seizure.

Varya positioned him so he wouldn't hurt himself, and waited. Then she called Professor Langford, who called the medical team back in. Varya and Kir met them at the research facility late that night. The scans were clear. The cancer hadn't returned.

"What, then?" Varya demanded.

"The treatment successfully destroyed the tumour. But it also appears to have caused problems with his Rest Time Chip," he explained quietly.

So, it was her fault. She was the one who had rushed the treatment through, who demanded it be carried out on a live patient before all the hurdles had been cleared. The hurdles were normally just administrative hoops that never showed up anything else they hadn't anticipated. Her research teams were nothing but thorough.

But the Time Chips. How could the treatment have affected them? It just wasn't something that had ever come up before.

"I think we can isolate the particular chemical which caused the reaction, test it out on other Time Chips to be certain." The doctor paused. He looked down at his feet. "It won't be a problem in future patients."

"And Kir?" Varya tipped her head, trying to catch his eye, trying to force him to look at her and tell her the truth, but make it a good truth. An easy truth. A certain truth.

He shook his head and met her gaze with pain and sorrow. "I don't know. It will take time to find a way to neutralise the reaction. And I don't think the young lad has enough time to wait. I'm so sorry."

And so, Kir was stabilised again and Elena went back into the Time Lock with him, with just hours to spare until her own Rest Time Ceremony. Kir sulked for days, asking about the moving people and why he couldn't go and play with the cat in the stairwell again.

At least, this is what Elena told her daughter when Varya finally came to visit them after six days of absence. By then,

Elena and Kir had settled into their routine again. Although Kir remained a little more sullen and cross than usual.

Varya ran her finger around the rim of her crystal vodka glass and relished the musical ringing it elicited. She was just starting to feel calm enough to consider getting up for a refill. The doorbell buzzed and Varya shuddered, both at the jarring sound and the concerning meaning that came with it. She wasn't expecting anyone. The doorbell buzzed again. This time she got up to answer it.

"Sebastian."

"Hey." He held up his hand in a half-hearted wave. Varya thought he looked tired, defeated. She still didn't want him in her apartment, nor in her life. His presence forced her to confront things in a more immediate fashion than she cared to. His physical proximity scrambled her mind and his scent distracted her. She stood, her hand on the doorhandle and her body blocking his entrance to the apartment, waiting.

"Can I come in?" he said at last.

"Why?"

He raised his eyebrows. "Because it seems a little odd to be having a conversation..."

"I mean, why are you here?" She cut him off.

Please fix our son, she wanted to say to him. Please don't judge me, yell at me, be furious with me. You have every right, but please tell me how to fix our son. Then you can hate me all you like.

Instead, she glared at him, free hand on her hip, as though this was all his fault.

"I came to apologise for the other night. I was a little hard on you and I'm sorry for that. I just needed to rule you out as a suspect." He paused and frowned at her unchanging stance and expression. "You understand, right?"

Varya nodded and took a step backwards. "You want a vodka?" she asked as he brushed past her.

"I'd love a vodka," he murmured.

She curled up beside him, drink in hand, bare feet tucked to the side, pretending a calm and relaxation she didn't feel. 'Numb' was the best she could manage right now. Sebastian seemed less able to hide his feelings. He sat awkwardly on the low sofa, long legs bent in front of him, back straight, glass resting on one knee, hand on the other.

"We found the two little girls who went missing," he started. He took a gulp of vodka and rested it gently back on his knee. Varya pictured the fortifying burn the liquid would make as it meandered down his chest, into his limbs. "One was a murder-suicide. The non-custodial parent." Another gulp. "The other had the same M.O. as Daniel. Looks like they didn't manage to leave enough life span to get her home safely first, though. The body was dumped in an alleyway, behind the Town Hall."

Varya tried extremely hard not to feel a thing at this news. She lifted her glass and tipped back the entire contents, flicking her head backwards and swallowing in one fluid gesture. But it didn't silence the voice in her head, which whispered, *Your fault. This is all your fault.*

Worse, Sebastian wasn't finished. He took a deep breath and looked at her directly.

"While the parents were identifying the body, we got a call about three more abductions. We have to consider the possibility they may be escalating operations."

She dropped her glass onto the carpet then. It stayed there, tipped to the side, empty.

"I'm so sorry," she whispered. "I'm so sorry." Great, hacking sobs that shook her shoulders started to gush out. She felt, rather than saw, Sebastian kneeling in front of her, his face level with hers. Her skin burned where he placed a hand on each of her arms and gently tried to pry them from covering her face. "So sorry, I'm so sorry," she kept whispering, developing momentum into a disturbing yet comforting rhythm. "All my fault, this is all my fault."

"This is not your fault, Varya. You're doing everything you can to get the time transfer tech ready." He'd settled for rubbing her tensed upper arms gently, trying to inject his warmth into her cold body. She stopped whispering but continued to sob. She leaned into him slightly, testing to see if the feel of herself against his chest would fracture her completely. His smell was so good, sweet and affirming. Familiar and safe. Sebastian put one hand on her back, then another. It felt so good, as though anything could be overcome.

"It's nearly finished," she muttered into her forearms, which still protected her face against his chest. "The time transfer tech, I think we're nearly there. Maybe a few more days, another week."

He touched her hair gently and smoothed a few strands down, brushing against her neck. Slowly, trembling, she drew her arms down and folded them around her own chest. She leaned her cheek against his shirt, aware but not caring that she was staining it with her tears.

"There, see? And there was nothing you could have done to help that little girl anyway, not without us finding the perpetrator to transfer the life span back from."

Varya nodded and started to pull away. The vodka was making her dizzy and the proximity to Kir's father was making the world spin too fast. Sebastian relaxed his arms and let her sit up straighter. Did he look disappointed? She wasn't sure.

"I should have destroyed the technology. None of this would be happening if I had."

Sebastian smiled sadly. He pushed up from the floor and returned to the opposite sofa, picking up his glass and taking a large sip.

"You don't know that they're using the unit you and Reg kept. I know you're very talented, but that doesn't mean someone else hasn't been studying what you did. It doesn't mean somebody else hasn't discovered what you discovered. It could simply be coincidence."

Varya frowned. "A coincidence that the M.O. is identical to the time thieves from ten years ago? That the second victim was my best friend's son?"

"It's not identical. Similar, but less precise. The child today, she had no life span left at all."

"Maybe they're just less theatrical, or less compassionate, than the last mob," Varya shrugged. "And the connection to me, what do you make of that?"

"Like I said, possibly just coincidence. You said, yourself, that you've been incognito these past years. Nobody mentions you in the media anymore, nobody at the research facility knows who you really are."

"Unless somebody found out."

Sebastian sighed. "Yes, unless somebody found out. But Varya, I think you're being a little paranoid, aren't you?"

She glared at him then. He hung his head a little and took a swig from his glass.

"I'm tired," she announced.

Sebastian nodded. "Of course, it's late. I could do with some rest myself." He stood and placed the glass on the little table next to the couch. "I'll see myself out."

"Let me know if there are any developments," she called after him.

He turned on his heel. "I'll call Connor?"

She shook her head. "You have my number."

"Okay."

"Okay, then. Good-bye," she prompted, when he didn't move.

As soon as the door clicked shut, she stood to refill her glass. She stared towards the spare room, where she knew Elena would be dosing Kir with Entiac to get eight hours of daily peace. As she sipped her third drink, she decided that she would use her own magic potion to get her eight hours tonight. The time tabs were a vice she wouldn't readily give up. She made a note to avoid telling Sebastian about them, even if she had to come clean about other things. For now, she needed to just wallow a little in her own guilt.

CHAPTER FORTY-FIVE

Elena

This time when I give Kir his Entiac I measure out a dose for this newcomer Daniel as well. We have little to say to each other and it is too much to ask him to stay in his room for eight hours at a time, doing nothing. He is still a child. He does not yet know how to fill the expansive hours. He seems relieved when I offer him a small plastic cup of liquid, just the right amount fuller than Kir's.

I tuck them both into their beds, leaving Kir's door open so I can hear if I need to go to him again. I sit in my comfortable chair and I count to one thousand. Then I steel myself and stand. My Varya has not visited as she should this evening. She is avoiding us. But she needs to know about Kir. She has been avoiding the inevitable for too long. It's time for her to face it. Though I know I don't need to, I hold my breath as I walk through the shimmering curtain.

CHAPTER FORTY-SIX

Varya

Varya was unsteady on her feet as she placed the two empty crystal glasses in the sink and reached for the top cabinet. Two paracetamols for her headache and two time tabs for her fatigue. As she placed the boxes on the counter, she heard a faint sizzling, followed by footsteps. She turned, her heart beating.

"Mama!" Varya stacked the paracetamol on top of the time tab case, guiltily hoping her mother didn't notice. "Mama, what are you doing?" Alarm replaced the guilt as she glanced at the clock on the wall. "You don't have much time left on your Chip." She walked forward and tried to turn her mother around, to return her to the safety of the Time Lock. Elena sidestepped her daughter and drew herself up to face her. Her several inches less of height did nothing to diminish her authority.

"Then I've got plenty of time to talk some sense into my daughter."

Elena pulled out a kitchen chair and sat down heavily. She nodded to the chair opposite her. Varya lowered herself into it obediently.

"What is it, Mama? What's happened?"

"Kir has had another seizure." She said it quietly and calmly but Varya shot up out of her seat and scrambled toward the door. Elena put her arm out to block the doorway. "He's okay for now; he's asleep." She pointed at the chair this time. "Sit."

Varya sat but turned to the side, her weight on the balls of her feet, ready to leap up again at any moment.

"I may not be a fancy scientist like you, but I know a thing or two about life. And that, in there..." Elena poked a finger towards the Time Lock. "That is no life for a child." She let this sink in for a moment. "He needs other children to play with, wind on his face, music in his ears. A frozen second lasting for many years, this is no life for anyone. This isn't a life at all."

Varya sat, fidgeting and gazing longingly at the doorway. "You don't want to look after him anymore," she said softly, without turning. "Okay, I'm sorry. I'll get someone else. Zoe has offered. She can look after them both. If you..."

Elena slapped her palm on the table. Varya flinched.

"Don't you dare misunderstand me, girl. You know that I would do anything for that little boy. I have done everything for our Kir." She sighed, sorrow outweighing her anger. "But I'm not sure that you're doing everything *you* can do."

"I'm trying, Mama. I really am."

"Have you asked him yet?"

Varya stilled. She wondered, if she stopped breathing altogether, whether her mother would go away and stop torturing her. It was much easier when she thought of the Time

Lock as a one-way door. Varya could leave whenever she wanted to, and her mother could not follow her.

"Soon. I will ask him soon. I just need a little more time, there have been a few complications..."

"Sweetheart, you're not listening to me," Elena said, this time with tears in her eyes. "Our little boy doesn't have much more time to spare. You need to make a decision."

"While he's alive there's still hope."

"While he's alive he's suffering and he's afraid, my dear girl. And by refusing to ask for help you're making him suffer even more," she said gently. "Either face his mortality brave-ly and comfort him at the end or play your final cards now. Otherwise he'll be gone, and you won't have a chance to say goodbye."

Varya nodded and swallowed, blinking rapidly.

"The time thieves are back, Mama." She turned to show her face—and with it the full depth of her fear and grief—to her mother. "It's all my fault and I have to fix it. I have to fix it first before I can get help for Kir. Then, I promise, I'll ask Sebastian for help."

Elena nodded too, wanting so fiercely to believe her daughter's words. Knowing that her daughter barely be-lieved them herself.

"I'm sorry, my Varya. I know that you feel like you're to blame for what these evil people do to children. And you be-lieve that Kir's illness is your fault. But just remember this: you are not the all-powerful God. You cannot take respon-sibility for such things. You are not the sun around which everything revolves. But you are Kir's sun, and he wants his Mama to be with him very much."

Elena glanced at the clock. Varya followed her gaze.

"I'll get some medicine to try to stop the seizures for a while. Zoe will help, I'm sure. You go back to the Time Lock now, and keep yourself safe as well," said Varya.

Elena stood and held out her arms to Varya. Varya walked forward and allowed herself to be enfolded for the second time that night. This time she found a sense of peace she hadn't with Sebastian. Her mother knew all her faults and all her secrets. She couldn't hide anything from her, not really, unlike Sebastian. Elena moved back and held Varya at arm's length. She looked at her for a moment, then shook her slightly.

"When this is all over, when you've cured our Kir, you'll need to find a way to let me go, too. Remember that."

Varya nodded and smiled weakly. "Not yet though, Mama. Not yet."

"Soon."

Varya waited for the tell-tale sizzle that let her know her mother was safely back in suspended animation. Then she walked over to claim her tablets and her time tabs and went to bed.

CHAPTER FORTY-SEVEN

Daniel

The Entiac was enough to make him drowsy but, try as he might, for what felt like many hours, Daniel just couldn't seem to fall asleep. His head felt heavy and fuzzy and his limbs were like lead. He considered getting up again, asking Elena for a higher dose, but the thought of getting out of bed was too exhausting. He was certain he'd just fall on the floor if he tried. He wondered if this ever happened to Kir, or whether the dose was more accurately calibrated for his small body. He wondered what went on in the younger boy's head each day that he was stuck in here, whether he wanted to get out and go home. Or maybe this *was* home. After all, he was just a little kid, he didn't know any different.

But the way he'd stood looking at the Time Lock's portal, after Varya went back through it. Shoulders slumped, head still. It was as if a switch had been flicked in the small boy. Daniel had stood in his bedroom doorway, watching him, unsure if he should call out to him or go to him.

"Kir?" he tried softly. "Kir, you okay?"

Kir's only response was to sink down onto the carpet, crossing his legs and settling in, never once taking his eyes off the shimmering curtain. Was he really waiting for his mother to come back so soon?

"Come away from there, Kir," Elena called from the kitchen.

Daniel stepped back into his bedroom, afraid to be caught staring. But Elena hadn't come.

"She'll be back again soon enough; you know she will. Come and have something to eat."

"I'm not hungry!" Kir shouted.

Daniel took one last peek at Kir, then crept down the hallway to the kitchen. He sat down at the table, watching Elena prepare the food that Marisa had brought for them. Tomatoes, cheese, and whole wheat bread.

"Is Kir okay?" he'd asked.

Elena turned to look at him briefly, frowning in surprise, as though she'd forgotten he'd remained in the apartment. She turned back to slicing the tomato, sawing thin segments directly onto the bread. Daniel noticed she only had two sandwiches set up on the board. She glanced at him again and reached for more bread. A slice of cheese on top of each collection of tomato, then she closed the sandwiches and plated them up.

"Kir misses his mother." Elena sighed heavily as she balanced all three plates in her hands and placed them on the table. "It's good that you're here. Good for him, I mean." She flicked her head towards the hallway. "Bad for you, obviously. But good for him. He will miss you, too, when you leave."

"But he'll leave too, one day, won't he?"

"Maybe he will. But maybe not. It all depends on what his mother decides." Elena seemed to speak to herself as much as Daniel. "He needs other children; he needs to live in the world. But his mother, she has trouble accepting the cruelty of the true world. She refuses to let the universe run its course, thinking she can always intervene to change the path of fate."

"She seems to be pretty good at intervening so far," said Daniel.

Elena glared at him. "Kir! Come and eat your sandwich! Right now!"

Kir's stomping footsteps approached down the short hallway. He stood in the doorway with his arms crossed. After a moment he stood on his tiptoes so he could see over the back of the chair, to find out what was on his plate.

"I don't like tomato," he announced.

"Yes, you do. You had it yesterday and you loved it," said Elena. "Now sit down and eat."

"I don't like tomato!" he shouted, punching his fists downwards and lifting his chin. He advanced on the plate then, shouting alternately, "I don't like tomato!" and "I don't like you!" Elena sat silently as the little boy picked up each sandwich quarter and flung it at the wall. Finally, he picked up the plate, hurled it on the floor and jumped on it.

"Are you done?" asked Elena, her lips pursed.

Kir flopped to the floor and started to sob, his shoulders heaving, struggling for breath.

Elena calmly stood and went to him, patted his head, and murmured into his ear before retrieving the sandwich pieces and putting them on a fresh plate on the table. She lifted Kir onto his chair where he sat, hunched over his sandwich, not eating.

Daniel had lost his appetite, too, though he ate mechanically so as not to attract attention to himself. This wasn't a happy place. And Kir wasn't a happy boy.

In his bed, he rolled over to face the wall and lazily pried his eyes open to look up at the print which adorned it. A wide, thin black and white printed photograph of a long, old-fashioned pier stretching off into the distance.

Kir had cheered up a little as the day went on and they'd headed outside for some fresh air and a walk. Daniel had looked around and realised how much the same everything was. He thought he knew his own neighbourhood and that it was pretty boring. Nothing happened except that people went about their business every day.

But this frozen world didn't even have that. In Daniel's world, the balls were different shapes and colours some days. The teams of kids would swap and come out at different times on different days. People would get new cars or put dents in old ones. In Kir's world, the children wore the same clothes and the same pose every day. The sun was always in the same position, the air was the same temperature, and the light made the same shadow patterns around the trees. The shadows didn't even dance in the wind. The whole world was still.

Daniel heard the creak of floorboards as Elena paced down the hallway, away from his room and towards Kir's. He waited a few beats before tracking the sound of her moving towards his own room. The door swished softly against the carpet as it opened. Daniel stayed very still until he heard the door close. Soon after, the warmth of the room, his own weariness, and the strength of the Entiac combined to finally lull his senses enough for him to slip into a synthetic sleep.

CHAPTER FORTY-EIGHT

Varya

The prototype time transfer device that her team at the Minor Miracles Foundation had built looked almost identical to the one she had searched the archives of Rest Time Corps for, albeit a little rougher around the edges.

"Stand by, ready to test," she warned.

Varya's hands trembled slightly as she typed in the coded sequences that would trigger the transfer of ten days' life span from Gamma mouse to Delta mouse. The mice twitched every now and then. They were sleeping, but still alive. They'd been dosed with a sedative to prevent them running about and shaking off the wires which attached them to one another.

This time it would work, she willed silently. She looked up at her colleagues peering into the side of the glass container before hitting enter on the keyboard. They all waited. Three minutes. That was the minimum amount of time that needed to lapse before they could re-test the life span of each mouse. For once, Varya wished she could speed up time rather than freeze it or slow it down. This was the eleventh live experiment in the past twenty-four hours. They were nearly there, though there had been problems getting the calibrations right. The first six experiments didn't work at all; there was no change. The seventh and eighth resulted in drained span from one mouse but didn't transfer it to the other. The ninth had killed both mice and the tenth had successfully transferred life span but had continued to drain the donor mouse entirely until it dropped dead. The recipient mouse was still happily running around its cage, and likely would be for quite some time.

"Ready?" asked Connor, holding a black wand-looking device aloft.

Varya nodded, not trusting herself to speak.

He tested the donor mouse first. Its life span was twenty-two days, ten fewer than it was three minutes ago. Varya breathed in sharply as he reset the scanner and moved it over the recipient mouse. The green numbers glowed – thirty-four days, exactly ten days extra. She blew air out in a great sigh and grinned. Connor grinned back then turned to face the other scientists who had crowded around to watch.

"Success!" he declared. A cheer went up. There were high-fives, back-slapping, and a sudden increase in chatter. Connor turned back to Varya. "You want to call Sebastian, or shall I?"

"It's okay, I'll call him." She picked up her phone from a nearby desk and carried it out into the corridor, where there was relative peace.

"Varya." Sebastian answered immediately. She ignored the strained note in his voice.

We did it, she tried to say, but it caught in her tense throat. She took a breath and tried again. "We did it. The time transfer tech is ready."

248 | REBECCA BOWYER

"That's... that's great. Thank you. That's really great news."
He sounded distracted. Varya frowned.

"Sebastian? Is everything okay? Has another child been...
has there been another abduction? Or..."

"We have a few leads, but we won't need the scanner just
yet. There's been another body."

Varya leaned heavily against the wall. "Oh, no."

"You'd better bring it over here anyway, so it's ready when
needed. I won't be here, but just leave it with..." his voice became muffled. Varya heard another male voice in the background. "Jonathon. Ask for Jonathon Wilde when you get
here. Don't entrust the tech to anyone else, okay?"

"Okay," she replied hesitantly.

"Varya, this is important. Don't trust anyone else. Only
Jonathon. Got it?"

"Yes, Sebastian. I'll leave now and bring it to Jonathon. I
understand."

"And Varya, are you sure you haven't had any contact with
Reg recently? None at all?"

"No. I already told you."

"No calls, no texts, not even a friendly beer?"

"No, of course not. I know what 'contact' means, Sebastian. I haven't heard from him or seen him since I left."

"And nobody else has access to your apartment? Nobody
else has a key?"

"It's not key-operated. It's coded to me only. And no, I
haven't given anyone else access."

"Not even Marisa?"

"No, she has scheduled times she comes in, and always
only when I'm there, although..." Varya trailed off, her scalp
suddenly feeling tight and cold. "She hacked the system one
time. Sort of as a joke. Met me inside the apartment. I got

so angry at her; she's never done it again." Sebastian was silent. "Sebastian? Why does this matter? Is someone trying to break in there? Are they... I mean, am I in danger?" Varya's mind raced, calculating the number of minutes it would take to get back to her apartment to check on the Time Lock.

"Why would someone want to break into your apartment, Var'?" he said quietly. "What are you keeping in there?"

"N-nothing. I mean, Marisa meant it as a joke. She didn't want to wait in the stairwell and..."

She thought she heard Sebastian sigh softly.

"Sebastian? What is this about?"

"I'm sure it's nothing. Just make sure you come directly to the Rest Time Corps headquarters and bring the time transfer tech. Ask for Jonathan. I have to go now."

He hung up and Varya made a split-second decision. The Rest Time Corps headquarters and her apartment were in opposite directions. She'd promised Sebastian to come to Rest Time Corps, but she had to make sure Kir and Elena were safe first. And Daniel. Zoe would never forgive her if anything happened to him.

"Varya?" said Connor. "Varya, what did he say?"

"I have to go. I have to go right now."

"And take the transfer tech to..."

"Yes." She brushed her hair out of her eyes and snapped the briefcase shut. "I have to take the transfer tech right now. I don't know when I'll be back." She paused. "Thank you for your help, Connor. You may never understand how much this means to me, but just know that it means everything. I'll make sure this technology never hurts anyone again."

Connor sidestepped in front of her, cutting off her exit.

"Varya, wait. Why does this feel like good-bye? Where are you going?"

"I'm going home to check on my little boy," said Varya. "Now get out of my way."

He stepped aside and she marched out of the research facility that she had built and run, fuelled by her own grief, possibly for the last time.

CHAPTER FORTY-NINE

Reg sat on Varya's sofa, directly over the impression made by Sebastian the previous night. A uniformed police officer snapped his cuffs securely then read to him from a tablet, pausing from time to time so Reg could nod his understanding. Reg was the first in the room to see Varya as she pushed open her apartment door. He looked tired, thought Varya. And old.

Sebastian stood with his back to the front door, writing notes on his screen with a stylus and speaking quietly to a colleague. He looked up when the colleague did; over his shoulder his eyes met Varya's. He murmured something else to his colleague and walked toward her.

"If you could wait outside for now..." he suggested gently.

"Why is he in my apartment? How did he get in without a..." Varya trailed off as she stared at Reg. Everything started to fall into place. "Marisa... is Marisa here?"

Sebastian shook his head.

"Mum?" she said. She started to calculate in her head how many hours she'd been away for; how many hours her mother might have been outside of the Time Lock for. How many hours she might have left until her Rest Time kicked in.

He pressed his lips together and flicked his eyes towards the kitchen.

"Mum!" she called out, a plea this time. She tried to walk towards the internal door separating the two rooms, but Sebastian stepped in front of her.

He shook his head. "Not yet. She's still being questioned."

"Questioned? Why are you questioning her? She has nothing to do with this, she's..." Varya tried to push him out of the way but he took her by both arms and steered her around.

"Let's go outside into the hall where it's a bit quieter. I can explain there."

Varya's head swam but she clutched tightly to her handbag as she allowed herself to be led out of her own apartment. She pressed her fingers against the shape of the scanner, nestled next to her screen in the bag's central compartment, reassuring herself it was still there. She wasn't entirely sure what use it would be now, but she had to have it. It was her security blanket. Something to bargain with, perhaps. Sebastian led her to the small padded bench seat on the landing.

"Did you know your mother was seeing Reg?" he started.

Varya shook her head. "No, I had no idea. She can't be involved with this, she wouldn't..."

Sebastian held his hand up. "We know. She wasn't directly involved. We caught the perpetrators earlier today. Reg swears he doesn't know them, but they seem to know him and have copied the tech he stole from Rest Time Corps. Fortunately, they didn't copy it particularly well. As we suspected, it's an inaccurate duplicate and not functioning the way it should."

"So, why is he being arrested? Why do you have him in cuffs?"

"Varya, he's still responsible for a serious theft. And that theft led—albeit indirectly—to the deaths of four kids."

Three kids, thought Varya. She studied Sebastian's face for signs that he knew about the Time Lock, whether he'd found Daniel.

"Have you notified the children's families yet?" she asked.

"Not yet. We'll get Reg processed and the others fully questioned before we make those calls."

So no, he hadn't found the Time Lock. Otherwise Zoe would have been one of the first people he called.

"How about the people they sold the kids' life spans to? Have you found them?"

Sebastian nodded. "Yes, we have. They've been taken into custody for receiving stolen goods. We're still trying to decide what else to charge them with, and what their punishment should be. We can't allow them to benefit from the proceeds of their crime. At the very least, we'll confiscate the additional life span they stole."

Varya pulled her handbag onto her lap, opened it, and handed him the black scanner.

"Is this...?" He turned it over, examining it as though he knew anything about the technology. Varya had to bite her lower lip to stop herself from laughing inappropriately.

"Yes."

"You figured it out? It works? That's pretty impressive." He weighed it in his hands. "It'll need to be destroyed again, though, after we confiscate the perpetrators' stolen life spans. It's no use to us now, with the kids..."

With the kids already dead, is what he meant to say.

"I'll hold onto it for now, if that's okay, while the higher-ups decide what to do with it," he said.

Varya's mind was already ticking over, trying to figure this bit out. She'd been so focused on getting Daniel out of immediate danger she hadn't planned ahead for the bit where her team actually succeeded in reinventing the time transfer tech and Sebastian's team succeeded in catching Daniel's life span recipient.

"Your mum said she did it for you, you know."

"Did what?"

Sebastian stared at her long and hard. "Asked Reg to steal the time transfer tech."

She frowned. "What? For me? That doesn't make any sense."

He shook his head. "No. It didn't make sense to me either." He stood up and stretched to his full height. "I'll need you to wait out here until Reg has been read his rights and removed to the station. Then I'll come out and bring you inside. You'll be able to talk to your mum then."

"You're not taking Mum into custody, then?"

Sebastian looked at her curiously. "No, we're not. She says she doesn't have long until her Rest Time. Maybe hours. We'll question her and then she'll remain here with you. It's what she wants."

Varya just stared right back at him as he returned to her apartment, her mind whirling.

If the time thieves had used the time transfer tech during the abduction of the children, it must have been stolen well before Daniel was taken. Why would her mother ask Reg to steal the tech before then? For herself? Did she hope to extend her own life span? It made no sense at all. Varya fidgeted and chewed on her tongue, hoping they would finish the questioning quickly.

It felt like hours, but her screen told her it was just seventeen minutes later, the door swung wide again, and Reg was led out by Sebastian's colleague and the uniformed officer.

"Varya," Reg nodded.

Varya looked at him, taking in his dishevelled appearance. Did he feel guilty for what he'd done?

"I'm so sorry, love," he said, as though he'd read her mind.

"I'm sorry, too, Reg." If it hadn't been for her mother would he ever have thought to try to steal the time transfer tech? None of this mess might ever have happened. The officers moved Reg along and they started the several storey descent down the stairs. Sebastian appeared at the door. The mess had thrown her in the way of him again, which wasn't all bad. She'd been meaning to contact him, to ask about Kir, she'd been working her way up to it. She just wanted to try a few more things, to make absolutely sure it wasn't something she could fix herself.

"You can come in now," said Sebastian. "Your mum's asking for you."

He disappeared back down the hallway. Varya followed him, closing the door behind her.

CHAPTER FIFTY

Elena

"Mum, you need to go back now."

My Varya is dancing around me like a toddler who needs to pee. If she could pick me up and throw me over her shoulder to put me back in the Time Lock, I believe she would.

"The boys won't be awake for hours yet. There is plenty of time."

Her eyes are desperate now as she checks the clock above my head. "How long have you been out here, Mum?"

I don't answer her. I wait for Sebastian's reaction, to see if she has told him yet. He looks very confused.

"What boys?" He looks to Varya. So do I.

"The children are out of danger now," I tell my Varya. "So, you need to keep your promise." I flick my head at this Sebastian. I feel sure that he will know the answers. He will be able to fix our Kir. Don't ask me to tell you how I know this. Some things, you just need to have faith.

"Please, Mum. How many hours?"

I shake my head. No hours.

"Minutes? You have minutes left?"

Now I turn my head to look up at the clock myself.

"Thirty-seven minutes, my darling girl. I have thirty-seven minutes left."

She comes to me then, throwing herself at my knees, tears in her eyes.

"Please, don't do this. I can't lose you both."

"You have what you need," I tell her, nodding towards Sebastian. His mouth opens and closes but he says no words. He is a sensible man sometimes. Perhaps he has grown through his grief.

"I need you," she chokes.

I know in my heart of hearts that this has never been just about Kir. It's about letting go of being able to control everything around her. She is a strong woman, this girl of mine, and for the most part, she asserts her will on the world with great success. But while she can leave Kir safely with me she will never swallow her own pride and admit her failings to Sebastian and ask for his help.

I take my Varya's hands. "Your little boy needs you. He needs his mum. And he needs his dad. And he needs you both to figure this out. Not at some point in the next twenty years. Now. He doesn't need to come out of there when you're a mirror image of me and he has thirty-seven minutes left with you. He's living his life now, and he needs to be out here in the world to do it."

"But what if you're... gone. And then I can't fix him. What then? He needs you, Mum, please don't do this."

"You can't fix him," I tell her bluntly. I narrow my eyes at our Kir's father. Varya turns to look at him, too. "But he can."

"Fix who?" says Sebastian then. "What are you talking about?" He looks a little frightened now, confronted with this strong woman brought to her knees, reduced to tears at the thought of her mother leaving. She never cried when he left, but he doesn't need to know that.

"Your son," I tell him, simply.

"My son is dead," he says, his mouth twisted. "Is this some sort of sick joke?"

"He's not dead," whispers Varya.

"What?"

"I said, he's not dead," she says, louder now. She turns to face him, wiping furiously at her tears.

"You told me he was dead." He is horrified now, puffing out his chest, not sure whether to fight or flee.

"You left him for dead!" And now she is yelling. As she should—she is right. I check the clock again and decide to let them have it out for a few minutes. They need this confrontation, the one they never had all those years ago.

"I couldn't stand to watch him in pain and to watch you in denial." He is crying now, remembering. "I wanted to let him go and be in peace. But you insisted on keeping him, on keeping hope, even when there wasn't any. Even when you were hurting our son with it."

He has hit my Varya where it hurts. With truth that cuts her to the core. Because this is exactly what she did. Kir was in a world of pain that the doctors couldn't keep at bay the whole time without killing him. The choice was pain and life, or death and peace. It's not a choice any parent should have to make for their child. Sebastian couldn't force Varya to choose death, so he left her alone to endure Kir's pain instead.

"He's alive?" he says quietly. I feel his anger dull to a throb.

Varya nods.

"But how?"

"A Time Lock."

"You've kept him in agony for all these years?" His anger rises again.

"No! No, of course I haven't. I made sure he was comfortable before he went in."

Sebastian sits down heavily.

"A Time Lock," he repeats, his head in his hands. "Why didn't you tell me?"

"They're not legal. It would have put you in an impossible position."

"Time Locks are theoretical. They're experimental, they're not illegal. They're outside the law. How did you even...?"

My Varya smiles a little then, unable to keep her scientific pride at bay.

"I figured it out." She shrugs.

"Clearly. But who looks after him? How do you feed him? How..."

He turns to me and remembers I'm in the room now. I smile broadly at him. The overlooked older lady that everyone forgot about. That nobody really noticed when I disappeared. They all assumed I'd had my Rest Time in sunny climates, just like we arranged. No funeral, no grieving, all my contemporaries gone within a few months.

"Your little boy has been safe with me," I tell him with a gentle smile. "Marisa helps a little. She brings the food. Not quite the same as my cooking, but it passes. Cooking doesn't work so well in the Time Lock. We're not sure why." I shrug. I miss cooking. I tried, early on. The vegetables would grow hot but not soften. The cake mixtures bubbled but never solidified.

"Sebastian, we found the cure for Kir's brain tumour. He came through the operation and treatment with no side ef-

260 | REBECCA BOWYER

fects at all." Varya is wringing her hands now. Sebastian and I both wait but she doesn't go on.

She has come this far, but her pride won't let her go further. She is all out of humility. I sigh and continue for her. "He still has a problem with his Time Chip. The treatment, it messed with it and made it go..." I wave my arms around a little, hoping Varya will interrupt me soon. I am quickly realising I don't have the right words for this conversation. "His little body, it didn't like the Time Chip anymore." Usually if I bumble my way through scientific terms for long enough, she gets exasperated enough to tell me what I need to know. Or what Sebastian needs to know.

"His body started to reject the Chip?" Sebastian offers.

"Yes!" I say. "And the seizures. He started having the seizures."

Sebastian looks to Varya. "This is what you wanted to ask me? About anti-rejection serums?"

Varya nodded, not meeting his eyes. "Connor said... said he thought you might know about one. We haven't been able to develop one that we can test in similar enough conditions to ensure its safety. I need to know it's safe."

Sebastian smiled then, a watery, teary smile. "You've cured the cancer?" Varya nods. "And so... he's still in the Time Lock because of the Chip rejection, the seizures?" Varya nods again. "But that's the only thing?"

"Yes," she whispers hoarsely. "And it's my fault. It's my fault because I rushed the treatment without the proper tests..." She's slumped at my feet now, twisted to face him. She flicks her eyes up to his briefly, trying to judge his reaction to this news.

He shakes his head in amazement. "Varya, you found a cure. You saved his life. That's incredible."

She moans. "I nearly killed him, Sebastian. I nearly killed him because I was rushing. I wanted it to be right. I wanted to *be* right. And it nearly killed him. I nearly killed our son."

He stood up suddenly. "Can I see him? Is he near? Who's looking after him?"

"Yes," says Varya.

"He's asleep," I interject. "Can you fix him?" I ask, annoyed that they have had this big long discussion, taking up my valuable minutes but still not solving the issue at hand.

"Y-yes. Yes, of course. I can fix him," says Sebastian, distracted. He's trying to focus on me at the same time as looking around wildly trying to find where his little boy might be hiding. But I need to know. I raise my eyebrows expectantly. "Yes, Connor was right. We've been advancing in the field of anti-rejection serum over the past few years. We have several different types, including one that was developed specifically to deal with organ transplants and blood transfusion cases. It's fully tested and operational. No side effects." He turns to Varya. "They did a blood transfusion as part of Kir's treatment?"

She nods. "Several."

He grins. "Well, there you go. That'll be what triggered it. The Chips are programmed to the recipient's genetic code. Transfusions and transplants can screw with them if the genetics are too different, even if the blood type matches."

"Okay," she says, barely willing to believe.

"I can fix him," says Sebastian.

"Okay." Her tears flow again. I think mine might as well.

"But can I see him first? Please?"

"Yes," she says.

I glance at the clock.

"Varya, my dear."

"Mum? Mum, how many minutes do you have left?" She puts her hand on my knee, her other on the couch, and pulls herself up to sit beside me.

I put my hands over her hand. "I have sixteen minutes left, my darling Varya." I look up to Sebastian. "Spare room down the hall, walk through the shimmery circle, then second door on the left down the hallway. Don't make too much noise. He's asleep."

Sebastian pauses, then nods and walks quickly out of the room.

"I need to say good-bye now," I tell Varya when he is gone.

She doesn't try to fight me this time. "Thank you. Thank you for..." She sobs. She hasn't prepared for this moment, but I have. I have had much time in that Time Lock to think about this.

"Sssh," I soothe. "Listen to your mother."

She nods.

"Our Kir, he has a long life ahead of him. Reggie, he measured Kir's life span for me."

"Is that why he took the time transfer tech? Reg?"

"Yes. I asked him to take a reading. I had a dream, a premonition, that Kir only had a life span of just seven years. I was so sure I was right. I didn't want you wasting away your own years trying to fix a child who would die soon anyway."

"But you were wrong," Varya said, a small laugh escaping along with her next sob.

I roll my eyes. "Yes, on this one, single occasion. I was wrong."

"So, how long does he have?"

"Barring catastrophe, he has a total of seventy-eight years of life span. He's already lived nine years, but only four years out here. The Time Chip, Reggie says it will let him live his full sixty-five years out here, it won't count the ones in the Time Lock. So, our Kir has had five bonus years." I grin, incredibly pleased with myself. My Kir will get to live for seventy years in total before his Rest Time.

"Good," Varya nods fiercely, then. "Good," she says again.

"Yes," I agree. "It is very good."

We both sit, silently contemplating Kir as a teenager; Kir as an adult; Kir as a father himself, maybe; Kir as an old man waiting for his own Rest Time Ceremony, a long time from now. I pat her hand.

"And now I have to let go of you. I will miss you, Varya. But I'll see you again one day, a long time from now, after your own Rest Time. And Kir. We'll all be together again, I'm sure."

"Oh, Mum, you know I don't believe in..."

"Hush. I will believe for us both. You can do whatever you like. Don't rain on my afterlife."

I hold my arms out to her for a big hug then. She comes into my arms and we hold each other fiercely, not looking at the clock, not checking the time. I know it is nearly time. I don't need the clock to tell me that. I breathe in the smell of my Varya's beautiful hair, remembering how soft it was when she was first born, how soothing it was to stroke my fingers through it. A damp crown of prolific dark hair, which all fell out soon enough.

I feel the first stage of the Time Chip's release. My limbs start to relax, and I feel Varya's silent sobs increase again.

"I love you, babushka. You take care of our Kir, won't you?"

It's the last thing I say to her as my eyes close.

"I love you, too, Mama. I'll take the best care of Kir that I can, I promise."

As the final stage of the Rest Time Chip releases I hear soft footsteps.

"He's so beautiful," Sebastian breathes as he comes into the room. I can picture him taking in the scene. My body slumped against Varya, silent sobs wracking her exhausted body. I apologise silently to her for causing her so much pain all at once. But this is the right way to do it. We both need to let go. This suspended animation isn't good for anybody.

"Oh, Varya, I'm so sorry," he says. It's the last thing I hear. As I slip out of this world for the last time, I'm barely aware of his warm hands. One on my back. I hope the other is on Varya's. I'm sure it will be. I thought he seemed changed. I'm sure he is. He'd better be, or I'll find a way to come back and haunt him.

Good-bye, my Varya.

Good-bye, our Kir.

CHAPTER FIFTY-ONE

Varya

Varya sat and held her mother and cried. Loud, wailing cries which released so many years lived with grief and fear. She stroked her mother's wiry hair and held her mother's still-warm cheek against her chest. She touched her mother's hands, so like her own, and placed them gently together.

Eventually, Sebastian helped her lay her mother out on the couch. Varya slumped to the floor beside her and held Elena's hand, her sobs almost spent.

Once all the sad tears had come, the happy ones followed. Sebastian took control and made three phone calls to arrange delivery of the anti-rejection serum for Kir. Varya didn't know what he told them, and she didn't care. All she knew was that her mother was gone. It was all she could focus on while Sebastian made arrangements.

Sebastian's next call was to Zoe, to tell her the good news—the recipient of Daniel's life span had been found and was in custody, and they had the means to restore his life span to him. He told her to come to Varya's apartment, that an ambulance would be arranged, and she could travel with Daniel to the Rest Time Corps medical facility, where his years would be returned.

Then he knelt down on one knee to Varya and placed his hand over hers.

"The nightmare is almost at an end, Varya. We're going to get our little boy back in the world and safe, by our side."

When she didn't respond, he looked at Elena. Varya hadn't taken her eyes off of her mother for many minutes now. He flexed his jaw and pressed his lips together. He withdrew his hand from Varya's.

"I have to ask you some questions, Varya, about your mum." He rocked back on his heels and stood; slipped a screen out of his pocket and sat on the couch across from mother and daughter. "They may be hard for you to answer, but I need to know, so we can decide what to do from here, okay?"

Varya didn't shift her gaze, but she gave a small nod.

"Was a death certificate prepared for Elena before she went into the Time Lock?"

Varya shook her head. "No."

"Good," nodded Sebastian. "That's good, there'll be nothing in the system then. I'm going to call an ambulance for your mum. They'll probably be here within half an hour or so, then they'll take her body to a funeral home."

"Okay," she replied dully.

"Zoe will be here very soon, as will the ambulance for Daniel. After that, an ambulance for your mum. Do you understand?" He paused.

"Yes, I understand." Her words came out in a quiet sigh. It was such a relief to allow someone else to be in charge for once. She looked up at Sebastian then. He had always been so good at taking charge. Now that he was here, she wondered why she hadn't called him before. Her stubbornness, her refusal to take the advice of her mother and Marisa, all these years. It suddenly seemed so silly. "Thank you," she whispered, throwing a glance of pain and gratitude in Sebastian's direction.

He smiled. "And within an hour or two a doctor will bring the anti-rejection serum for Kir."

She withdrew her hand from her mother in alarm, shocked out of her numbness. Kir was no longer safely tucked away with her mother, locked in a bubble together. Her heart pounded loud and fast, her hands started to shake.

"No, you can't let them find him, they'll take him away, they'll..."

"Ssh..." Sebastian swooped back to her side and cut her off, putting a finger to her lips. "Nobody's taking him away. This particular doctor owes me a favour. She'll keep quiet until we've decided what we're going to do about Kir."

"She won't take him away?" Tears streamed down Varya's face again. She felt so vulnerable, so uncertain. When Sebastian put his arms around her and pulled her head against his shoulder she didn't resist.

"No, she won't take him away. I promise."

Varya swallowed and blinked at her tears, sinking into her ex-husband's warmth. The father of her son. "But the doctor will make Kir better. And he can come out of the Time Lock."

Sebastian pressed his cheek against the top of her head. "Yes."

Varya nodded once and pulled away from him. She settled back into gazing at her mother, touching the end of her own finger to the end of her mother's fingers, one at a time.

"Okay, then," she said at last.

She was barely aware of Zoe arriving. Zoe wrapped her arms around her friend and offered her condolences, but only briefly. Her attention was stolen away a few moments later when the ambulance for Daniel arrived. Zoe led them into the Time Lock and then followed them out again with Daniel on a gurney, still sedated. Varya lifted a heavy hand in farewell.

Sometime after that—maybe minutes, maybe hours—Sebastian came to tell her the next ambulance had arrived, was she ready to say goodbye for now? Was anyone ever ready to say goodbye to their mother, really? Even if you knew the end was coming, even if you were given a specific year, day, time and location? Varya didn't think she could ever have really prepared for her mother's death. But still, she stood aside for the paramedics, obediently waiting in the kitchen while they loaded her up and took her away.

"Drink?" Sebastian asked her when the apartment was quiet again.

She shook her head, no. Her mind was foggy enough and she needed it to be clear before Kir woke up. Realisation dawned that she would be doing this part alone. Elena had always been there, to help with Kir, but now she wasn't.

She wondered whether Kir would even remember his father. She would have to explain to him that his grandmother was dead. Thoughts crashed into each other until she felt thoroughly overwhelmed.

"Marisa should be here," she said. "For Kir, I mean. He's very close to her."

Sebastian picked up his screen again. "I'll call her now."

Marisa arrived at the same time as Dr Osborne, a matronly medical professional who had clearly spent more time with unconscious patients than conscious ones. Sebastian led the small party into the Time Lock as though he'd been crossing the threshold for years.

Dr Osborne held both hands up to the shimmering curtain. She might have raised an eyebrow, Varya wasn't sure—she couldn't see from her position tailing behind her—but she definitely paused and cocked her head to one side before she strode through.

Varya and Marisa crowded the doorway, Sebastian folded himself down onto Kir's small desk chair. They all watched with bated breath while the doctor set up her equipment and checked Kir over.

"It's best if he stays here in stasis until after the serum is administered," explained Dr Osborne, her back to her audience. "In case he goes into anaphylactic shock. It'll give me more time to resuscitate if needed."

Varya squeezed the hand Marisa offered until Marisa protested.

"Hey," she muttered. "Blood supply. Bones. Both important components of my hand, let's not damage them, yeah?"

Kir was still blessedly sedated when Dr Osborne slid the needle into a tiny vein on the back of his hand. Varya watched him closely. Did his hand twitch, or was that just her blinking? Did he seem paler than he had a moment ago, or was that just the light?

"Now, we wait," said the doctor, perching herself on the end of his bed.

After twenty minutes with no sound except for Kir's soft snoring, Dr Osborne checked his pulse for what seemed like the thousandth time. She nodded.

"He seems stable. You can try removing him from stasis if you like. I'll stand by outside with the resus kit, just in case."

Sebastian moved towards the bed, but Varya was already there. She pulled back the covers, hooked her hands under her little boy's arms and gently lifted him up, holding him closely to her chest. His sleepy head flopped against her shoulder and she wrapped his legs around her hips, hugging him to her. Without a word, she moved out of the bedroom, down the hallway and straight through the portal. She paused on the other side for a moment, her entire body rigid as she waited for the worst to happen. But Kir's small body remained soft, warm, and still against her, his chest rising and falling in sync with hers.

"Bring him in here," Dr Osborne called from the living room.

Varya followed her voice and sat on the couch opposite the one her mother had lain on so recently. The doctor indicated the cushions next to Varya with a sweep of her hand and pointed to Kir. Varya shook her head and wrapped her arms around him protectively. Dr Osborne shrugged and disappeared into the kitchen, returning with a kitchen chair which she deposited in front of Kir and Varya.

"We'll check his vitals every five minutes for thirty minutes. If his body is going to reject the Time Chip, we'll know by then."

Varya blocked out everyone and everything in the room and focused on Kir's heartbeat, feeling it pulse through his chest. She wasn't relying on five-minute checks. She noted every pulse and every breath her son took for the next thirty minutes.

Sebastian sat next to her, his arm draped protectively around her, watching.

It was well after midnight by the time the doctor pronounced Kir stable and left the apartment, assuring Sebastian of her continuing silence both over the identity of her patient and the nature of his affliction.

Marisa made her exit at the same time, promising to come back in the morning.

Varya stayed where she was, continuing to mark Kir's heartbeat, his now-sweaty head resting against her shoulder. Her eyes became heavy and dropped closed. Sebastian cloaked mother and son in a blanket and dimmed the lights. Varya dozed fitfully until the dawn light started to creep in through the unshuttered window. She felt the weight shift from her chest and opened her eyes.

"Mummy?" croaked Kir, staring at the window in wonder. "It's darker outside. There's no sunshine."

The corners of her mouth pushed wide even as tears spilled from her eyes.

"Yes, sweetheart. It's dawn outside, the sun's only just coming up. Daddy fixed you. You're all better now."

Kir looked around, taking in his changed surroundings.

"Where's Nanna?"

Varya tried to speak but choked on her tears instead.

Kir looked at the window again, craning his neck to try to see up and out, into the world. He turned back, his gaze settled on his mother, his nose less than an inch from hers.

"Can we get a puppy dog, Mum?" he whispered. "A moving puppy dog?"

Varya laughed and hiccupped, wiping at her eyes. "Sure, why not. Let's get a puppy dog."

CHAPTER FIFTY-TWO

Marisa

Marisa arrived at the apartment late in the afternoon, bearing the ingredients for burgers. She stood outside the door, her hand poised to knock, and smiled. She leaned her ear closer to the door and listened to the happy sound of Kir whooping up and down the hallway; Varya calling after him, a light warning tone in her voice. She straightened, pressed the doorbell, and waited.

Varya opened the door wide. "Hey," she grinned.

"Hey," said Marisa, grinning right back. She stepped across the threshold and pushed the door shut behind her. "How're you holding up?"

Varya rubbed her neck, just below her earlobe, and winced. "Happy. Sad. Tired."

Marisa laughed. "Bundle of energy, isn't he?"

"Marisaaaaa!" shouted Kir, jogging into the room with his arms stretched wide, narrowly missing walls and furniture. "I'm coming in to land!" He flopped himself down on the floor and rolled onto his back, so he lay over the top of both of her feet.

"Pilot, I've seen better landings from a flight of stairs. Now, move off the runway. I've got burgers to cook." She shook her food-laden bags over his head in mock disgust. Kir giggled in delight and rolled off. Varya sank down onto the couch as Marisa went to put the groceries away. When she came back, she stood, leaning against the wall, watching Kir roll around and around the floor.

"Has he slept at all today?"

"Not since he woke up this morning," said Varya, rubbing her eyes.

"Have *you* slept at all today?"

Varya shook her head and chuckled softly. "No. We've been out most of the morning, watching the moving people and the moving cars and the moving buses."

"And the moving puppy dogs!" said Kir, mid-roll. He came to rest near Marisa. "We're getting a puppy dog! A moving one!"

She raised her eyebrow in amusement. "Is that so?"

"But not today," said Varya.

"But not today," echoed Kir, a serious frown on his face. He perked up suddenly. "But maybe tomorrow!" And then he rolled away again.

"So, what happens now?" asked Marisa softly.

"I don't know. I never thought this far ahead."

Marisa nodded and inhaled deeply. She moved over to the couch and sat next to Varya, squeezing her hands between her own knees.

"Your mum did, though."

"How did she find Reg? That was you, wasn't it?"

Marisa watched Varya's face carefully, trying to assess whether she was looking to allocate blame, or simply trying to understand.

"Yes, that was me. We were both worried about you, and Kir." She paused, bracing for a backlash. Varya remained silent. "We never meant for the technology to fall into the wrong hands."

"I know." Varya smiled weakly. "You're not the first to wreak havoc with the best of intentions."

"The path to Hell..."

"Yes, paved with good intentions." Varya turned to Marisa. "Daniel's fine, by the way. Zoe called this morning. They pulled the life span restoration procedure off without a hitch."

She sighed in relief. "Good. That's great news. What happens to the thieves now?"

Varya bit her lower lip hard and replied bitterly, "Death. Sebastian just called with the news. He says the evidence is clear and an example will be made of them. If they plead guilty, they'll be allowed an early Rest Time. Painless. If they don't, and they're found guilty at trial..."

"Hanging," said Marisa.

"Or firing squad."

"Any of those would be too good for them. Hanged, drawn and quartered would be what I'd go for." Marisa surprised herself at the venom in her voice. "And Reg? What will happen to him?"

Varya grimaced. "Sebastian's working on having the charges reduced. The powers-that-be are keen to charge him as an accessory. He thinks they'll be satisfied if the real culprits plead guilty, though. Reg should be able to fly under the radar and slip away fairly quietly. Especially as Sebastian intends to point out to them today that if they charge Reg and it goes to trial there'll be mud that sticks to Rest Time Corps. They'll be even more keen to avoid that, I imagine."

"That sounds like everyone else taken care of, then. Now you need to get yourself and Kir out of reach as soon as possible."

Varya frowned at her. "I know. But not without Sebastian. I'm thinking Canada. Maybe New Zealand. We've travelled to both before, he liked them."

Marisa's voice was strained. "For a holiday, he liked them, not to live. And what if he doesn't want to leave?"

"I can't separate him from his son again," said Varya lightly. "I was wrong to do it the first time. I should have known I could trust him."

"You did what you had to do to keep Kir alive," said Marisa firmly.

Varya looked at her blankly then, as though she didn't see her. Marisa sighed softly, recognising quickly—from long experience—that she wasn't going to be able to get through to her today. Varya had made up her mind and there would be no budging her.

"If he won't go, and if you change your mind about leaving without him, look inside Kir's closet, up the top, a blue shoe-box towards the back. Everything you need is there." When Varya didn't respond, Marisa stood and rolled her shoulders, trying to release some of the tension. "I'll get dinner started and then leave you to it. You must be exhausted."

Varya reached up and took Marisa's hand in hers. "Thank you," she said, staring into her eyes intently. "Thank you for everything you've done for us."

Marisa looked down at her hand in Varya's. She squeezed it gently, then let go. "Just doing my job, boss."

CHAPTER FIFTY-THREE

Varya

That evening, Varya sat with Kir until he fell asleep in his old bed back in their apartment. With each stroke of her knuckle down Kir's soft cheek his questions became slower and shorter.

"Can I download nine-years-plus games now or still only ones for four-year-olds? 'Cause that's not fair if I can't 'cause really I'm sort of nine even though I look four."

"Can I watch television again tomorrow?"

"Is YouTube still a thing?"

She answered a few of the questions—no, yes and yes—and hushed others. In her own mind she picked off the issues underlying each query that she would now need to deal with. Her brain started to ask itself questions that she couldn't even find the answers for. "How will you explain Kir's sudden reappearance? Which year will he start in school? Will you need to move to another city? Or another country?"

Kir's eyelids were almost completely closed and he'd started to snore softly now. He shuddered in the throes of falling asleep and opened his eyes halfway again.

"Mum?"

"Yes, sweetheart?"

"You'll be here when I wake up?"

"Right next door, in the next room."

"And Dad? Is he going to stay too?"

Varya hesitated mid-stroke. Just a small glitch before she smoothed it over and kept moving. She felt, rather than heard, a presence behind her left shoulder.

"I'll be here, little man," said Sebastian.

Kir's eyes flew wide open for a moment as he smiled and shifted his eyes from one parent to the other and back again.

"Okay, good." He gathered up Yappy Dog in his arms and rolled over to face the wall. Varya laid her hand on his back and waited for his breathing to deepen. She tensed as she felt the warm pressure of Sebastian's hand on her shoulder. The smell of his cologne brought back so many memories. And so much guilt. Sebastian patted her gently and left the room, closing the door halfway behind him to block out the hallway light. Varya continued to watch over her son. Tomorrow he would be a day older. In three months, it would be his birthday. But which year would they celebrate?

Now the Minor Miracles Foundation's questionable—okay, illegal—method of funding was exposed. She was sure Sebastian wouldn't turn her in, but now that her own background was common knowledge, there would be higher scrutiny on the Foundation. Returning to selling time tabs was far too risky. She could put pressure on previous donors to continue the stream of cash in return for her silence, but that would put herself and those close to her in great danger. Safety and peace were what she craved now. A small house in a small neighbourhood with a small job. Maybe moving cities wasn't such a bad idea after all.

Varya shifted and realised her left leg had fallen asleep around the same time as her son. Listening for Kir's breath one last time, she stood and wriggled out her pins and needles.

In the living room, Sebastian sat with his legs wide and his elbows on his knees, hands clasped. He looked up as she came in and flicked his head in an invitation to sit beside him. Varya deadpanned him, annoyed at his attempt to guide her even in her own home. She sat in the matching armchair, legs and hands folded.

"You can sleep in the spare room. There's a bed made up," she said into the silence. "Extra blankets in the cupboard."

Say something, she silently pleaded. She felt the pull of the empty, cushioned seat next to him, could almost feel the warmth of his thigh next to hers. They'd been so happy, so right for each other. They'd fought, of course they had. People like Sebastian and her were never meant to be dependent on somebody else. They didn't need each other in the way that some couples seemed to. She could survive perfectly well without him; in fact, she had. For five years now. She told herself she could survive for the rest of her life alone, as long as Kir was close. But right now, the primal scent of him was wafting over the short distance between them.

She nodded and leaned forward, as though to stand.

"The other kids, their life spans have been restored," he said to the rug, not looking at her. "But it could have been so much worse."

Varya swung forward again and this time stood up fully, placing her hands on her hips and facing Sebastian. Suddenly the smell of him aroused only anger in her.

"It could always be worse. That's life, Sebastian." She waited, spoiling for a fight. This was familiar territory; it was why their working relationship was so powerful but their personal one fraught with runaway fireworks. She would come up with a radical idea to trial; he would pick it apart and tell her why it was a terrible idea and could never be made to work. She would defend the idea; he would modify it. The final result was always better than the sum of its parts.

"None of this would have happened at all if you'd just let go to start with."

"Let go of our son's life, you mean?" said Varya, simultaneously fighting back tears and the urge to slap him.

He looked up at her then, pain evident in his grey-blue eyes. Varya noticed lines on his face where there hadn't been any before. She had been looking at him for days since his surprise appearance but hadn't really seen him until now.

"Yes." His response was barely audible. He looked away then and mumbled something to the side table.

"I'm sorry, I didn't hear..." she started.

He met her eyes then. "I'm sorry," he said, clearly and firmly this time. "I'm so sorry for not believing in you."

She stood, too stunned to say anything. Her whole body started to shake. The tremble started in her elbows and crept up her arms and into her shoulders. Her chest concaved once, then twice. Then the tears began again. She felt warm, strong arms fold her into a solid wall of comfort, but she couldn't allow herself the relief.

"I killed a child," she hiccuped between sobs. "More than one."

He didn't let her go, instead he put his hand over the side of her head and gently pulled her close to his chest, where he rested his cheek on her crown.

"You didn't kill those kids."

She pulled away from him and turned away, wiping her nose with her sleeve. "No." Her chest tightened with anger, though to whom it was directed she had no idea. "I killed them. If I had destroyed the tech like I was supposed to, if I had let go of Kir like you told me to." She placed her hands on Sebastian's chest and pushed him away. "Don't you understand? Other people's sons and daughters have died because our son lived."

Sebastian clenched his fists, his body defaulting to a fighting stance. He inhaled and exhaled heavily, forcing his muscles to relax.

"How am I supposed to live with that?" Varya sat down suddenly, her head in her hands. She rocked and keened quietly, wary of waking Kir. Sebastian sat beside her.

After a while he said, "I could tell you that it doesn't work like that. I could tell you that we make the best decisions we can with the information we have at the time. And, I think, you did exactly that. You couldn't have foreseen what your mother did. She and Reg couldn't have known that he was being followed. I could tell you that you should stop feeling guilty about it." He put his hand on her arm, but she pulled away. His grip tightened, refusing to yield. "But I'm not, Varya, because I know it won't help you."

She stilled.

"I think," he started, stroking her forearm with this thumb. "No, I know that Kir will now have one of the most overprotective, anxious mothers that ever walked this planet. I know that you will spend the rest of your life trying to repay your perceived debt to those kids' parents." He laughed wryly. "And, if you continue trying to repay that debt with your work at the Foundation, you'll also *save* the lives of countless kids."

Varya had stopped sobbing. Sebastian took both of her hands and tried to put his face in her line of vision.

"Varya."

"Mmm?" she sniffed. She let him take her hands, but she couldn't meet his eyes just yet.

"Thank you. Thank you for completely ignoring everything I said. Thank you for not letting go of our boy."

Varya let out another sob and leant into him. "I've missed you so much," she whispered. "And I really need some tissues."

He laughed, a slightly strangled sound, and she looked up and smiled. She saw he was crying now too.

She wiped her eyes with her sleeve again. "I'll be back in a minute."

She brought him soft, aloe vera-infused tissues from the bathroom, sneaking a peek in at the still-sleeping Kir on her way past. Clutching the box of tissues to her chest, she watched Sebastian from the doorway. He was tapping things into his screen, frowning. It felt like such a relief to forgive and to be forgiven. To put herself in his hands again and feel her stomach bottom out and her mind start to freefall. Everything was so black and white for him, so certain. She envied his ability to make his own peace and walk away from his son; then to return five years later and walk back into his life with no sense of guilt. Varya bit her lip. He had walked away, from their dying son. And from her. And yet, she was the one who seemed to hold all the guilt, all of the pain.

"Here you go." She held the box out to him as she sank down on the couch next to him.

He took a proffered tissue and placed it on his lap. "Thanks. I just have to..." He trailed off and continued to tap on his screen. Varya checked his face. The tears had dried.

"Kir and I, we can't stay here."

"Mm-hmm, I'm nearly finished, they just need to know..."

"I think we should move to Canada."

He looked up then, mid-tap. "What?"

"Or New Zealand." She looked at him, expressionless. "You could come with us."

"What? Why?"

Varya pursed her lips and shook her head slightly.

"Seb, we can't stay here. How will we explain Kir just suddenly reawakening from the dead?"

"We'll just tell them the truth." Sebastian swiped at his screen a little and held it up to her, the lines a blur to her tired eyes. "I've already started trying to explain it. I'll file a report, we'll answer some questions, that'll be it. Var', they won't arrest him for being alive."

Varya laughed softly. "Well, that's something."

Sebastian swiped again and went back to his tapping. "And you'll be able to stop work and look after Kir properly. You can both come live with me."

Varya bit her tongue and dug her thumbnails into her fingers. She kept her voice even.

"Hmm. And what about the Minor Miracles Foundation?"

"Connor can run that, can't he? Surely Kir's more important."

"Maybe *you* could look after Kir while *I* go back to work."

He stopped swiping and looked at her as though she'd suggested he take up pig farming and pipe smoking.

"Varya, I can't just leave my job. I'm part of a small team of specialists that keeps our country safe, that maintains civil order and ensures we don't exceed our resources. That's..."

"More important than Kir?" she offered.

"That's not what I meant." There was anger in his tone, but also pain.

"You could do important things to keep Canada safe."

"Canada isn't my country."

"No. It's not, but your country murders its own citizens when they reach their expiry date. Canada does not."

"My country's citizens sacrifice their place on this earth when their time comes so that others may flourish." He looked hard at her and stood, towering above her.

She smiled and pushed herself up from the couch. She lightly gripped his hands, rigid by his sides, and stroked his palms lightly with her fingers until they relaxed a little.

"I'm sorry, you're right. We'll stay and work things out. I'm just tired and... overwrought." She smiled, head bowed, then peered up at him sideways. "You're staying, right?" she asked. "I-I mean just for tonight, in the spare room. I didn't mean..." She held her breath as he leaned towards her and gently kissed her forehead. "It's just that I'm... really tired. I'm so very tired."

"Yes, I'm staying. I thought I could make us pancakes in the morning." He smiled.

She shrugged. "Well, actually, I've taught myself how to make pancakes. I'm pretty sure they're better than yours. But you can give it a shot, I suppose." She raised her eyebrows and looked directly into his eyes, trying not to think about how her face was probably red and blotchy with dark semi-circles on her cheeks where her make-up would have run.

"I've missed you too," he said, giving her a half-smile. "Damn, I'm tired too."

"How about we have a drink, a toast to our new future, and then get some sleep."

"Sounds like a plan."

She kissed him this time, on the lips. They were warm and dry and the smell of him made her hungry.

"I'll be back in a few minutes."

Varya padded out to the kitchen to prepare the drinks. Sebastian went back to replying to urgent messages of national importance.

They sipped imported vodka and talked about old times—when Kir was a baby, when Kir was a toddler, when they first met. Never about the time thefts; never about his illness.

When both their glasses were empty, Varya left him to finish up a couple of things on his screen. Then she checked on their boy one more time. There he was, back in his bed as though he'd never left. She pulled the cover up to his chin and stroked his soft hair with her open palm. He sighed deeply and rolled over.

In her own bedroom, alone, she changed into pyjamas and fell into bed. Varya slept deeply for the first time in five years.

CHAPTER FIFTY-FOUR

Marisa

If you'd asked me, I could have told you what Varya would do before it even happened. I knew she wouldn't stay. I don't know Sebastian well, but I know his type and they're infuriatingly predictable. He thinks everyone should accept their fate, and sacrifice whatever they can for our great and glorious country. Varya, on the other hand, doesn't have a single belief that she won't happily beat to death in favour of her one obsession—protecting her little boy. Ain't no way she was going to let them use Kir as a guinea pig for the next sixty years.

Here's what I think happened that night. I think Varya dosed both Sebastian and Kir with Entiac, the night she slipped away with their little boy. Sebastian would have been sleeping like the proverbial baby when she woke up and packed her bags. She would have taken the bags down to the car first, then come back up for Kir and carried him down in the elevator.

Then she took the documents from the shoebox at the top of the wardrobe and drove east, deep into the back roads

285

of Gippsland, and off the grid. Nobody would look for them there. And besides, the government doesn't much care if they occasionally lose a few people. The new economy means that less really is more, so long as we can keep our population decline fairly steady. And I mean, really, why would you want to go anywhere else? Most of the rest of the world has at least the same problems as we do, usually worse. It's not like you can escape your Rest Time Chip anyway. Once that sucker's inserted at birth it's not coming out again while you're alive. No, it's going back the other way, back into the system, that people have trouble with.

Disappearing into a tiny, dispersed community of people all trying to live outside of the strict government rules, using the fake IDs Reg, Elena and I had organised for her and Kir, was a piece of cake.

It's a shame about Elena, you know, a real shame. I'll miss her.

I didn't hear from Varya for a whole week after she took off. Had the bloody cops on my doorstep daily, no thanks to Sebastian, who came in here damn near bashing down my door.

"Where's my son?" he demanded, standing in that cocky legs-spread, arms-tensed stance guys like him have.

I just blinked at him slowly a few times while my brain caught up. I slotted all the puzzle pieces into place pretty quick-smart though. Took all the self-restraint I had to not burst out laughing. Good for you, Var'. That's what I was thinking—good for you. I put on my best sweet-submissive-woman face and asked him, "Are you okay, sir? What's happened?" Like I had no idea, like I barely remembered who he was.

He didn't believe me, of course, that I didn't know what he was talking about. I was a little hurt, I have to say. I was putting on my best performance, after all.

A couple of times over the next day or so, I tried to head out and shake the cops who stalked me, but they were sticky bastards. I got as far as the corner store a couple blocks over before I gave up. Grabbed some snacks and headed back home to wait.

It took a whole week.

Text message from an unknown number to my special, unregistered soirée client phone. It's the old-fashioned kind, no data connection. A 'dumb' phone.

"Here are the coordinates if you care to join us. Be discreet and be certain. You won't be able to go back."

I grinned, then dismantled the phone and took a hammer to the SIM card. You know, just in case. Can't be too careful.

Spent a few days tying up some loose ends. I still had my time tab display stock, which I didn't fancy trying to smuggle out of the city with me. Moving a few tabs around the inner suburbs for wealthy clients was one thing, but driving them through the outer suburbs where I could be stopped for anything. Well, that's something else entirely. Seemed a shame to just throw them out, though. Popped into the women's refuge and donated the whole lot. You should have seen Lenny's face: "I'll have to get me some new Georgette Heyer novels," she told me. I told her it was the last batch of tabs she'd probably ever get. "Spend them wisely," I told her. She smiled. "Maybe I should read a real classic romance, then. Like, you know, *Twilight* or something." I just snorted and told her to scram before I changed my mind.

Okay, so there was just one loose end to tie up, really. What can I say? I live a simple life.

After that it was my turn to head east. I still had to break into Varya's apartment one last time, though, to grab my fake ID. Getting past the cops stationed outside wasn't easy. Sebastian was always a bit delusional. He had to have known she wasn't coming back—why bother with surveillance? But I got in there eventually, found the shoebox, right where I'd left it. Just my passport left in there, along with some spare cash. 'Estella Ramirez' is my new name. It means 'star'. Elena's idea, but I like it.

With a bit of luck, Sebastian will have bought into Varya's chattering about Canada and New Zealand and is putting out feelers to look for her and Kir there. I trust he'll eventually get distracted by an issue of great importance to national security and leave off searching. He'll accept the fate that's been handed to him and get on with the job. He's done it before, after all.

We're all happily settled out here in the sticks now. I won't tell you where. Just picture us—Varya, Kir, Reg and me—in a little town not far from the beach, knocking back a few bottles of beer at sunset. Okay, so Reg and me knocking back beer. Varya's more a mojito kinda gal and Kir loves his kiddie pineapple sangrias. Varya was right. They let old Reg off pretty quickly after they realised that whatever they threw at him would come back to bite the government.

You still can't hold Varya back from work. Connor's taken over running the Minor Miracles Foundation officially, but paperwork and job titles never stopped Varya. She spends a large chunk of each day in the back room with the fan going, tapping away at her laptop. I have no idea what she's doing. Research? Blackmailing rich people to raise funds? I know she's in touch with Connor, though, and I know the Foundation's still pumping out cures regularly.

Reg and me, we look after Kir and share the cooking. Reg is kind of like the grandpa Kir never had, and it turns out he knew Elena better than any of us, so they have fun telling each other stories about Nanna, may she forever rest in peace.

Kir will start school next year and then I really will get into my early retirement properly. Maybe I'll take up surfing.

In the meantime, I'd say we're all pretty happy down here. Life is slow and easy, and the views are fairly spectacular. It feels like we've got all the time in the world, really.

Take care of yourself out there. And may your time be plentiful.

ABOUT THE AUTHOR

Rebecca Bowyer lives in Melbourne, Australia with her husband and two sons. She can be found writing about books, reading and writing at www.storyaddict.com.au.

Stealing Time is her second novel.

Connect with Rebecca Bowyer:
    Twitter: @rebeccabowyerau
    Instagram: @rebeccabowyerwriter
    Facebook: /rebeccabowyerwriter

OTHER BOOKS BY THE AUTHOR

Maternal Instinct

www.ingramcontent.com/pod-product-compliance
Lightning Source LLC
Chambersburg PA
CBHW050028120726
47903CB00006B/1960